I0547615

TIME FOR LOVE
Explicit Content

By Linda Mayo
All Rights Reserved

Published by Linda Mayo
Printed in the United States Of America
Copyright @2021
Linda Mayo
ISBN: 978-0-578-92709-1
Cover design by:
SelfPubBookcovers.com/FrinaArt

TABLE OF CONTENTS

CHAPTER 1

FORGING AHEAD

Beth walks into the publishing company's lobby with a sense of apprehension, having no clue that this meeting would transform her world forever. Receiving a call regarding a particular assignment was a bit of a surprise. She didn't expect it as her one book didn't appear to meet the publisher's expectations. She knows her time with them is limited. If she was being honest with herself, she despises the books they are launching. With that in mind, she presses the elevator button for the top floor.

Stepping out of the elevator, she heads toward Mr. Lawson's office. Catching his head lowered, she pecks lightly on the door. He glances up gesturing her to enter. Glancing back down, quickly marking his spot, he says, "Hello, Beth. Grab a seat."

Accepting the chair directly across from him, she smiles uncomfortably, saying nothing.

He seizes her silence as an opportunity to get straight to the point. "Beth, I have an assignment that you may find interesting. We've received a written invitation from the well-known Vanders family to submit a proposal for a novel on their family history. Mrs. Vanders has been unwell and wishes to chronicle their lives from an inside view. This might be right up your alley." He hesitates, assessing her reaction.

Feeling uninspired, but desiring to maintain an impartial attitude, she responds, "You have my attention. Can you offer any additional details?"

"Yes. It would mean spending two weeks at the estate interviewing family members. Mrs. Vanders will evaluate your research to determine if you get the publication rights for the biography."

"Two weeks at the estate?" She repeats while contemplating the idea. Considering the possibilities, she decides it could be an adventure. However, the pressure to produce under such intense scrutiny would be unsettling, to say the least. "Tell me more," she asks Mr. Lawson for more details.

"Yes, two weeks. You must take proper attire to participate in the events common with their lifestyle. I understand they have a ballroom in the estate." He declares this with enthusiasm in his voice. "If you find yourself struggling, you can always contact me to come to your aid. We could skype, or schedule a business lunch. I've been informed that you'll have full access to the residence as well. If there is an urgent matter, we could make a quick phone conference if the conversation is brief."

"Why are you selecting me?" She observes his facial expression to see if he's uncomfortable answering.

Hearing her question, he answers truthfully. "To be honest, I don't have anyone else available during that period of time. Two weeks is quite a commitment for one feature. Plus, with no guarantee of the publication rights, it's not something I can ask my biggest authors to do. I assumed you have no fires in the oven at the moment. I felt it would work for you. Of course, I would pay you a two-week salary. I think it would be a great opportunity to associate with the Vanders on their level and terrain. Plus, not to sound chauvinistic, but your beauty will fit right in with the exquisite family. Have you ever seen Mrs. Vanders?"

"Not personally, but I have seen photographs of her. She's stunning."

"Precisely! So is everyone else in that family. Even the men are strikingly handsome." Hesitating, he watches for symptoms of interest. "So, what do you think?"

"I guess I could try it. When would I go? Do you have any specific instructions I need to follow?"

"As I stated before, you'll stay for two weeks at the estate. Take business attire and gowns for evening events. The magazine won't be able to cover your expenses until we acquire the booking. Sorry about that. Do you own a few gowns you could take?"

Her mind goes over her wardrobe. She concludes she has a couple of dresses that might work. She'll attempt to get out of every event she can, stating her commitment to writing. "Yes, I have a couple of gowns that would be adequate. I won't be there that long."

He stands, saying, "Okay, arrive at the estate first thing Monday morning." Holding out his hand for a shake, he offers, "Good-luck, Beth!"

Startled by the abrupt conclusion of the meeting, she asks, "I don't need to sign an agreement or contract?"

"No. It's after you get the green light that we'll negotiate the contract."

Getting the message that the meeting is over, she shakes his hand then turns to leave.

Feeling a little less than enthusiastic, she's relatively suspicious of Mr. Lawson. "It's not big enough to give to an established writer." She repeats this fact to herself, accepting the declaration and breaking it down to a fact that she doesn't seem successful enough."

I suppose after the meager sales of her book, she could understand why. However, she wonders if the company put any effort into marketing her book. Their "successful authors" have representation everywhere she looks. On the other hand, it's as if her book doesn't exist. She did find one of her books on a bookshelf once. It had a "Reduced Price" tag on it. She ponders the question. "So, why am I taking an assignment with him?"

Arriving home, she devotes the next few days packing for the two-week excursion. She has plenty of business attire. It's the gowns she is less assured will meet the criteria.

Inserting them in the garment bag the night before her departure, she tells herself that she's not going there to impress with her wardrobe. She's going there to do a story that may develop into a book. She focuses on that and nothing else. Deciding she has everything packed, she showers, then settles in to sleep, not realizing that tomorrow her life will change forever.

Rising early the next day, she loads her car and locks up the apartment. Stopping by Starbucks to get coffee, she knows everything is in order for her extended leave from home. She still ponders if she has forgotten anything. A quick stop for her daily dose of caffeine, with cup in hand, she turns the key in the ignition and backs out of the parking lot.

An hour later, she pulls into the Vanders estate. Taking in the lengthy driveway, she marvels at the magnificent landscape and its grandiose display. The scene is stimulating her creative juices and her approach to the biography. Pulling up to the main entrance, she gets out of her car and opens the trunk to get her luggage.

Before she turns, a gentleman approaches and states, "Please, Miss, let me assist."

She spins around hearing his remarks. "Thank you." He removes the large suitcase as she grabs the cosmetic case, and closes the trunk.

He guides her up the steps and to the front door. Parking her luggage in the entryway, he shifts to take her cosmetic bag to lay on top. Facing her, he says, "This way, Madam."

She walks behind him as he escorts her to a luxurious space with exquisite furnishings. There's a lovely sofa placed squarely in the heart of the room. Unacquainted with expensive furniture brands, she observes a cream-colored chenille sofa with antique legs and arms that have gold accents. A chaise lounge with a matching duvet draped over the bottom is positioned in front of the massive fireplace. He directs her to take a seat on the sofa.

She smiles, replying, "Thank you."

"Mrs. Carlyle, the estate director, will be in shortly. May I get you something to drink?"

She studies him and sees he has a very pleasant nature and smile. Smiling back, she replies, "No, thank you."

He turns to leave as Mrs. Carlyle enters. She initiates orders at once. "Frederick, please take Miss Olsen's luggage to the Ribbon Room."

Acknowledging with a slight head nod, he seizes both bags from the corridor.

Rising, she places a smile on her face. Beth holds out her hand to Mrs. Carlyle. "Thank you."

Mrs. Carlyle is struck by the refinement of this youthful girl. Beth's height is around five-six or five-seven. Her eyes are a striking sea blue with lush dark lashes that underscore the blue of her eyes. Her long blonde hair cascades down her back. Her lips are full with a natural shade of lipstick. She notices beautiful white teeth as Beth smiles, holding out her hand. "Welcome, Miss Olsen. I have instructed Frederick to take your luggage to the Ribbon Room. I expect you'll discover your accommodations suitable for the work you will perform here. I'll assign you an assistant to whom you can approach for anything during your stay."

"Thank you, Mrs. Carlyle."

Beth notices the formality in their conversation. She adds nothing to the discussion that is not required. Her intention is to keep her eyes and ears alert, gathering everything she can to support the biography.

Frederick walks back into the room.

Looking at Beth, Mrs. Carlyle speaks. "Frederick will take you to your quarters. I have placed an itinerary on your desk, so please review it, making certain you arrive at events on time."

"I will. Thank you, again."

Leaving the room, they head for their destination. Frederick leads her to a grand staircase that extends to a lengthy corridor on the second floor. The carpeting is thick and plush. On each side are two stands with art pieces and beautiful large framed pictures of exquisite landscapes above each. Everything she sees reeks of money. Frederick stops at a door and turns the doorknob.

Entering the room, Beth is overwhelmed by the lavish luxury. The room is cream with various shades of blue ribbons everywhere. The ribbons look as if they are stitched into the draperies, bedspread, and even on the cushion of the desk chair; but, in reality, they are part of the material itself. The blue-shaded ribbons match in arrangement. Mouth agape, she eventually says, "This is stunning."

Smiling, Frederick leaves her suitcases in front of the closet. He turns to her motioning toward the bags, "Your assigned assistant will be in shortly to unpack your belongings." He shows her the call button on the phone for any needs.

As Frederick leaves, she thanks him, then closes the door. Turning back to the room, she roams around checking out the details. The sheer vision and planning behind each detail in the décor is mind boggling. It was professionally designed, of course. Smiling, she runs her palm over the material of the spread and decides that blue is now her favorite color.

A tap on the door startles her. Opening it, she finds a young woman clothed in uniform at her doorstep. Since Frederick had revealed the need for an assistant, she recognizes her to be just that. She lets her in, moving away from the doorway.

"Hello, Miss Olsen. My name is Stacy. I'll be your assistant during your stay here. Please call me if you require anything." She says pointing to the phone on the desk. "Lunch will be served in 20 minutes in the dining hall. Will you be wearing your present outfit, or do you require assistance with your selection?"

Caught off guard, she asks, "What do you suggest I wear? Is this a formal business luncheon or a private lunch with Mrs. Vanders?"

"It's relatively informal. What you have on is fine. Mrs. Carlyle has arranged a private lunch with you and Mrs. Vanders today, a get-to-know-you event."

"Okay, great. I'll wear this then. Let me freshen up a moment, then I'll be ready to go."

Nodding, she then eyes the luggage. "May I put your clothes away while you ready yourself?"

Glancing at the unopened suitcases, Beth asks, "Are you certain you don't mind? I can unpack them myself."

Stacy smiles, then says, "Please allow me. It will provide me something to do while you freshen up."

Grabbing her cosmetics bag, she goes to the adjoining powder room. There's a section set up with a counter, a chair, and a light-up mirror specifically for makeup and hairstyling. The bathroom is enormous.

Freshening her face, she fluffs her hair. Returning, she finds that her belongings are sorted and put away. Peeking at her watch, she sees its time to go. Walking toward Stacy, she says, "Thank you. I really appreciate your help."

Opening the door to the hallway, they leave. Beth follows Stacy as she takes the same corridor they took when coming to the room and heads downstairs. Reaching the bottom floor, they turn toward the rear of the estate. She's escorted to a grand dining area with tall regal chairs sitting at each end of an expansive table. She notices that another woman has already been seated at the end near a window. Stacy escorts her to a seat directly across from her. Feeling slightly apprehensive, she's glad when a beaming smile appears on the woman's face. The friendliness is comforting.

The staff departs. The woman introduces herself as Rachel Fensworth. Beth shakes her hand and introduces herself. Just then Mrs. Carlyle enters to announce that Mrs. Vanders won't be joining them for lunch as planned. She sends her apologies for the last-minute change. A guided tour of the estate has been arranged for you in her absence. She will see you at dinner this evening." Mrs. Carlyle pauses for a response.

Rachel thanks her, then replies, "Please, thank Mrs. Vanders for her hospitality."

Beth adds, "Please tell her we look forward to meeting her."

Mrs. Carlyle nods, and leaves the room.

After the food is displayed before them, Beth grabs her plate and prepares her selection. She assembles a chef salad. Rachel does the same. The ingredients are fresh and tasty.

Rachel asks, "When did you arrive at the estate?"

Beth replies, "Two hours ago. What are you here for?"

Rachel explains, "I'm writing an article on the Vanders family history."

Surprised by the revelation Beth says, "So am I."

Rachel gets a startled look on her face and asks, "What magazine are you with?"

"I'm not from a magazine. My book company received an invitation to write a biography of Mrs. Vanders. They've asked me to draft an article on the family first. If it passes her scrutiny, I'll be allowed to pen the book. It's basically a test at first. If I don't receive permission to publish this book, my publisher will most likely drop me." She shrugs her shoulders to emphasize her frustration.

"That's a lot of pressure," Rachel says and states her own dilemma. "If my history piece doesn't get accepted, although my boss didn't specifically say so, I suspect I could lose my job. It looks like we're both under some strenuous demands. I'm here for several weeks, so I hope it all works out."

Beth agrees knowing a lot is riding on their visit. The fact that they both have the same time frame to stay, plus the arrival and departure similarities, sounds suspicious. These next fourteen days will be high stakes for both. She hopes Rachel is not her competition, and that a magazine article will not override the book needs.

Continuing lunch, they talk about their lives, and are shocked to realize they live near each other. New York is so big, for them to be that close is uncanny. It's amazing to learn that they're living in a nearby neighborhood, yet their paths have never crossed. Both agree that after the assignment, they should make plans to meet for drinks and discuss their new adventures.

CHAPTER 2

HISTORICAL REVIEW

With lunch completed, the two go on a lengthy tour of the Vanders estate. The event begins in the room where Beth had arrived. The guide is Mrs. Carlyle. She accompanies them from room to room, quoting historical information and detailing random artifacts. They enter a room devoted exclusively to portraits of family members dating back to the early 1600's.

One portrait catches Beth's eye. The subject is indistinguishable from Rachel! Perceiving Rachel's discomfort from her staring, Beth looks back at the portrait, examining the details. The figure is of Adrianna Vanders. She and Rachel could be identical twins. Both have jet-black hair with alarmingly similar features. The gray-blue eyes with thick long lashes, the perfect small nose, and full luscious lips are merely the beginning of the qualities they both possess. Their flawless oval faces with high cheekbones are a dead match.

Not aware of the stirred interest Beth and Rachel have over the portrait, Mrs. Carlyle excuses herself for a phone call.

Beth hesitates, but asks Rachel, "Did you know you looked like Adrianna?"

"No. I must admit I'm just as perplexed as you."

Beth asks, "Is that the reason they selected you to do the article?"

"No, I guarantee my boss would have gloated about that fact, if he had realized."

They both stare at the portrait. Adrianna is positioned on a white regal armless chair. Her deep blue silk evening gown looks exquisite as the skirt cascades down the sides of the chair. Her posture is straight, with her hands folded on her lap. She's captured from an angle with her head tilted slightly upward toward her right shoulder. Her long, slim arms are covered by the long-sleeves. The bust of the dress is low enough to show a pushed-up cleavage, implying the corset begins below the chest as was typical for the time.

As they move to the next portrait, Beth finds it just as alarming. Adrianna is seated on a small sofa with her husband, Chad Grayson. They make an impressive couple. Chad is holding Adrianna's hands in his. His strong chiseled jaw line and dark piercing eyes envelop the onlooker. He wears a black tuxedo, which exudes a mysterious presence. The slight grin on his face accentuates deep dimples that draws the onlooker into a smile. Beth stands dazed as she absorbs this gorgeous man. She pulls herself away from the portrait to see Rachel is just as captivated by the handsome man.

Mrs. Carlyle returns to continue the tour breaking them away from their sole focus of the portraits.

Beth notes particular details mentioned at each location. Completing the initial two floors around four, she returns to her room to review her comments. She is meticulous with taking notes, so she examines them with a critical eye. Adrianna and Chad Grayson are of considerable interest at this stage.

A knock on the door takes her attention away from work. Opening it, Stacy announces that dinner will be served in an hour. "Will you desire my services, Miss?"

Feeling insecure, Beth asks about the appropriate attire.

"Dinner is semi-formal. I noticed a dress earlier when I unpacked you that would be suitable. May I show you?"

Beth realizes she's making Stacy stand in the hall. She backs up, opening the door wider for her to enter. "Of course. Thank you, Stacy." Following her to the closet, Stacy pulls out a navy-blue knee length dress. She picks up the navy-blue matching shoes to go with the dress.

Beth thanks her for the suggestion, but is somewhat disappointed. This was the outfit she was considering as formal, not semi-formal. Boy, does she have a lot to learn about the elite society. Accepting the dress from Stacy, she heads toward the dressing room. Stacy tells her she will return in 45 minutes.

True to her word, Stacy knocks on the door exactly 45 minutes later. Beth takes another glimpse at herself in the mirror. She's satisfied with the look. Walking to the door, adjusting her dress just out of nervousness, she opens it. Beside Stacy stands a smartly dressed gentleman. Stacy introduces him as Joshua. "He will escort you to the formal dining room."

Beth takes his outreached hand and shakes it. "It's very nice to meet you, Joshua."

He grins as they shake hands. "This way, Miss." Holding out his arm for her, she places her arm under his as they begin the trek to the dining room.

She spots Rachel already seated at the table as they join the festivities. She is ushered to the chair next to her. Beth takes a seat mouthing a thank you to Joshua. He acknowledges with a nod and walks away. She looks at Rachel and declares, "Wow, what formality! I feel like a fish out of water."

Rachel giggles and responds, "Me, too."

A commotion commences from the direction of the door where men and women are entering the room. Soon the table is full of strangers laughing and seating themselves as if they're regular participants of the extravagant atmosphere. Brief silence looms over the table. The gentlemen stand when a stunning woman arrives. Beth recognizes her from the basic research she has conducted so far. It's Mrs. Vanders. The regal woman makes her way toward their table. Rachel looks at her, producing an expression of fear. Without saying a word, Beth nods in understanding.

Seated at the head of the table, Mrs. Vanders can view everyone. She scans her way down the right side, then to the left to see who is in attendance. As Beth watches, she sees Mrs. Vanders' facial expression varies with each person she acknowledges. When Mrs. Vanders reaches her, she smiles warmly. However, her expression changes visibly as she looks at Rachel. Shock is evident on her face. Beth sees her struggling to compose herself and move on. Regaining her composure, she exchanges a pleasant smile with Rachel. Beth can tell the reaction unnerved Rachel. Feeling sorry for her, Beth reaches over and touches her arm to comfort her. She smiles at her with a silent moving of her mouth, "Thank you."

The waiters serve the course of the meal in stages. Beth and Rachel chat during dinner. Everyone is enveloped in their own conversations, which allows them to talk to each other. Acknowledging both are fish out of water comforts them. When dessert arrives, it's a deep chocolate cake with warm cream poured over it. Rachel takes a bite and moans as the warmth hits her tongue. She looks at Beth and delivers a muffled, "Delicious."

Beth performs the same extravagant muffled delicious. They laugh, finding enjoyment and delight in each other's company.

Mrs. Vanders clinks her fork on the rim of her glass bringing the chatter to an immediate stop. Rising, she introduces Beth and Rachel, informing the guests about their assignments. She requests that all be available sometime this week to answer questions for their research. She tells Beth and Rachel that each person at this table is connected to the Vanders. You may ask what you wish. Everyone will offer complete cooperation.

With that, she excuses herself and says good night to the group. Everyone gets up and exchanges hugs, then Mrs. Vanders exits the room. Others follow her exit and leisurely leave the dining area. Some head toward the main door to exit the estate, while others go off into an adjoining room to socialize.

Beth and Rachel are escorted outside to a veranda where they order red wine and stay until ten o'clock chatting and enjoying the beautiful night. A mild breeze ruffles Beth's hair as she sips her drink, finding it soothing and relaxing. The two discuss Rachel's resemblance to Adrianna.

Rachel asks, "Did you see Mrs. Vanders' face when she looked at me?"

"I did. Rachel. You could tell it startled her."

"When I saw that, I didn't know how to react. The only thing I can determine at this point, is that she had no clue what reporters they had selected. If she had known, I probably wouldn't be here."

Beth says, "Rachel, you look so much like Adrianna. Could you be a long-lost relative of the Vanders? Is there anything in your family history that may connect you?"

"Well, if there is, I'm not aware of it. I hope this doesn't influence her desire to have me here. She could summon me to leave tomorrow, assuming I'm an imposter."

Beth ponders the statement for a moment then responds, "I don't see that happening, Rachel. If anything, they will choose to learn more about you. You have a leg up on me." She smiles and clicks Rachel's glass, hoping this knowledge comforts her in some way.

Rachel replies, "No, Beth. We're in this together." Draining their glasses, they decide to retire for the night. Parting ways, they say goodnight.

Arriving back at her room, Beth grabs her notebook to document everything she has observed. The one thing she is best at is reading people. She feels sorry for Rachel, but she still thinks Rachel's looks will carry her a long way in this adventure.

Starting to sense fatigue, she remembers the itinerary for tomorrow and how early her day begins. Rubbing her eyes, she gets up and takes a long hot shower. Dropping into the gloriously comfortable bed, she's asleep within seconds.

CHAPTER 3

DISCOVERY

The alarm goes off way too early. Beth rolls over to reach for her phone and presses the snooze button. Coming out of the fog of glorious sleep, she stretches and yawns. Jumping up, she goes over to the desk to get the itinerary and a pen. Crawling back under the covers, she props her pillows up against the headboard, and with a pen she marks the itinerary with special notes of her own. Feeling confident and ready to dive into the interviews, she turns off the snooze and starts readying herself for the long hours on the schedule.

Her first day of interviewing begins with members of the immediate family. She has designed the questions to understand the associations and relationships of the family. The family business is an empire. It surely takes more than one person to make that happen, so she digs deep into the role each person plays in the family. She finds family members forthcoming offering many details.

She's most captivated by the two brothers. Being a red-blooded American girl, she can't help but be attracted to both Grayson and Alex Vanders. Each has a hint of arrogance that emanates when they walk into the room. Grayson has an air of "I know you want me." It's a bit of a turn off for Beth because of his assumption that she would fall all over him with admiration. There is a distinct difference between the two brothers.

Beth is beautiful. She's used to men from all walks of life hitting on her. Grayson's self-importance doesn't impress her in the least. Squashing his self-indulging rambles, she turns the conversation over to his role. "What is your role in the Vanders empire?"

He stops mid-sentence to speak about his business acumen and the many companies they own. To her surprise, he has a very high-ranking position in the Vanders banking institutes. His demeanor changes from arrogant to serious. Beth can tell he takes the aspect of business as nothing to be flippant about. He makes it clear that this article should focus on the overall success of the businesses and not the details of particular successes or failures of each person.

He states unequivocally "Your readers admire the Vanders, and I expect you to support that premise."

Stopping him in his tracks, she says, "First, this is my article, not yours. This article will go where the interviews lead me." She looks at his surprised expression and feels good about putting him in his place. "Furthermore, if I'm not truly honest about all things Vanders, then I may as well leave now."

Grayson finds himself in new territory. A woman has never stood up to him like this. He has an empowering personality, so this 'put me in my place attitude' from Beth was rather amusing. "Okay, don't say I didn't warn you. If you start minimalizing those associated with the Vanders, you will give yourself a one-way ticket out of here."

She wants to reply harshly to that smug, arrogant pompous ass, but refrains from doing so. Looking down at her notes, she looks back up at him with an indifferent expression and says, "Thank you for your time, Mr. Vanders. I think I have everything I need for your part of the Vanders family."

"Wow," he thinks to himself. I have just been dismissed. Smiling, he stands and says, "It's been a pleasure, Miss Olsen. I look forward to your article."

Putting an artificial smile on her face, she says, "Would you mind sending in Alex on your way out?"

"Certainly. Good day." He turns to leave, looking back as he opens the door.

Beth could see he is about to turn back. She starts marking on her sheet so he wouldn't see her watching him. Her heart is pounding fast. On second thought, maybe she shouldn't have gotten so irritated with him. She had not been very professional by showing her irritation with him. Any good reporter never tips his or her hand. Thinking back, she can't figure out at what point the interview went to hell.

Alex Vanders walks in. Pushing Grayson out of her mind, she begins her interview with Alex immediately. While he carries the same aloof demeanor, there is a kindness about him that his brother lacks. The interview is interesting and goes smoothly. Beth discovers that he, too, also has a major position in the family business. However, his business division is strictly led by his immediate family. She probes him with many questions to see if he has been granted the position because of the family, or his business acumen. In the end, she determines it's both. His father has taken Alex under his wing preparing him to take over. His answers are very structured providing details of his great business deals.

Feeling quite satisfied with the day's interviews, she packs up. She goes straight to her room to expand on her notes while the interviews are fresh in her mind. Having eaten only half a sandwich earlier, she is feeling quite hungry and can't wait for dinner.

At dinner, Beth and Rachel share notes. Rachel asks, "What angle are you taking for the article?"

Beth replies, "I'm still working that out." She shrugs her shoulders. "I'm just gathering facts at this point to see where it leads me."

Rachel says, "I'm doing the same. I'll stay hibernated in the library for the next few days to focus on the story. I have quite a few pictures if you need any. Mrs. Vanders had Mrs. Carlyle take me to the library where there are tons of family books. In fact, Mrs. Vanders showed up today after all of my interviews had been completed."

Beth asks, "She did? What did she say?"

"We discussed my resemblance to Adrianna. Then she spoke about the library and the many books in there of the Vanders family. I'll show you what I found in the library, and if you want to go with me to see the books, let me know."

Beth replies, "Yes, I would love to see the pictures and the books. By the way, I don't think you can stay cooped up tomorrow evening. There's a ball tomorrow night that we are to attend. I just received the invitation right before I left my room."

Surprised, Rachel says, "I didn't notice an invitation in my room."

"I saw Stacy leaving my room, so she told me all about it. She said she would lay the invitation on my bed," Beth explains, before taking a sip of water.

Rachel says, "I didn't look around. I ran in, threw the books on the desk, and then changed. Is it formal?"

Beth has a concerned look on her face and says, "Yes, and I have nothing to wear for such an extravagant affair."

"I brought some formal wear per my boss's instructions. I have several outfits if you want to look through mine.

"Could I really? That's so nice of you!" Beth exclaims as relief pours over her.

Rachel smiles at Beth. "Absolutely. I'm sure there will be only one ball while we're here."

Beth replies, "I sure hope so. I'm not cutout for this extravagant life style."

"I'm not either, but I will enjoy myself. I wonder how many handsome single bachelors will be there?" She giggles and says, "If there are a lot of handsome men, I'll just have to suffer through it."

Beth laughs out loud. She covers her mouth to muffle it. "You're crazy Rachel, but oh so much fun."

As dinner ends, Rachel and Beth go to their rooms to organize their notes. Beth still has an uneasy feeling about her encounter with Grayson earlier that day. She regrets her coarse nature with him. There's something about him that she finds offensive, but she can't put her finger on it. It's almost as if he wants her to feel inferior to him. If there's one thing that she can't stand, it's arrogant men. For her, it's almost a hobby to put them in their place.

Beth is a graduate of Yale University. She has been around wealthy men for most of her adult years. However, she avoided them and focused on her studies, graduating top ten in her class. Although she never engaged in their extra-curricular activities, she understood their self-important attitudes to know they felt themselves better than her. She was there on a scholarship, and most of them probably knew that. Her self-preservation kept her from experiencing their lifestyle.

Over the years, she had many preppy guys ask her out, but she blew them off thinking they pitied her. She never took the time to get to know them or allow them to know her. However, the task at hand has really given her another opportunity to finally understand and know the thoughts of the wealthy. Graduating in journalism, she should have been more open to learning about their culture. It would have assisted in the path she has chosen for her life. If nothing else, she would at least have known how to function here among the rich and famous.

Putting away her laptop, she takes a shower, and snuggles under the covers. Even though the negative experience with Grayson is on her mind, it doesn't prevent her from falling sound asleep. Before she leaves this estate, she promises herself she will get the brand name of the mattress. No matter what it costs, she will get one for home.

CHAPTER 4

BEAUTY AND EXTRAVAGANCE

Beth spends the next day in the library. The knowledge she assembles is astonishing. Analyzing the Vanders history, she finds the angle she wants to focus on to make her book unique and one of a kind. She prefers to take the road less traveled. What is it that motivates the Vanders to be such a tight-knit family? And who owns the esteemed position of leader?

First impressions tell her Mrs. Vanders is the matriarch. She wishes she had met Mr. Vanders. Did Mrs. Vanders become leader after his demise, or had she always dominated the family?

She carries a bunch of books back to her room and settles in for a reading session. She is well into her second book when a tap on the door forces her to reluctantly stop reading. Placing a bookmark, she lays the book on the desk. Rubbing her eyes, she shuffles to the door. Opening it, she's presented with a rack of clothes. Stacy motions her to grab one end so she can roll it into her room. Beth pulls as Stacy pushes. Once inside, she inquires, "What's this?"

"Mrs. Vanders wanted to offer you a selection of gowns to choose from for the ball this evening. She has selected these from one of her favorite designers. Search through them and select the one you prefer. If there's nothing that delights you, we have another rack in Miss Rachel's room."

Surprised, to say the least, she thumbs through them. "It's incredible. The sizes are on point. How did they know my size?"

"I unpacked you, don't forget." She adds, "I took the liberty of investigating. We're always prepared for our guests' needs."

Browsing, Beth replies, "I'm at a loss for words. This is incredible. I have never seen such beautiful gowns."

Stacy offers an understanding grin. She holds out the skirt of a dress. "Mrs. Vanders is such a lovely person, Beth. She is constantly thinking of others and their comfort."

"I can see that. Each dress comes with matching shoes! She constructs the complete outfit."

"That's not all," Stacy says, smiling. "Once you select your outfit, an attendant will appear to do your hair and makeup."

With an exclamation of disbelief, Beth asks, "Really? That's inconceivable to me."

Focusing on her favorite, Beth selects a cream-colored gown that will conform to her body. It has sheer layers that tumble down the back, leading to a flawless fit. The heels are a shade darker in the same color. Holding the gown up in front of her, she twirls, feigning a waltz.

Stacy is swept up in Beth's enthusiasm. Getting lost in the drama, she laughs, seeing Beth's excitement over the dress. However, glancing toward the clock, she says, "Beth, it's getting late. You should take a shower and get ready for the next phase of preparation, which is makeup and hair."

Beth hangs the garment back on the rack, then dances her way to the bathroom. Excitement is overwhelming her. She feels like Cinderella going to the ball. She just hopes her night ends better than Cinderella's.

After a brief shower, she dons the outfit and crosses over to the massive mirror. She looks stunning! She embraces the look, running her palms over her hips, she knows the gown was created just for her. Absorbed, she's startled when a knock on the door brings her to notice the hour. "That must be hair and makeup."

Stacy opens the door. A woman pushes in a cart full of accessories for the creation of Cinderella. The woman goes to Beth, spinning her around to study the dress. She maintains a hasty, "I can work with this," then pushes her cart to the dressing room.

They morph Beth into a radiant beauty. Once ready, she is awe-struck at her reflection in the mirror. The makeup is flawless. Not at all excessive, just perfect. The blue of her eyes looks bluer than normal against the dark liner and mascara. The neutral lip color, called "Naked," is a shade deeper than her natural lip color. She watches how the makeup is applied, making mental observations of brand and shades. She decides to wear her hair down. Changing anything from the ensemble would be a tragedy. Turning around to observe the final look, Beth is ecstatic.

Stacy stands back, studying her. "Beth, you're gorgeous! You could be a model. You're so beautiful."

Beth exclaims, "This is a dream, Stacy. I have never been catered to like this."

"You're stunning."

Beth says, "I have to show Rachel." She leaves her room, going down a couple of doors to Rachel's room. Knocking rapidly, she anxiously waits to get Rachel's reaction to her transformation. When Rachel answers, she gasps in amazement.

Rachel's in a deep green gown that has a train behind her. Beth couldn't decide where to look first. Her makeup is just as perfect as her own. Rachel's black hair and gray-blue eyes are perfectly sculpted to illuminate her already stunning beauty. Breaking the shock of the moment, Rachel pulls Beth in, closing the door.

"Oh, my goodness! You look beautiful! Did you have a stylist too?" Rachel turns her around to examine her hair.

Beth replies, "Yes! I can't believe what they did to me. It doesn't look like me. I don't even recognize myself."

Rachel gets Beth to spin. "You have the perfect build for this gown."

Beth tells Rachel how gorgeous she looks. They are giggling with excitement when there's a rap on the door. Rachel opens it to discover both Frederick and Joshua are there to usher them downstairs. Stacy is there with a small purse for Beth, and Rachel grabs hers from the bed. They take the arms of their escorts and begin their evening. There's excitement in the air.

Guests are already gathered in the ballroom. It's as if they're late, but the guests take no notice of their arrival. They observe in silence as others mingle. Pulling on the arm of another, a woman both had interviewed earlier approaches their table. She introduces an acquaintance with her, pointing out what Rachel and Beth do for a living. She explains their presence at the estate.

After a brief exchange of pleasantries, she hurries on, while others promptly follow. Both make comments back and forth about the exquisite gowns. Requests for dances later from gentlemen are plentiful.

Noticing the crowd merging in one direction, Rachel and Beth follow. They are seated for dinner and the feast begins. The meal is delicious. Beth turns the food over with her fork, deciding not to overindulge with the tight clothing. Taking small bites, she concludes she should get something in her stomach before alcohol.

The music begins just after dinner. The evening starts with a low volume, then becomes louder as the night moves on. Mrs. Vanders is the first on the floor for a dance with a dashing gentleman. Her husband had passed two years ago, so Beth knew this was not her husband. She watches intently for intimacy between them. Mrs. Vanders is caught up in the luxurious waltz rather than her partner. Beth finds it remarkable that this woman has pancreatic cancer and can still move around the floor as if she is in perfect health.

Beth and Rachel move to one of the standing tables. The first person to join them is Grayson Vanders. Feeling uncomfortable, Beth looks at the floor. Instead of approaching her, he maneuvers to Rachel. Rachel had not interviewed him yet, so she didn't know who he was. Just then, a gentleman approaches and asks Beth to dance.

Relieved by an interruption, she places her hand in his as he walks her to the crowded floor. Staying away from Grayson seems like a splendid plan to Beth until she gets over their earlier unfortunate encounter. Once on the floor, she and her partner dance to a slow melody that calms her nerves.

As she returns to the table, Rachel grabs Beth's arm and asks, "Do you know who that is?" Before Beth could respond, she states, "Grayson Vanders."

Deciding she should react, she replies, "Yes. He's the son of James and Erica Vanders."

"Yes!"

Beth watches Grayson mingling with others. She grudgingly admits that he's incredibly handsome! Depicting admiration for him for Rachel's benefit, she states, "He's gorgeous."

Rachel replies, "Yes, he is! I felt like a fish out of water again with that sophisticated, exquisite man!"

"He was certainly in to you. He was holding you tight and gazing intently as you danced." Beth tries to display enthusiasm for the match, but her thoughts only return to his arrogance.

Rachel, still mesmerized by him, says, "He did Beth, and he smells wonderful! I love his cologne."

Both girls giggle.

Rachel admits, "He is way out of my league, though. I could never travel in his circles."

Beth replies, humorously, "Hey, miracles happen. Just ask Cinderella."

Rachel laughs. "What about you? I noticed you were dancing. Did you meet anyone that appeals to you?"

Beth looks at the crowd. The one she would be interested in is in the arms of another. She nods toward him exclaiming, "He's a fine specimen." They chuckle.

Their table is frequently visited during the night. Lots of laughter and conversations are happening at once. Beth notices Grayson has planted himself beside Rachel. She can tell there's genuine interest there.

Noticing older couples departing, Rachel calls it a night. Beth follows her lead. As they are delivering their good nights, Grayson pulls out his cell phone to ask for Rachel's number. She shares it, clarifying that he could not contact her during her assignment. He concedes to her terms, entering her number.

As Beth announces their departure, Alex, Grayson's brother, asks if she can remain for a while. "I'd like to get your number."

Witnessing Rachel giving hers to Grayson, she thinks, why not? At first, she's let down with the lack of attention during the night. But by the night's end, he has made his presence known to the point of pushing other guys away to seize possession of her time. He's handsome, so she's enthralled with his interest. Once she shares her number, he asks her to take a walk. She declines politely, taking Rachel's initiative to retire. Disappointment becomes evident on his face, but he refrains from insisting.

Entering her room, Beth takes one last glimpse of herself in the mirror. Hating it's the end of Cinderella, she removes the gorgeous gown. She climbs into the shower, hating to scrub away the perfectly applied makeup. As she crawls into bed, she realizes that the rich and famous couldn't care less what day of the week it is. It's almost midnight, and tomorrow will be another hectic day. Despite the long day ahead, she falls asleep with a smile on her lips. It was a lovely evening.

CHAPTER 5

SEEING A PATH LESS TRAVELED

Stirring the next morning, Beth is surprised at her excitement over giving Alex her number. However, he's remarkably handsome and rich, so it's understandable. Both of these qualities have always made her suspicious. Attending Yale, avoiding the elite, she wonders now if she hadn't been a little prejudiced back at school.

Just because someone possesses money, doesn't mean they lack empathy or manners. Wealth doesn't systematically make you a spoiled brat. Alex was unusually attentive during the last part of the evening. She could picture this leading somewhere if she breaks down her barriers and lets it happen.

Unable to contain her giddiness, she dresses quickly and bolts to Rachel's room. Who better to share her joy than Rachel, who is also courted by a rich eligible bachelor? Knocking on Rachel's door, she pauses, then hears, "Come in."

Beth rushes in. Closing the door behind her, she jumps on Rachel's bed, squealing happily. She considers her actions and reflects, "What has gotten into me?"

Propping her pillow against the headboard, Rachel says, "You don't have to tell me you're happy."

Beth laughs. "I had an amazing time last night. I've never been to such a formal event."

"Me, either. Considering the décor, plus the estimate of those attending, it had to cost a fortune. Yet, they functioned as though it was an average evening."

Swooning, Beth replies, "I could learn to embrace this lifestyle."

Rachel responds, forcing them back to reality. "We shouldn't write as if we're outsiders. The article should read from the family's perspective. Our audience needs to understand their world.

"You're right," Beth says, suppressing her enthusiasm a bit.

Rachel asks, "Beth, did you share your number with any of the guy's last night?"

"Yes, I gave it to Alex."

"I did too. I urge you not to see him until after the two weeks are up. It may not bode well if we mingle with our subjects beyond our professional investigations."

Beth agrees. Coming to her senses, she acknowledges, "I'm glad you're here to keep my feet on the ground. I may have messed up royally. I was assuming it was an inside track."

"No. I suspect Mrs. Vanders would be extremely unhappy with us."

"You're right." Beth shrugs with disappointment. She knows turning down the date means calling the whole thing off. Relaying that, she asserts, "He may never call after that."

"Then he doesn't respect your profession and isn't worthy of your time."

Beth pulls her thoughts together and acknowledges, "You're right. Well, if I'm writing this book, I should begin the summation of its content. We only have two weeks, so I have plenty to accomplish between now and then.

Returning to her room, she closes her door and walks over to her desk. She commences by searching through all the photographs. However, a brief tap on the door interrupts her thoughts. She opens it to find Stacy with a tray of food.

"Miss, you didn't arrive for breakfast this morning, so I thought I would bring it to your room."

Backing up to let her in, she thanks her. "You're too good to me, Stacy. I wish I could take you home with me."

Stacy smiles as she sets the tray on the edge of the desk. "Will there be anything else, Miss?"

"No thank you Stacy, this is more than enough." Lifting the cover over the food she adds, "In fact, I won't be attending lunch today either. I'll only attend dinner."

"Are you certain, Miss? Would you prefer your lunch served here as well?"

"Honestly, Stacy, I rarely eat this much. Being a light eater, I feel like we're constantly going to meals. I'll be a horse by the time this assignment ends."

Stacy laughs. "I understand. I could request a diet of your choice if you like."

"No, I'm good. Thank you, though. I appreciate all you do for me."

Stacy nods and smiles. "Please let me know if you need anything."

Thinking over her day's plans, she adds, "I'll need assistance with my attire for dinner. Any recommendations?"

"I'll return an hour before dinner to assist."

Smiling, at Stacy, she responds, "That's perfect. Thank you!"

Getting back to her books, she devotes the day to unearthing the family history and to identify who's who. Adding her notes from interviews, she gets to know each person on an individual level. Grouping and dissecting relationships is part of the fun for Beth.

Around two, her eyes begin to burn. Rubbing her eyelids, she trudges to the bed to relax for a bit. Falling fast asleep, she encounters a strange dream. She's standing on the veranda outside. There's a heavy mist in the air. She spots a figure advancing toward her. She assumes it's Alex. As the figure gets closer, she still can't make out who it is. The person suddenly seizes her and begins kissing her.

At first, she's stunned. His lips search hers, exploring and intensifying. She succumbs to his advances when his tongue searches hers. Passion explodes in her, and she pulls him closer, folding her arms around his neck. The kiss is full of sexual tension and ignites a fire in her. He dramatically pulls away and steps back. To her horror, it's Grayson Vanders!

Startled enough to wake up, she finds her heart thumping in her chest. She's delirious and disoriented. What just happened? Why the hell would she dream of Grayson Vanders for heaven's sake? Feeling a surge of confusion, she stays in bed, trying to calm herself. She doesn't understand why she would have this dream. She loathes him. He's not her type. No way, no how!

No longer able to tolerate her thoughts of Grayson Vanders, she gets up and washes her face, then runs the brush through her hair. Unable to comprehend or capitulate to the dream, she turns to work to erase the image from her mind. Diving back into her studies, the research of the Vanders continues. She steers clear of the topic of Grayson Vanders!

At dinner, she's tired. Reading all day, sorting facts, and doing deep analysis can be exhausting. She puts the research out of her mind for tonight and concentrates on relaxing with some wine. Taking the glass from the tray, she glances to see Alex approaching.

"Good evening, Beth. How are you?"

She replies, "Honestly, I'm exhausted. I started early this morning with my research and didn't stop until right before dinner."

"You look beautiful."

Smiling, she responds, "Thank you, Alex."

He asks, "Do you think you could find some time after dinner to have a drink with me privately?"

Cautioning herself, she recalls Rachel's advice on not associating until after the assignment. She answers, "I don't know if that would be wise, Alex. I'm still working for Mrs. Vanders."

"Just for a brief drink?"

"Well, I guess that couldn't hurt."

He kisses her on the cheek and says, "Good. I'll catch you after dessert." He leaves to take his place at the table.

Rachel approaches, smiling at both of them as Alex leaves. Giving her a hug, they both turn to be seated. Mrs. Vanders is in her customary spot at the head of the table. After a moment, Beth glances at Rachel. Instead of being her chatty self, she has scarcely uttered a sound. She can see something is wrong. "Rachel, are you okay? You haven't said a word." She sees hesitation in Rachel's answer.

"I've had a long day of research. I'm a little fatigued and out of sorts. I think I'll make it an early night."

"Okay, I hope you feel better. I'm meeting Alex after dinner."

With a look of admonition, Rachel says, "That's not a good idea, Beth. You don't have that long here. I would concentrate on the article. Don't get drawn into some exciting romance that may not last, or undo what you are attempting to do here. You can meet him after the two weeks are up."

"That's precisely why I'm meeting him tonight. I want to explain that to him. I need to focus on my writing. After that, we can see where it leads."

Rachel asks the legitimate question, "You couldn't just tell him here?"

"I don't want anyone to overhear us, so we need a more private setting." Beth feels Rachel is being overcritical, but continues to listen.

"Okay, but I would make it brief. Sorry, I realize I'm giving advice you probably don't need or want, but I like you and I want you to get this book deal. What we do here these two weeks will influence our future."

Knowing Rachel is right, she replies, "Got it. Thanks."

Rachel expresses a grin. Changing the subject, they assess their findings of the day to compare notes during the remainder of dinner. Beth can still detect something is not right with Rachel. She appears unfocused and not herself at all. When they move to leave, Rachel excuses herself, using complaints of exhaustion. Giving her a brief hug, she notices Alex motioning for her. As she walks away, Mrs. Vanders approaches Rachel. Beth takes this opportunity to slip away.

Alex leads her out to the veranda. She takes in a deep breath. The night air is crisp and clean. It's 72 degrees, a cozy temperature for outdoor lounging. He motions for her to sit on the outdoor sofa. As soon as they are seated, the staff places drinks on the outdoor bar. Alex excuses himself and retrieves the glasses. To her surprise, it's precisely what she drinks. She looks at Alex and inquires, "How do they know what I want to drink?"

"The staff observes and makes notes on the parties that dine here."

"What if I don't want what I had at dinner?"

"Then you tell them what you desire, and they get it."

Beth doesn't want to sound unaware of how the wealthy live, so she attempts to make a joke. "Well, I suppose I could drink both."

Alex laughs.

"I mean, I wouldn't want it to go to waste or anything."

"You're adorable, Beth."

Adorable. She ponders that remark in her head and decides she will take it as a compliment and not let her insecurities get the best of her. Does adorable mean, naïve? She replies, "Thank you."

"I'm glad you could break away to spend some time with me," he pauses, then adds, "I would like to spend a lot more time with you, Beth."

Instead of feeling the butterflies in her stomach, Alex's words are not sitting well with her. She isn't sure if it is his tone or the manner of saying it that troubles her. He sounds too available, and his words lack sincerity. "Thank you, Alex. As I mentioned before, I'm not available until after this assignment is over."

Clear frustration is displayed on his face. He counters, "What does your assignment have to do with us spending time together?"

"I'm here for business. This is a remarkable opportunity for me, I won't do anything to jeopardize it. I'm here to do a job, not date one of the family members."

Grudgingly agreeing, he concedes. "I get it, but I can defend us if needed."

"No, Alex. I am committed to my work. If you still want to see me after I complete this job, then call me."

He can see she is not backing down on her decision. "Whatever is best," he says sullenly, taking a last swig of his drink. "Well, be sure to let me know when the assignment is over." Getting up, he says, "Good night then."

She is somewhat taken aback by his childish response. She watches him as he turns to walk away. As a spoiled little rich boy who didn't get his way, he doesn't look so attractive. Her interest in him died in that moment.

CHAPTER 6

FACT OR FICTION

The next morning, Beth wakes up feeling rejuvenated. She pulls on her workout clothes and jogging shoes, preparing for a run around the grounds. The physical exertion feels incredible. With beads of sweat running down her face from her demanding run, she returns to her room and sprints to the shower. Dressing, she leaves for the veranda, where breakfast is being served. Rachel is already there.

She glances at Rachel and discovers she looks better today. With a smile on her face, she is back to her old self. They discuss the enormous amount of food being served every day. Laughing, they agree that by the time they leave, both will have gained ten pounds. Rachel admits she's been declining meals because it's just too much.

Rachel has a ton of news to share with Beth. The two agree that sharing notes is a good thing. Both want to tell the same story with little variance in detail. "What we write about the family should match. Whatever spin each version has on the info can be writer specific," Beth suggests, and Rachel agrees. Beth is impressed with what Rachel has uncovered and responds, "I didn't know that. That's good!"

As they leave breakfast, they decide to work together to examine all of their notes. Rachel has scheduled interviews tomorrow with various members to get their perspectives on the hierarchy of the family. Who does what, and who is the driving force of their wealth? While reviewing their notes they consider the questions they want to ask each member. This will allow each person to boast of their connections in the family line. They agree to meet in the library in half an hour.

It's entertaining to learn other's perspective as we go through one another's information. It sparks a new point of view and brings up different questions to research. Both agree that with each adaptation, they enhance their probability of publishing.

The door opens and Stacy enters with a rolling cart of food. "Excuse me ladies, I noticed that neither of you attended lunch or dinner. I thought I would bring your dinner here."

Both stare at each other, then at the clock. They burst into laughter. Beth says, "Oh my! Did we miss two meals? Where did the day go?"

Rachel gets up and thanks Stacy while removing the lid on the tray. The aroma permeates through the room. Rachel says, "I'm starving!"

Both grab plates, filling them with the glorious pasta dripping with red sauce, meat and cheese. The garlic bread was just the added calories they didn't need, but each grabbed one anyway.

Beth says, "How did they know I'm addicted to pasta?"

Rachel laughs as she retorts, "They know everything! By now they know what you drink, what size clothes you wear and, I venture, they even know your bra size."

Beth, being facetious, asks, "What bra?" They howl!

The next day over breakfast, Rachel suggests that Beth should attend her interviews. They deliberate the fact that she has none scheduled. Interviewing together would serve them well. Beth jumps on board with the idea.

To her bewilderment, Rachel changes some facts they had previously uncovered last night. "I'm confused. Did you go back to the room to research after we retired last night?"

Rachel replies, "Certain things troubled me about Chad Grayson's history. What we missed in the grand story is the degree of involvement the Grayson's had in the Vanders' financial successes. They were wealthy in their own right."

Pondering that view, Beth agrees. They walk into the room where the interviews begin.

At first, Beth sits quietly taking notes. As time progresses, she adds questions when Rachel pauses. At a point, they are feeding off of each other getting into more details from each interview. Each time one would come up with a great question, it inspires another major question from the other.

In the end, Rachel asserts, "Beth, you are an excellent interviewer. I can't wait to read your book."

"Thanks. So are you! For each question you proposed, I had to cross one off my list. We think alike. If I don't get this book deal, I may consider doing an unauthorized biography."

Rachel assures Beth that it's a done deal. Having seen Beth's research, Rachel is sure there's no way Beth won't get the assignment. Plus, Beth's personality is compelling.

"I think Mrs. Vanders will have a sense of confidence in you, just as I do."

That evening at dinner, the two continue to discuss the interviews and their points of view on who were the genuine leaders of the Vanders. Both arrive at the same consensus that Mrs. Vanders makes all the vital decisions. The fascinating fact is that, no one seems to object. All have the greatest respect for her and relay their concerns regarding her illness. Everyone hopes that she can beat it, quoting she's a tough lady.

It doesn't go unnoticed by Beth that Alex is a little chilly toward her this evening. Those actions only reinforce her resolution not to see him after the assignment. The adage 'looks are skin deep' definitely lend merit in this situation. He is handsome, but his charm stops there. The evidence of his greatness is fiction in her view. He is more like Grayson than she first assumed.

Rachel says goodnight promptly after dinner. Feeling wired from the exciting day of interviews, Beth decides to go to the veranda for an after-dinner drink. Walking to the bar, she requests her customary glass of red wine and takes a seat on the edge of the veranda that overlooks the estate and river. She leans back in the chair, laying her head comfortably on the headrest. In a trance of peacefulness, she's startled by a voice that comes out of the darkness.

"Hello, Beth."

She jumps slightly, shifting to see Grayson Vanders. "Oh, hello."

He reaches down and touches her shoulder, "I'm so sorry. I didn't mean to startle you."

Trying to calm herself, she shrugs her shoulders. "Oh, that's okay. I was just appreciating the serenity of the night." She privately hopes he is not about to ruin it.

"Do you mind if I sit with you?" He nods his head toward the seat beside her.

She points to it and says, "Help yourself."

As he sits beside her, he's close enough that she can smell his cologne. It smells manly, awakening her senses to his presence. The dream of him kissing her comes to mind. She begins feeling awkward, finding it challenging to think of something to say. She remains silent, waiting for him to start the conversation.

He peers at her and ponders her thoughts. He begins, "You know, I realize we may have gotten off on the wrong foot."

Trying to play coy, she responds, "Oh? Why do you say that? I think we perfectly understood each other."

Seeing she's not going to let this be easy, he continues, "I may have come off a little harsh during our interview. It's just that I'm protective of my family, knowing not everyone does or says things in our best interest. Many go for scandal rather than highlighting the hard work it requires to be what we are today."

"To begin with, if I get to pen this book, it will be Mrs. Vanders who reads, approves and authorizes its content."

Smiling, sheepishly, he adds, "Yes, and that is why I'm trying to apologize. It was not my place to make the remarks."

She comes back, "You're right." She sips her wine while looking over the edge of her glass.

He asks, "What is it about me that rubs you the wrong way?"

"Let's just say you're correct. You didn't provide a great first impression. I'm a writer and it was insulting for you to tell me how to conduct my career."

He leans very close to her face and studies her intently. "Tell me how can I make amends?"

"Just let me do my article without judgment that I am less than you. You nor your family can make or break me."

Stunned by her sharp tongue, he lays his hand over hers, "I'm very sorry if I gave you that impression."

His touch causes her to think back to the dream. She looks at him and for a moment feels the attraction she had in her dream. She nervously jumps up and states, "Well, it's late. I have an early day tomorrow. Let's just forget our initial encounter and start fresh. Good night, Grayson" She scurries away before he could acknowledge. As she rushes up the staircase, she ponders his apology. Was it fact or fiction? Was he truly sorry?

CHAPTER 7

THE DEPTH OF REALITY

The next evening at dinner Beth can see Rachel has something on her mind again. She notices Rachel staring in mid-air with a dazed look on her face. "What's up Rachel? What's going on with you?"

Rachel pulls herself out of it, then replies, "Nothing." She continues with, "Oh, I sent my article to Mrs. Vanders earlier today."

Beth is surprised. "You did? That's great. I didn't know you were that close to finishing."

"I went with my gut. If I keep it, I will go on and on with edits. Sometimes I tend to spoil my stories if I change too much. I felt it was time to get her perspective. We don't have that much time left. I wanted to have the time to correct it if she isn't happy with it."

Beth thinks over the idea then says, "I get that. That actually may be a good move. Do you think after a day or so, I could give her what I have?"

"Sure. I don't know why not? I've read portions of it. Your writing is captivating. You drew me into the story right away."

"Great. I think I will go up tonight and add some last-minute details. I'll give her time to absorb your article, then I'll give her mine."

Moving to the veranda, they lounge on the long sofa. Rachel says, "Did you notice Mrs. Vanders didn't come to dinner tonight?"

Beth replies, "I noticed. Maybe she is so engrossed with your article that she can't put it down."

"That, or too annoyed to look at me to tell me it sucks!"

"You don't believe that any more than I do."

"I know. I'm just nervous about it."

As they are making their way to their room, they run into Frederick. Rachel pulls him aside to ask, "Frederick, is Mrs. Vanders not feeling well this evening?"

"Quite the contrary! She requested dinner in her room tonight to read your article. She was eager to get started on it."

"Oh, I see. Well, I hope she provides some feedback for me. I welcome her reaction."

He offers her confirmation. "Rachel, you can be confident she will let you know her thoughts."

"Thank you, Frederick. Good night."

Walking back to Beth, Rachel turns to go to the veranda. Passing the bar, she motions for another round.

Once seated, Alex approaches. "Good evening, ladies."

Rachel is wired now and is the first to respond, "Good evening, Alex."

Without asking to join them, he seats himself beside Beth. Beth is cautiously friendly. Grayson arrives as well, adding to the group. He asks if he can join them, motioning to the seat beside Rachel.

He sits as the server places a drink in front of him. Beth notices the server doesn't inquire, but simply places the tall glass without hesitation. Gosh, they are so spoiled. However, she notices Grayson politely thanks him. He looks at Rachel and says, "I was counting on you still being around. I didn't come to the last function, so I wasn't certain I would see you again, at least not here. I still have plans to contact you once you leave."

Rachel replies, "I wrapped up my first draft today and gave it to Mrs. Vanders for review. If she approves, I will leave by the end of the week."

He offers her a petulant face and says, "Not before we've discussed plans, I'm sure."

She smiles in response, but doesn't bother initiating the plan.

It doesn't take Beth long to notice the change in Rachel's demeanor towards Grayson. Rachel simply doesn't seem excited about his presence anymore. She has always been clear about having nothing between them until she leaves, but this is more than that. Watching Grayson's face, she can tell he has noticed too, but seems intrigued instead of disillusioned

He feeds her some bullshit. "You're unique, Rachel. You're mysterious. Something in short supply around here."

Beth is more interested in listening to their conversation than conversing with Alex. She overhears Rachel say, "I'm here to do an article. I'm not here trying to snare a husband." Rachel hesitates then says, "I'm sorry. Maybe that was a little harsh."

"No, no. Your frankness is refreshing."

Luckily for Beth, another gentleman has joined the table, taking the chair across from them. Now, she can listen to Rachel and Grayson without anyone noticing.

"Poor Grayson, Beth thinks. "Last night, I put him in his place, and now Rachel has served him again." She almost feels sorry for him, but it doesn't look like he cares that much. If he does, he hides it well. She suspects he considers Rachel a challenge he will ultimately win.

The next morning, Beth gets a quick call from Rachel saying Mrs. Vanders has requested that Rachel join her for breakfast. Nervous and excited, she says to Beth, "Wish me luck."

"Good luck, Rachel! Come to my room the minute you leave her. I want to know what she thinks." They hang up the phone, and Beth waits with anticipation. It's hours before Rachel gets back to her.

With relief and euphoria, Rachel taps on Beth's door. Beth opens it within seconds. She grabs Rachel by the arm and says, "Get in here! I've been dying to hear."

They sit on Beth's bed. Rachel pulls out the manuscript and shows her the notes Mrs. Vanders made. With exhilaration, she says, "She loves it! She said she didn't want to change anything in the storyline. Just some simple notes and additions that would round it out in details."

Beth is feeling a little jealous that Rachel has gotten through the hard part, and she hasn't. It makes her a bit skittish about her own work. She confides this to Rachel, who replies, "Beth, you're a better writer than me! She will love your work." None-the-less, Beth is happy Mrs. Vanders likes it because she cares about Rachel. Moreover, they have composed the same general story with different approaches, which means it is highly likely that Mrs. Vanders would like her work as well.

Rachel confesses, "You may be mad at me, but I told Mrs. Vanders that you would do a tremendous job sharing the warmth that lies beneath in the book. I shared your insight, and that you have asked all the right questions. Your strength lies in perceiving things from various angles and being able to document those in beautiful words. I told her you should tell the Vanders story, especially her story."

Beth is speechless. "Rachel, why would you put yourself out there like that?"

Sincerity crosses Rachel's face. "Beth, you have become a dear friend to me. I am proud of our work and will support you no matter what. Your work is authentic and special. No one can deny that I have no fear in upholding my view of that."

Beth gets up and hugs her. Feeling her eyes well up with tears, she says hoarsely, "Rachel, thank you so much for that. It means everything."

Rachel replies, "Beth, there's more." She draws back and says, "You need to sit back down for this."

Beth worries. "Okay. What's going on, Rachel?"

"Beth, just hear me out. What I am about to reveal to you will sound crazy! I expect you to say you don't believe me, but because I consider you a dear friend, I need to tell you!"

Beth sits, allowing Rachel to begin a story that is so out there, she stays silent until the end.

Rachel begins. "When we first came here, Mrs. Carlyle gave us permission to roam the estate. I became intrigued by the portrait of the woman that looked like me. I wandered to the third floor, where I found a room filled with old clothes. I looked around, and in an old bureau, I found the dress that Adrianna had on in the portrait. It's in pristine condition. I was unable to stop myself, so I put it on. There's a standing mirror in the room. I walked in front of it, and I saw the image of Adrianna I looked exactly like her, Beth! I began dancing around like I was at a ball. When I twirled around, everything went black."

Rachel stops and gazes at Beth. "Go on. I'm listening." Beth encourages her to continue.

"When I came to, I was back in 1914."

Beth screams, "What?!"

Rachel begins walking around the room. She tells Beth that when she awoke, instead of being in that room, she was in a hotel in Virginia. "I had just pulled myself off the floor when Chelsea, my assistant, came in the door, calling me Adrianna."

"Sorry, what?!"

"She was pushing me to finish getting ready. I didn't know what to do, so I followed suit. Once ready, they pushed me outside to a carriage where my mother and father were waiting for me. It was Christmas, and we were headed toward a gala. Adrianna's parents couldn't tell that I was not their daughter. I was afraid to admit it myself. They might think I'm insane, or worse yet, that I must have hurt the real Adrianna."

She pauses and looks at Beth. Beth just stares with her mouth agape. "Go on."

"At the gala, I met Chad Grayson. Oh, Beth, he is so handsome. He's a better-looking version of Grayson Vanders." She stops speaking, as she thinks of Chad and swoons.

Continuing, "Anyway, that first night, I met Grayson and Adrianna's best friend, Celeste. No one knew I wasn't Adrianna. I must be a brilliant actress because I pulled it off. After that night, I went back to New York, on a train, mind you. Not an airplane! It was the longest trip." She pauses and looks at me. "You still with me, Beth?"

Unable to utter a word, Beth nods.

"Beth, I have been back and forth to the past many times. Do you want to hear something shocking? I'm engaged to Chad Grayson."

Beth couldn't take it anymore. "What?! Rachel, what the hell are you talking about? This doesn't make sense. Let me get this straight. You are engaged to a man that has been dead for what, 40 years?"

Rachel sees Beth panicking and tries to calm her. Grabbing Beth's hand, she says, "I know it sounds absurd, but I'm telling you the truth, Beth." She tells her everything that has transpired during her visits to the past.

"Beth, please put on your writer's hat and examine this from every angle. I needed to tell you. You are the best at rationalization. Help me through this. I must decide whether to go back permanently to be Chad Grayson's wife, or stay here."

Moving her mindset to the plausibility of this whole phenomenon, Beth asks, "What do you want? Do you want to go back?"

She replies without hesitation. "Yes. Beth, life with Chad overrides any life that I have here. I really love him. My parents died in a car accident five years ago. I have no family here. I have nothing to lose."

Beth says, "What about your job?"

"You're right. I need to be respectful and give my notice there." She makes a list of things she needs to do. "I need to end my lease. Mrs. Vanders' payment will take care of anything I have here. I have no dating life whatsoever, so nothing to wrap up there."

Beth could see that Rachel has no ambiguity about the past being her future. "Wow, Beth. I just realized my life here sucks! I can wrap up my life in a matter of hours and no one would notice I'm missing."

Beth reminds her of Grayson Vanders. "He's clearly interested."

Rachel replies, "I could never feel for him as I do for Chad Grayson. The resemblances are evident in their physical appearance, but there is something about Chad that would always override my heart for Grayson Vanders."

Beth says, "I get that. Once you gave your heart to Chad, Grayson had no chance."

Rachel states, "Don't get me wrong, Grayson Vanders is a catch. I think any woman who grabs the heart of that handsome man is lucky. I think Mrs. Vanders has kept the family on the straight and narrow. He has good values and has been trusted with many Vander businesses. He is a success story in his own right. I just happen to love a certain lawyer who is over a hundred years old."

They both laugh at the absurdity of the statement.

"I can't believe you're able to go to the past. I keep trying to picture it, but it escapes my common sense to do so. You are asking me to imagine the impossible. Maybe I need to take some creative writing courses to remove myself from factual writing into a world of what-ifs."

"Beth, I strolled down the streets in 1914, and I still can't believe it. How can I expect you to believe it? I feel as if any minute I'll wake up from a dream to discover I have imagined all of this. All I know at this moment is, I belong to Chad Grayson, so 1914, it is!"

Beth and Rachel go to the room where it all happens. She shows her the dress she dons and the mirror she twirls in front of. Beth asks, "Do you think any other dresses would work?"

Rachel thinks it over before replying, "Honestly, I wouldn't want to take the chance of ending up in the wrong place. This dress is the one that always takes me to Chad."

"Okay, thinking this through analytically, I would love to witness it, but I wouldn't want to disturb your travel in any way. My being in this room when you leave may interrupt something. Let's record it. We'll set up a camera in the room and watch it after you leave."

Rachel agrees with that plan.

"Rachel, does Mrs. Vanders know about all of this?"

"Yes. She told me Adrianna came here years ago. She was aware of time travel."

"This is insane!" Beth blurts out.

Rachel replies, "I know Beth, but you have to be there."

Beth replies, "What is real anymore? After this, I'll be damned if I know."

Rachel smiles and contentedly says, "I know."

CHAPTER 8

THE TRUTH

Beth leaves the room feeling confused and thoughtful. One moment she thinks Rachel has lost her mind. The next, she feels jealous that Rachel has found a love that surpasses time. How romantic! Her life feels mundane and boring in comparison.

Later that morning, Rachel leaves to give her notice at the magazine. It's also a big day for Beth. She finally gathers the courage to submit her article to Mrs. Vanders. She knows her piece possesses a different twist than the one Rachel submitted, so she prepares herself for any outcome.

Finding Frederick, she asks him to deliver it to Mrs. Vanders and to tell her it's the first draft.

He nods his head slightly, then heads toward Mrs. Vanders' suites.

Taking a deep breath, Beth tries to exhale the tension from her body. It doesn't work!

When Rachel returns, she decides she wants to let Mrs. Vanders know their plans to record her disappearance from the room. They gather to discuss it. Rachel plans it down to the minute. Heeding Beth's advice, she has decided to go back to determine if Chad Grayson is truly her destiny.

Pulling a plan together, Rachel suggests that an old paper and pen in the antique desk may help Beth and Mrs. Vanders communicate after she travels back in time. Beth agrees, "It's worth a shot."

Rachel plans on putting those items inside the desk when she returns to 1914. They've established that part of the plan will work, noting it may exist in the desk for years waiting to be discovered. However, for them, it'll only be a day.

They set the camera in the room upstairs. Rachel, Beth, and Mrs. Vanders discuss all scenarios. If they never hear from her again, that signifies her capacity to travel back and forth in time is over. If the letters inside the desk doesn't cross over time, they will never know what happened.

Rachel hugs Beth and Mrs. Vanders before they leave the room. All points examined, Rachel puts on Adrianna's gown and stands in front of the mirror. Twirling, she blacks out and vanishes.

Beth and Mrs. Vanders wait for an hour before entering the room. Finding it empty, they grab the camera and take it downstairs. Beth inserts the chip into her laptop, hitting play. She sees Rachel disappear into thin air. It's as if she dissolves into fragments before her eyes as she disintegrates. It's unnerving to watch. Beth gets up and paces the floor. "Oh my God! I can't believe what I just witnessed."

Turning to Mrs. Vanders, she asks, "Can you believe that?"

Mrs. Vanders smiles. "I can believe that. Beth, I need to share something with you."

Beth takes a seat across from Mrs. Vanders, considerably concerned with her seriousness.

Mrs. Vanders says, "You will need to record this conversation. The impact will provoke you to overlook some details I'm about to reveal."

Pressing record on her laptop, she sets up the camera again, arranging it on the coffee table between them. Still witnessing the solemn look on Mrs. Vanders' face, she instructs, "Okay, continue."

Mrs. Vanders begins slowly. "At Rachel's age, I was terribly unhappy with life. I concluded the course I was on was a disappointment."

Beth asks, "The same restless emotions Rachel has had with her life?"

"Yes, precisely." She continues. "I was bored. After observing my best friend find love, it set me on a course of dissatisfaction with my life. I began retreating from activities and events that were normally exciting for a debutant of my age. Eventually, I left for Europe, hoping I would discover a life there that would satisfy me. Unfortunately, that would not be the case. When I returned, miserable and disheartened, I discovered the area upstairs."

She looks at Beth and nods, confirming it's the same room that Rachel found to enter the past. Continuing, she adds, "I discovered an unfamiliar pen in a desk and read ramblings that made no sense to me. The letters were all about my life and marriage to Chad Grayson." She pauses, expecting a reaction from Beth.

When Mrs. Vanders pauses, her facial expression signals Beth is missing something. Rerunning her words in her mind, it clicks. "Oh, my God! Are you Rachel in the future?" It was the only thing that made sense.

Recognizing that Beth doesn't quite get it yet, she proceeds. "I read what had happened to Rachel in this room. I saw the future clothes laying on a chair. The concept that perplexed me was that it had not yet happened based on the dates she penned on the paper. It was to happen very soon, though. My curiosity got the best of me. I put on the future clothes and did exactly what Rachel said to do in the letters."

Beth asks, "So you have traveled to the past as well?"

Smiling, she answers, "No, I have traveled to the future."

Beth is becoming frustrated because she can see Mrs. Vanders believes she should be connecting something, but what?

"Maybe if I reveal my actual name, you'll understand." She hesitates, watching Beth's face. My real name is Adrianna Vanders "

Stunned, Beth is speechless. Not able to find words for what she just heard, she stammers, "What?"

Mrs. Vanders continues. "I'm Adrianna. When I put on the future clothes and turned in front of the mirror, I landed in the future. When I awoke, I believed nothing had happened. I put my clothes back on, and I left the room.

Feeling faint after reaching the second floor, I collapsed. I was roused by someone holding my hand. I gazed into the eyes of the most handsome man I had ever laid eyes on. Nathan Vanders, my husband, is the person who discovered me. Of course, Frederick knows, but that's all."

"Oh, my God. You're Adrianna!" Beth gets up and paces the floor. "But you told us about finding Adrianna years ago. Why did you lie about that?"

"I couldn't let Rachel know she would become Adrianna in the past. I didn't go back, so she had to. If Adrianna was not in the past, it would alter the future history of the Vanders. I had made my choice to stay when I came here years ago. I suspect that is why Rachel kept ending up in the same place and time as when she returned. That's when and where I left. Does this make sense?"

"Okay, let me track this back. Basically, you and Rachel have traded places in time. You arrived here, so it was crucial that she go back there." Looking wearily at Mrs. Vanders, she asks, "But wouldn't you be related to Nathan? How could you be together knowing that?"

"Very few people know this, but Nathan was adopted." Continuing, she answers the rest of Beth's questions. "Yes, I was hoping with great anticipation that Rachel would fall for Chad and thank God she did. You have no idea how elated I was when I saw Rachel for the first time in my dining room. I almost fainted. The reason the portrait of Adrianna looks so much like Rachel is that it actually is Rachel sitting for the picture."

Beth exclaims, "Holy Moly! But how did Rachel know to go to that room, to travel back to the past?"

"I offered subtle hints. Sharing the history of the estate, I revealed tales that a specific room could take you back in time. I told Rachel to roam the property at her own leisure, hoping she would discover it. I didn't know how much of a part I could play in pushing her to it without it affecting me. I was mindful not to provide direct information. It had to happen to her without my direct influence."

"Tell me about your life here. How did you explain your existence?"

Mrs. Vanders' face turns dreamy. "It was Nathan who managed it all. For a long time, he kept me a secret. His family was often away traveling, so it was simple to have me around. We exchanged stories about our lives and grew close. He fell in love with me, as I fell for him. The support staff just thought Nathan was sneaking a girl in, except for Frederick. Frederick misses nothing around here." She smiles. "Ultimately, after I was comfortable living in the future, we snuck out of the house and he brought me in one day as his girlfriend. His family was ecstatic that he had found someone polished and obviously well bred. We never told a soul about any of it."

Beth, still in awe, asserts, "So you fell in love with Nathan here, and Rachel has fallen in love with Chad there." It was not a question, but an observation. She prompts a suitable point, "But, what if Rachel had not fallen for Chad?"

"I was indeed torn about that. I knew Chad Grayson to be a womanizer. I wanted no part of him. But when Rachel informed me, after one of her returns, that she had fallen for him, I was relieved. I wanted to cry. Her nature, being from the future, considered him a challenge. In fact, she knew precisely how to put him in his place instantly. Her stories of their relationship almost made me like him. Chad was not for me. He was appropriate for her. My Nathan was my world, and I have no regrets."

Beth's career as author and editor had to know more. "What about your family? Did it sadden you to leave them?"

"I won't mislead you. I missed my father most of all. I returned to visit him once or twice. I justified my absence by taking a lot of trips. If you recall, Rachel arrived in the past right after one of my trips. In December of that year, my family whisked me off to attend a celebration in Virginia. That's when she first met Chad. If I recall accurately, I knew when she mentioned their meeting, it was the same day as when I had left.

I don't know how this time travel works. I thought we were in separate times opposite of each other, until she came to my home. The last thing I recall before waking up here in the future is being in the hotel room in Virginia. I have yet to determine how she could be here with me on each occasion she returns. I assumed we had to be in opposite times since we are the same person. I feel so close to Rachel. Staring at my own face peering back at me is, shall I say, disturbing?"

"But why didn't you tell Rachel who you are? It would have made sense to her why she needed to be in the past."

"I couldn't interfere with destiny. I wanted it to be her decision, her fate. Luckily for me, she embraced the past. She is so smitten with Chad Grayson. Again, I don't understand it, but when I analyze the portrait of them together, I see love. I don't think I could let this continue without witnessing that. I also needed to be certain she was okay with the strain of the trips." Mrs. Vanders pauses to think.

"One thing that started to develop with my trips back was that I began to be weaker on each return. Sometimes, when I would turn facing the mirror, it wouldn't work. It took me quite a few times that last time. I realized I couldn't take the chance, or I may not make it back to spend my life with Nathan."

Walking to the gallery, the two examine the portraits. "I was always apprehensive of them. I assumed it was me and that it destined me to return and leave Nathan. I despised those portraits for a long time. It was not until time went on and Nathan and I married that I found peace with them. I couldn't figure out how I could be there and here. I never sat for those paintings." She pauses, further reviewing her life. "Nathan and I never had children. We didn't know what cheating the past could cause to our offspring. I wish we had now. It was not until Rachel showed up that all the pieces fell into place. You will never understand the comfort I found in her presence. Never having children didn't bother Nathan. His devotion and love for me overshadowed all possible relationships I could have had in the past."

Beth sighs. "Destiny showed up at your front door."

Mrs. Vanders laughs. "That's why you're a great author. You have such a play on words. Speaking of that, we should talk about your book. Since you're in the fold now, of course I will authorize permission for the biography of the Vanders. You'll need to keep all of this out of it. I read your article and am particularly impressed with your vision and spin on our story. Are you onboard to do the book?" She waits for reassurance from Beth.

"Of course, I will do it. "Pausing, she adds, "Mrs. Vanders, I would never breathe a word about any of this. Who would believe me anyway?"

Mrs. Vanders laughs. "You have a point there. I would like to extend another opportunity to you."

Beth studies Mrs. Vanders face, and for the first time sees that she is truly Adrianna. How had she missed this before? She's an aged Adrianna, but the features are unmistakable. She asks, "What opportunity?"

"I would like to work with you on a fictional novel about Adrianna and Rachel, excluding the Vanders name of course."

Amazed, Beth has shock written all over her face. "You want this documented? I would speculate that's the last thing you would want."

"Again, this is a fictional novel. I would require you to publish it in another name, of course, so there would never be a connection. I'll see that the book is marketed and produced by a reputable publishing company. Not the one you are with now. Are you presently under an exclusive contract with your company?"

Beth is elated. Her excitement is overwhelming as she breathes in deeply. "No, I'm under no contract. In fact, if I didn't obtain this assignment, they alluded that my association with them may be over." Beth is astonished at the opportunity that has just landed at her feet. "You would do that for me, Mrs. Vanders? Get me a new publishing deal?"

"Yes, but I'm also doing this for me. As I leave this world, I need closure. I could never talk about this with anyone other than Nathan. Frederick and I agreed we would never mention it and never did until now. I want to record it, how it transpired, what became of all of us. If nothing else, it unquestionably confirms that there is such a thing as time travel. Unfortunately, only a few of us can validate this as fact."

"Do you think I could time travel, Mrs. Vanders?"

Mrs. Vanders hesitates with her response, but replies, "I have no idea. I would suppose if Rachel and I could, why couldn't you? I, however, don't know for certain. I know the clothing we both wore back and forth is gone. If Rachel ever returns, we could request that she put it in the room for you. I also can't determine if the connection between Rachel and myself gave us the capability. Only you making an attempt will answer that question."

Beth leaves Mrs. Vanders, dazed by all the information they shared. She climbs the stairs to reach the room. Walking around, she examines everything. She studies the mirror, the antique gowns, searching for clues to answer questions circling in her mind. She moves to the desk, recalling that Rachel said she would leave the pen and paper. She slowly opens the secret drawer. To her amazement, there's a note from Rachel. She opens it and reads.

CHAPTER 9

A CHANGED FUTURE

Finding the note is a surprise, but a welcome one. After what she has witnessed in the video, she couldn't imagine how Rachel could be okay. Unfolding the delicate paper, she draws a profound sigh of relief as she reads its content.

It informs them, "Beth and Mrs. Vanders, I've successfully made the trip. I thought I should write at once to find out if our experiment of communication will work. I'll be remaining in the past. One more return should tie up my life there. I want to marry Chad. We're genuinely in love. See you soon. Miss you, Rachel."

Beth races from the room to locate Mrs. Vanders.

Mrs. Vanders holds the note to her chest and weeps. "After years of speculation, I have answers of how my absence affected our history." To understand that Rachel will stay in the past to be Adrianna is heart-wrenching for her.

Rachel is taking over her identity as Adrianna. While this arrangement is best, she considers how Rachel will have her parents as her own, and that stings. She apologizes to Beth and excuses herself.

Beth understands how overwhelming this must be for her. She reacts, "Take all the time you need."

The next morning Beth is having breakfast alone when she spots Rachel entering the room. Excited to see her, she rushes to her and shrieks, "Rachel!" The two embrace and walk to the table together. The staff places a plate in front of Rachel. She selects a moderate amount of food, then faces Beth with a tortured expression. She's on the verge of tears.

Beth is eager to catch up with her. "Tell me what's happened. Why are you back so soon?"

Rachel pours out her story, emotions running high. "Beth, I told Chad everything. He looked at me as if I had lost my senses. At first, his silence gave me hope, but suddenly he announces he is concerned for my wellbeing. I knew it was over. I should never have put it out there as I did. It was too much at one time. I'm so heart broken."

"Stop now. Don't jump to conclusions. He may send you a note to come home."

"Beth, you wouldn't say that if you had seen the expression on his face. I honestly don't think he will."

Beth replies, "Rachel, there are details you're unaware of. Additional information has come to light that we weren't previously privy to."

"Like what?"

Beth searches the room for anyone that could overhear. "It's not my place to explain. Ask Frederick to let Mrs. Vanders know you're back."

Rachel is perplexed but says, "Okay. Honestly though, what could she say now that we haven't already discussed?"

"Well, perspectives have shifted. See her as soon as you can."

Leaving breakfast, they take a stroll around the grounds. They catch Frederick on their way out. Rachel asks him to let Mrs. Vanders know she's returned.

He nods and responds, "Yes, Miss."

Beth tells Rachel what it looked like when she traveled back. "It's as if you split into fragments. Piece by piece you vanished."

"Wow. Can I see it?"

Beth replies, "Sure, let's go."

They enter Beth's room. She pulls out her laptop and turns on the recorded event.

"My God, that's incredible. I understand now why all of my strength is zapped when I arrive."

Beth agrees with her assessment. A knock on the door interrupts their conversation further. Beth gets off the bed to answer.

It's Frederick. He looks at Rachel and announces, "Mrs. Vanders will see you now."

Beth returns to the bed and closes the lid on the laptop.

Rachel replies, "Thank you, Frederick. Where is she?"

"She's in the sitting-room."

Rachel glances at Beth and asks, "Catch you in a bit?"

"Sure. I'll be around."

Two hours later, Beth is summoned by Mrs. Vanders to come to the sitting-room. Arriving, she finds Mrs. Vanders perched on a chair gazing out the window. She motions for her to be seated. Both are facing the window. There's a small table between them.

Mrs. Vanders says, pointing to a glass on the table, "I took the liberty of ordering you iced tea."

"Thank you." Glass in hand, Beth takes a light sip.

Mrs. Vanders begins. "Beth, I presume Rachel has informed you of what has transpired with Chad. Am I correct in assuming that?"

"Yes, Mrs. Vanders. She's extremely upset with the way he accepted the news."

"It's a reasonable reaction. Time travel is not exactly an everyday event."

Beth asks, "Do you think Chad will contact her?"

Mrs. Vanders ponders the question for a bit. "It's complicated. My concern is, will he be able to, even if that is his desire. I realize we can communicate, but will he know how?"

"That's a good point."

After a few thoughtful moments, Mrs. Vanders turns to face Beth. "Let's discuss you for a minute. What are your intentions now that you have my endorsement for the book?"

"To be honest, I'm just taking one day at a time. Being here has provided a whole new perspective on my existence. Seeing you and Rachel living a destined life provokes me to ponder my own course in history and what I want to make of it."

Mrs. Vanders smiles. "Excellent, so while you are hypothesizing, your future, I wish to include other images to those visions."

"Okay, I'm listening."

"First, I've extended an offer to Rachel to move in with us here at the estate. I would like to expand that same offer to include you."

"What? Why would you do that, Mrs. Vanders?"

"I expect you already know why I would present it to Rachel. Beth, she is me in the past. We possess an attachment and depth that no one else could understand. It's as if I am helping myself when I support her."

"I get that, but why me? We have no connection at all."

"Beth, because of my situation, Nathan and I didn't have children. We were hesitant because we were tempting fate as it was. You and Rachel have become like daughters to me. There's a desire to make your dreams come true."

Beth is overwhelmed by the confession. "Mrs. Vanders, it means so much to hear you say that, but I want nothing from you. To know that you welcome me is gift enough."

Mrs. Vanders nods in understanding. "Hear me out. I've acquired your publishing company."

Beth gasps. "You did what?"

"Yes. I purchased it. I have already signed the documents. They're with my legal team to iron out the details and close the sale. It will be co-owned by you and Rachel."

Unable to speak, Beth just stares at her.

Mrs. Vanders laughs, then continues with her ideas. "Rachel can run the magazine portion of the business while you lead the book publishing side of it. You'll be responsible for editorial and publication offers, designating what to publish."

Again, Beth is at a loss for words. This is an enormous responsibility. She is wondering if she is indeed qualified?

Mrs. Vanders continues. "I will tap Grayson to control the financial aspects of the business. He has been tremendous in upstarts and has consistently built them into profitable ventures. He's a genius in finance, having led our banking division for years."

Hearing this gives Beth pause. "Oh, I'm not convinced that would be a good fit. To be honest, Grayson and I don't always see eye to eye."

"With the divisions separate, that shouldn't be an obstacle." She looks intently at Beth, wondering where all of these ambiguous feelings for Grayson are coming from. "It's fascinating that most women fall at his feet, but you haven't." Mrs. Vanders then declares, "Opposites attract."

Beth doesn't want to sound ungrateful for the opportunity, so she smiles and responds, "Of course, but there could never be an attraction there." Changing the subject, she asks, "What does Rachel think about this plan?"

Mrs. Vanders sees the value of the question. "She's confused right now on what her future entails. She has accepted my offer to move to the estate, and my business proposal, if you're on board. As mentioned, I would like you to move to the estate as well."

"Thank you, Mrs. Vanders. This is more than any girl could ever hope for. Of course, I accept."

Mrs. Vanders laughs. She asserts, "I can't wait to see what your publisher thinks of you being his boss."

Both laugh more than they should.

That evening, everyone retreats after dinner to the designated area for dancing. It's Friday, and indulging in a few more drinks than normal, seems to be the theme of the night. Beth and Rachel select a table far enough from the crowd to discuss their new venture. However, before they can get into details, Grayson Vanders approaches. Still not comfortable with him, Beth excuses herself to join Mrs. Vanders. Not long after she leaves, she sees Rachel and Grayson walking onto the dance floor. Feeling somewhat envious that she hasn't found romance, she watches them. She must admit, Rachel doesn't appear to be enchanted by the extremely handsome suitor. A sense of sorrow takes over her for Rachel. She realizes when you love someone, no one else will do.

It's not helping that his features are identical to the man you can't have. He's a perpetual reminder of her lost dream.

"Would you like to dance?" She glances up to see Alex holding out his hand for hers.

Uncertain of her desire to do so, she resolves to, despite her common sense. She takes his hand and quietly follows him to the floor. As she keeps her distance for the very slow dance, she notices they are in proximity to Rachel and Grayson. Rachel has her head on his shoulder with her eyes closed. Grayson is peering over the top of her, looking directly at Beth. Their eyes meet. For a moment, they gaze at each other.

Alex interrupts their focus by asking, "How have you been, Beth?"

She turns her face to meet his. "I've been doing well. How are you?"

"I've been rather busy. I just recently returned from Europe on a business trip."

"That's nice. Did you relax and enjoy yourself while you were there?"

"No, these trips demand all of my time. I would like to take a vacation one day, to appreciate some free time. Would you consider an excursion together?"

Her mind struggles for a respectful answer. She comes up with, "My time is about to become less available for vacations."

"I heard about the publishing company. What did you and Rachel do to warrant such an extravagant gift?"

His question sounded cynical to her. "What are you suggesting?"

"Don't you find it bizarre that Aunt Andrea bought a publishing company for you and Rachel?"

"No, in fact, I don't. Mrs. Vanders is a profoundly thoughtful person. I'm confident if you review the many years spent with your family, she has been just as generous to you."

"That's just it, the term missing with you and Rachel is family."

Rage growing in her, she leans back and declares, "Mrs. Vanders is a warm, caring person who has made this family what it is today. I wouldn't challenge her authenticity or her decisions, as most of them have benefited you immensely. She has sincerity and thoughtfulness that many of the male members of this family lack." With those remarks, she storms off the floor.

Going back to her table, she picks up her glass and devours it. Holding it in the air, the waiter brings her a new one.

"Is everything okay, Beth?" Mrs. Vanders can clearly see Beth is agitated.

Not choosing to let Mrs. Vanders know what an ass Alex is, she replies, "No, just getting a little tired."

Mrs. Vanders smiles, knowing very well that the answer has a hidden meaning. Touching Beth's hand, she maintains, "All will be well. You have much to look forward to."

Holding up her glass in agreement, she takes another drink. Finding her way to the lady's room, images of her prospects invade her mind. She convinces herself that there's a bright future ahead. While washing her hands, the lighting makes her examine herself, analyzing the changes since arriving at the estate. After mastering the application techniques from their makeup artist, she's doing a better job at emphasizing her qualities. The concentration of mascara over her thick lashes and perfectly shaded eyelids makes her look hypnotic. The fresh approach emphasizes the blue of her eyes. Her long blonde hair is full, flowing effortlessly down her back. The one thing she has always loved about herself is her straight hair. The natural shade of blonde allows her to be free of dyes, giving shine to its healthy texture. She moves her fingers through her long locks and moves on to freshen her lipstick before returning to her table. As she makes her way through the crowd, Rachel runs up to her waving a piece of folded paper. Beth sees she's elated.

Rachel yells over the music, "He loves me, Beth! He loves me. I'm going home."

Opening the note, Beth reads Chad's beautiful words. Holding it to her chest after reading it, she smiles. She couldn't be more thrilled for her. While admitting she will miss her very much, she can see the happiness Rachel has discovered in the past. She must constantly recognize this is best for her. She will miss her newfound friend. Not wishing to be selfish with her own concerns, she wonders what this means for the business. If Rachel isn't here, who will run the magazine?

CHAPTER 10

GIVING IT ALL

The next few days are about setting up for a new future. Beth leaves immediately. She enters the first phase of the transformation of her existence by giving up her apartment. Moving into the estate makes her apprehensive. The dramatic changes have so many implications. Hell, it's like she's no longer Beth Olsen. Coming and going from the estate, she feels like a Vanders. They handed her a suite in the south wing. It comes with a walk-in closet big enough for ten wardrobes. In fact, she chuckles thinking that it's the size of her cramped apartment.

The bed is in a private room of its own. The living area is enormous. It includes a sofa, chair and gas fireplace. There's a table that can accommodate four and a kitchenette that has a coffee pot, microwave, stove, and full-size refrigerator. There's a private office decorated in a black and white theme as well. The walls are a brilliant white, containing a black desk and chair. She identifies this as symbolic for black pen and white paper. She twirls around with her palms in the air, feeling more enthusiastic about her future than ever before!

Closing the acquisition of the publishing company goes without issue, much faster than expected. Tomorrow, they will take possession. The next morning, they are to go into the office. Mrs. Vanders asks her to join her for breakfast. Together they review the itinerary for the day.

Mrs. Vanders says, "Beth if you have no objections, I would prefer to go to the office with you today. Me accompanying you will demonstrate that you are to be accepted and in charge. There will be no doubt to any of those facts when I leave. I took the liberty of having your office decorated. It was in poor taste as it was. I didn't want you to be disappointed. Of course, if you decide it's not to your tastes, please redecorate. Grayson is also meeting me there to go over my expectations for this venture." Seeing Beth looking somewhat overwhelmed, she reassures her, "Beth, today is just for announcing your position. After that, this business belongs to you. You may run it as you see fit. With Grayson in charge of your finances, you won't fail." She lays her hand on Beth's for reassurance.

"I sure hope you're right, Mrs. Vanders. I'm a writer. I'm not accomplished in running an organization for profit."

"You don't need to worry about that. Grayson will support you." Each time she hears his name, the more she fears this will be a fight to the finish between them. They just don't get along.

"Beth, I made some revisions to the final acquisition of the company. I told you that this was for you and Rachel. Well, Rachel will not be returning, so I altered that. It will be co-owned by you and Grayson."

Panic lit up her face. Feeling herself blush red as the heat rolls from her neck to her face, she looks down to calm herself. "Mrs. Vanders, I know I should be grateful for what you have done for me, but I explained to you that Grayson and I don't get along. This will not work out well for either of us."

"I understand that, Beth. The first thing you do when running an organization is to put aside all personal feelings. You'll be collaborating on business decisions, not personality differences. He will respect his boundaries, as you will with him. I should have discussed this with you first, but I wanted to get closed on the business deal and get Grayson to be invested for personal reasons as well. This is the first business deal he has owned. All the other ventures he has been on are under the Vanders umbrella. This one will be his to cultivate and grow."

She looks at Beth's panic-ridden face and almost feels sorry for her. She lays her hand over Beth's, "It will be okay, dear, I promise."

"Let me make sure you understand who I am, Mrs. Vanders. You have witnessed me as a submissive writer who has been actively seeking to pursue the rights to your book. I am, in actual life, particularly demanding in my expectations. I had to work hard to get the scholarships to Yale. I am a motivated person endeavoring to accomplish a dream to be equal to those more fortunate. If Grayson and I butt heads, I will only bow when his decision has been proven better than mine. I will not accommodate him in any situation because he is a Vanders."

Mrs. Vanders' smile could not have been wider. "Good. We understand each other. I would expect nothing less. Beth, all I require of you is your best. You must put personal sentiments for Grayson aside during business conversations. How you feel about him after working hours is for you and Grayson to work out."

Feeling reassured, Beth gets back to finishing her breakfast. They leave for the office within the hour.

Driving into the garage of the twenty-story building, Beth's heart begins to pound, creating an anxious nervousness that envelops her. After entering the building and, stopping on the twentieth floor, she steps out of the elevator. This is where Mr. Lawson's office is. No sooner than the thought enters her mind, he walks out of his office. Feeling awkward, she says, "Hello, Mr. Lawson."

Holding out his hand to her, he replies, "Hello, Miss Olsen." He turns to Mrs. Vanders and says, "Welcome, Mrs. Vanders."

"Hello, Mr. Lawson. It's very nice to meet you. I have heard great things about you. Would you please put us on your schedule, let's say, in an hour?"

"Of course, Mrs. Vanders. He turns to the receptionist. Please book me," he glances at his wristwatch, "at 9:00 for an hour." He looks at Mrs. Vanders to confirm an hour will suffice.

"Yes, that would be fine. We will meet in Miss Olsen's office. Thank you."

Beth follows Mrs. Vanders to a gigantic office. A large oversized desk sits in front of a massive window overlooking New York. Beth has heard about the offices on the twentieth floor, and their opulence. Mr. Lawson's office is right after exiting the elevator. She has never gone beyond his. Only the owners and top executives were seen on these floors. She wants to pinch herself right now. This can't be happening to her. In her dreams, she knew Yale would open doors for her, but she hadn't known what path she would take to get there. Writing is a passion of hers that she wanted to investigate before committing to a career path. Walking into this office, she now has every part of the dream for her future realized.

Mrs. Vanders sees the mesmerized look on Beth's face and beams. "This is all for you, Beth."

Looking at Mrs. Vanders while trying to suppress the tears welling up in her eyes, she walks around the office touching everything. The immense conference table at one end of the office can seat ten. She twirls back to Mrs. Vanders. "I don't know how I will ever repay you for this."

"Be successful. That will be payment enough," she says.

Beth runs over to hug her. "I'm sorry. I know this is not professional, but I can't help myself." A tear drops from her eyes as she lets go.

Seeing this, Mrs. Vanders knows they have made the right decision. She's showing a vulnerability that will make her strong when needed.

Distant conversations are growing closer, so Beth pulls herself together, wiping the tear from her cheek. Walking to the desk, she lays her purse down. Keeping her laptop, she also grabs a notepad and pen off the desk just as Grayson and Mr. Lawson enters.

Grayson goes over to kiss Mrs. Vanders on the cheek. "Good morning." He then turns to Beth, and says, "Good morning."

Beth replies, "Good morning, Grayson." She points to the large conference table and asks, "Shall we get started?"

Everyone gathers at the table, dragging out laptops and iPad. Mrs. Vanders begins with Mr. Lawson. "Mr. Lawson, I'm confident you have been advised that this company is under new leadership. It is now co-owned by Beth and Grayson." She looks first at Beth, then Grayson.

"Beth will be over the book publishing division, while Grayson is over the finances and the magazine division. Grayson has concluded that since the finances themselves are a full-time responsibility, he would like to appoint you to run the magazine division. I recognize that's not a part of what you have been contributing to the company, but we feel it calls for your expertise to develop that division. Does that move meet with your approval?"

Mr. Lawson looks from Beth to Grayson, then Mrs. Vanders. "I have always thought the magazine division was weak and required some guidance, so I think I can take on that challenge. How much leverage will I have in the decision-making process?"

Grayson dives in. "You, Beth, and I will have meetings to determine courses of action on each division's needs. While you will have total liberties running it, as co-owners, Beth and I will have the ultimate say. I don't see this as being any different from your responsibilities for the company thus far."

He looks at Beth, then at Grayson. "I think I can live with that. Thank you for considering me for this important role. I won't let you down."

Smiling and feeling satisfied, Grayson stands up and shakes Mr. Lawson's hand. Reviewing the course of action for the new leadership changes, the meeting wraps up after an hour.

Before terminating the meeting with Grayson and Mr. Lawson, Beth says, "I would like to set up an individual meeting with each of you. I will require two hours of your time." She looks at Mr. Lawson, "Please prepare a presentation regarding the current status of my division and all active publishing's along with their history. Please have sales stats and current earnings of each."

Mr. Lawson replies, "Certainly." He gathers his laptop and leaves.

Beth looks at Grayson. "Please provide me the current status of our finances and your prediction for the course of action going forward. I need to understand where we are to identify our destination for the future."

Grayson looks surprised at her aggressiveness to press forward. In fact, he finds her intriguing in this new light. Agreeing, he claims, "I will require at least a week to dig into the books to establish where we are."

Beth picks up her laptop and says, "Thank you. That will work. I'll need the same amount of time to meet with Mr. Lawson. Be sure to apprise me of top selling books and those that are lagging in sales. I will need to match your figures to his." She looks at Mrs. Vanders. "Would you like to tour the offices with me?"

"I would love that."

Grayson leaves, and Beth goes to the phone to dial Mr. Lawson. "Mr. Lawson, would it be imposing on your time to provide a tour for Mrs. Vanders and me? The meeting we requested when we arrived can be used for this tour."

"No, not at all. I'll be right there."

They take a two-hour tour and meet all the employees. The company was more staffed than she realized. Shaking each person's hand, she introduces herself and Mrs. Vanders. Getting back to the office, she has no clue what to do next. She looks at Mrs. Vanders and asks, "Now what?"

Both look at each other and laugh.

Mrs. Vanders responds, "Well, we have had a highly productive morning. I am heading home. This company is yours, Beth. Do what you want. If you have had enough for one day, let's head home."

Beth looks around her office and replies, "I can't believe this is all mine." She corrects herself, "Mine and Grayson's."

"Well, believe it. I thought you handled yourself very well today. You clearly have a business mind and aptitude for strategic planning. You have outdone yourself, and I couldn't be prouder." Turning to pick up her purse from the conference table, she says, "I'm heading home. Do you want to stay or leave with me?"

Beth looks around the room, beaming. "I think I'll stick around to see if I can get I T to set up my computer. I'd like to dig around a little on my own."

Mrs. Vanders hugs her and says, "I will see you at dinner then. Enjoy your day. Call for the car when you're ready to leave." Turning, she looks back at Beth, "Don't stay too late. You have the rest of your life to get into it all."

Beth smiles, "I know, but I'm so excited about this. I can't wait to dive in!"

"I'll see you later, then." Mrs. Vanders leaves the office.

Beth twirls around to look out of the massive windows. The skyline's view is spectacular. Mrs. Vanders had mentioned if she and Grayson didn't like the office's location, they could relocate at Mrs. Vanders expense. Looking at this view, that would be the farthest thing from her mind. Holding her face in her hands, then looking up again, she vows to herself, "I will give this everything I have. I am committed to giving it my all."

Her thoughts go to Grayson, "Some things will be more difficult than others."

CHAPTER 11

MAKING IT WORK

Each day becomes an adventure Beth appreciates. She arrives before anyone else in the office and leaves last. She powers through the company information to identify the path to successful execution. Finding that her book had not been marketed appropriately will be a tough conversation with Mr. Lawson. Agreeing and disagreeing with decisions thus far, she finds herself eager to dismantle them. Her goal is to build up specific sections of her division. She schedules her first private session with Mr. Lawson.

He arrives precisely at 10:00 a.m. How ironic that she has her head down when he pecks on the door. Looking up, she gestures for him to come in. Saving her work, she shifts to face him. "Would you mind closing the door?"

Mr. Lawson turns back to close the door. This is giving him an uneasy notion that she needs privacy for this meeting. Unable to foresee how this conversation will develop, he follows her lead to the conference table. He takes the chair directly across from her.

Beth asks, "How are you this morning, Mr. Lawson?"

He smiles and replies, "Please, if you are comfortable, may we address each other by first names?"

She smiles, "Of course." She pauses, realizing she doesn't know his first name. Continuing to smile, she adds, "I'm sorry, but I've only known you by Mr. Lawson. What is your first name?"

"Oh, sorry, Kevin. My name is Kevin." She perceives he's tense. How interesting it is to see the shoe on the other foot. "Kevin, I want this meeting to be open and honest. I will put forth questions and concepts that may or may not agree with what has transpired in the past. I need your honest feedback if you disagree and why. That will simply benefit me in grasping how publishing works from the marketing aspect. Do you think we can do that? Considering our current structure, you don't actually work for me. You report to Grayson. So, anything you share will merely support me in getting my feet wet. I would be incredibly grateful for the guidance."

He accepts her remarks with a surprised expression on his face. "I'd be happy to answer anything I can."

"Okay, then. Let's get started." She opens her laptop. They begin taking notes as they move through a mountain of charts, graphs, memos, letters, and communications between authors and the company. As they examine each topic, they discern what criteria they applied to decide to publish a book, and what marketing practices they currently use. The question inevitably arises as to why her book wasn't marketed the same as others. Seeing the question makes Kevin uncomfortable, she adds, "I have no resentments here. I just need to understand the premise of the decision."

He nods his head in understanding. "At the time of your book's announcement, we were releasing a major author as well. She was one of our top successful writers, so we were compelled to invest highly into the advertisement of her novel."

Leaning back and crossing her arms, she hesitates before responding. "I see. Is it a practice to invest in certain authors while other authors get limited exposure?" She could see this was causing him discomfort again.

"I was provided a budget. I needed to invest appropriately in what has historically been successful over new authors."

Leaning forward, she states, "I see that as not supporting the new authors who could have gone to a publishing firm who would invest in their future. Don't you select the publications by investment opportunities? If we don't truly invest, the outcome will be the same failure."

He sits in silence for a moment, then answers, "Beth, if you are planning to operate in this fashion, I am eager to work for you. As an executive of the firm that employed me, I needed to follow their stipulations and desires. I followed the guidelines provided by the company. I will do the same for you."

It's a great response. She asserts, "Good. That's an answer I like." She goes to the next slide on her laptop. After two hours, she brings the meeting to a halt. She tells him she's waiting for Grayson to get back to her on their financial status. She may need to meet with him just a couple of more times to clarify and assist her with certain items. She stands after stacking her papers. Holding out her hand, she shakes his, and thanks him for his time. As she escorts him to the door, she asks, "How's it going in the magazine portion of our venture?"

"To be honest, I find that sector of the business fascinating. It's a lot of fast-moving parts. The need to constantly have articles ready on a short deadline is exciting. This may be what I'm better suited for. The team is quite enthusiastic and ready for the challenges to satisfy the demand."

Very much pleased with his answer, she replies, "That's great news. I'm glad you're comfortable with the move. Has Grayson been actively involved yet?" Scolding herself inwardly, she is frustrated that she is asking about him. She can't stand him.

"We had a meeting with the entire staff, and he laid out his expectations. He says once he gets the financials squared away, he wants to observe the brainstorming sessions for features."

Knowing the magazine and its array of topics, it would be entertaining to observe. Hesitating on the compliment, she says it anyway. "Grayson is brilliant. He'll bring much to the table, I'm sure."

Opening the door, Kevin says, "I agree. I've been in quite a few sessions with him. So far, his ideas are on target without having had any magazine experience prior to this."

As he walks through the door to leave, she follows Grayson's lead. Going back to her desk, she calls her administrative assistant to come in to her office. Once there, they examine her calendar, which has been filling up quickly. Together they schedule meetings with the various departments, then one for the entire unit. Getting that established, she begins the itinerary for each. Laying out her expectations, she drives her vision.

The meetings are a roaring success. The excitement is palpable and energizing. The team expresses their likes and dislikes of the past operations, giving her inspiring ideas from their input. She states clearly, "Today we cannot stay in the past of paper book publishing. We need to advertise our books in various venues, such as downloads and audio. Each author we sign will get the same budget for marketing. All writers get a fair and equal chance for success."

One member of the team says, "You can't know how delighted we are to hear that. We get the creators to come aboard, then let them down when we don't invest in them."

"Thank you, James. I agree. I expect to see this higher investment into more wide ranges of success than just relying on a few of our principal authors. When seeking new writers, we must caution them that self-publishing doesn't get the proper marketing that we offer. To make money, we must spend money."

Feeling quite satisfied with the meeting's outcome, she's about to end the session when a hand raises for a question. She points at the person to go ahead. The woman asks, "I was in charge of your manuscript. We didn't give the proper attention your book needed. May we republish that, or at least re-market it now?"

Feeling herself blush, she replies, "All authors are treated justly. Yes, but be sure you're doing this for the right reason. I want to be straightforward with you. I thought my book was under marketed as well. If that is your reason, then proceed. If it's because I'm your new boss and the work is not as desirable as I assumed it was, don't do it. You will throw away good money after bad. What's your name?"

Happy with the answer, she responds, "Jessica."

"Okay Jessica. Let's get it back out there if you think we should. Your director will fill you in on the reassignment method for submitting proposals for new manuscripts. I have established a form to request a new publication. That submission will travel through a committee who reads it, then provides feedback with a vote to publish yes or no. These will be volunteers from the community who love to read. Readers will get free editions of every book published with us in their perspective field of interest. We will contract a company or hire individuals who will do the readings for our audio works."

Seeing the excitement in their faces, she declares, "We are blasting into the future. Anyone having ideas about how we publish, my door is open to you. I don't want anyone to feel unheard or dismissed for fresh ideas. Each concept will be scrutinized on its merits." She looks around and asks, "Are there any further questions?"

No one lifts their hand. "Perfect, thank you all for your valuable time." She laughs then throws her hand in the air and yells, "Back to work!"

The crowd disburses as Beth gathers her things. She hears clapping behind her. Turning, she's face to face with Grayson. Feeling her face turn red, she asks, "Are you mocking me?" Mad at herself for always getting defensive with him, she struggles to calm herself.

"Quite the contrary. I thought your lecture was amazing. Do you have time for a meeting regarding finances?"

"Do you need to do it today? The only thing I have open is lunch."

He smiles. "That's a sly way of asking me to lunch."

She stares at him incredulously. "Are you kidding me right now? Are you hitting on me?"

"No, but it sounded like you were hitting on me."

"Not in this life." She storms past him.

He chuckles, "Okay, okay. I'm sorry."

"You should be. This is business and I want no crossing the line from you, Mr. Don Juan."

He laughs heartily at her remark. "I consider that a compliment, even if you didn't mean it that way."

She snarls, "You would."

He accompanies her to her office, then asks, "Are we leaving now for lunch?" He glances down at his watch.

"I don't think we need to meet. Put what you need in an email. I'll respond when I get time."

Getting serious, he counters, "Look, if you want to carry off those big speeches you make, you should know whether our finances can accommodate them."

Dropping her things on her desk, she acknowledges, "Okay, let's go." Opening her desk drawer, she grabs her purse.

He walks over and lays his things on the conference table.

They ride the elevator to the garage in silence. As they enter the garage, she says, "The estate driver dropped me off. Do you have a car here?"

He clicks his remote, and a dark gray Bentley lights up. She shouldn't have been surprised that he would drive such a vehicle. Although, she has seen him in quite a few at the estate. She doesn't comment, trying to cover her lack of experience riding in such a lavish car. He opens the car door for her. Well, at least he has manners. As she gets in, the fresh leather smell is all-consuming. She loves it.

Sliding in beside her, he starts the engine. Pulling from the garage, he takes a right, heading east. Driving only a few blocks, he pulls up in front of a large building. Immediately a valet walks out from behind a podium. Again, it's not surprising that he would go for the most expensive place to eat.

"Good afternoon, Mr. Vanders."

"Hello, Charlie." He throws the remote in the air for Charlie to catch.

Charlie catches the remote like he's an expert baseball player, swiping his hand right to left in the catch.

Entering the lavish building, he guides her to the hostess. Her smile widens as she sees Grayson. "Good afternoon, Mr. Vanders. Your seat is this way."

Grayson replies, "Thank you, Darci."

Darci seats them in a secluded area with no tables close. Removing the extra silverware, she asks Beth for her beverage preference. "I'll just have an unsweetened iced tea, please." Beth expects her to ask Grayson as well, but she doesn't. The server returns with their tea. After a quick look at the menu, they both give their order.

Grayson gets down to business immediately. "I've reviewed the finances of the company. The previous owners were operating on limited funds. This caused them to be lean with decisions for publications."

"I pretty much got that message from Kevin and the staff during our meetings. How bad off are we?"

"We would go nowhere if we were operating off of what this business has. They were barely afloat."

Beth feels disappointment taking over. "This was a poor investment, I guess."

"Well, if it functions like the past, yes. But we are now operating with capital. Our plans to be more creative in our decisions should turn it around."

"Where are we getting the capital?"

"Aunt Andrea, of course."

Shocked at his easy mannerisms regarding Mrs. Vanders' funds doesn't sit well with her. "Mrs. Vanders has already purchased the business. We can't ask her to support a failing business as well."

Grayson gets a little annoyed with her naïve ideas. "Did you really think this was a thriving business that someone would be so willing to sell? Mrs. Vanders investigated and reviewed their portfolio before she purchased it. She wants us to build this company into a successful entity. We can't do that without funds to do so. She knew what her total investment would be to give us a fighting chance. It's up to you and me to make this company profitable."

Taken aback from his directness, she concedes to not understanding the scope of Mrs. Vanders' investments.

His come-back is, "That's why she put me in charge of the finances." Realizing he is being an ass, he tries to support the comment with, "She understands our strengths. I'm not a writer. I couldn't write a book if my life depended on it. I will need to trust you in that area of the business. In fact, I have no clue how Kevin will do leading the magazine. I may need to come to you when I have questions regarding a decision he's made. I'm so tied up in financials right now. It will limit the time I can give to the magazine. Are you willing to assist in those areas when needed? This is our company together. I know we both want it to work."

As she's about to respond, the server brings their order. They eat as they talk about the next steps. They share their views regarding why the company was floundering. When Beth asks why Mrs. Vanders would invest in a failing company, he tells her that's her way, buy cheap and invest. It's what's made the Vanders fortunes. Investing in unsuccessful companies means getting them at a bargain price, then she builds them into empires. He says, "Truthfully, she's been wanting to get into the publishing business for a while. She can use the platform to guide the public into the images she wants."

Getting that, she feels less opposed to taking a handout. She states those thoughts out loud.

Grayson corrects her. "Beth, my aunt gives no one a hand out. You'll need to work hard to make this work. She watches and knows everything. If she sees you're not putting in the work, she'll cut you loose quickly. If this venture fails, she'll have learned the lesson not to trust you financially."

Feeling extremely insecure at this point, she says, "I don't understand why she would give it to me then. I have no experience in a publishing company. I can easily fail."

"Not with me, you won't! Beth, my aunt scrutinized you thoroughly. She knows you went to Yale graduating top of your class. She knows your complete history. Reading your article, convinced her and me that you had it in you. Her decision to do this wasn't made without facts to back them up. We are going to make this work." He glances at his watch, then motions for the server to bring the check. He signs the ticket, then stands to leave.

Grabbing her purse, she quietly rides back to the office. Knowing now the faith Mrs. Vanders is putting in her makes her dig deeper when she returns to the office. She gets down to running the ad for readers, instructing how the interviews should go, and what to look for. She describes to the staff how the voting will occur. She gets started with the marketing department on the new website for the company. She runs a strategic announcement in the magazine about the new owners and their vision, asking for authors to submit their work for publication. The new name of "Olsen-Vanders Publications" is announced. Only days after the announcement, reporters were hounding Beth and Grayson for interviews. She let Grayson select who would get the honors.

Three days later, she's escorted into a studio with lights everywhere. Grayson places his hand on her back as they walk to the couch, that is set up before a single chair. He feels her shaking and comments, "It's okay. Just let me do most of the talking if you're not comfortable." The angle of the couch puts both in direct view of the camera. Nodding to his comment, she says nothing. Admitting she's scared to death is an understatement.

Once seated, the host comes in, stopping at the couch to shake their hands. "Hello, Grayson. Fancy meeting you here again." Grayson smiles politely. He turns to Beth to shake her hand, "It's nice to meet you, Beth."

"You, as well," she comments.

She recognizes him from his show, "The Facts." Realizing she's on such a popular show elevates her stress. She becomes queasy from nerves. Taking deep breaths, she tries to calm down. Grayson looks so relaxed. It's as if he is at home on the sofa.

Grayson catches her looking at him, and notices how pale she has suddenly become. He moves his hand on top of hers to calm her. He whispers, "It's okay." He pats her hand, then keeps it there until he feels her shaking subside. As the interview begins, it takes on a life of its own.

John Fargos begins the interview. "Good evening, audience. Today we are speaking with Beth Olsen and Grayson Vanders. The two are partners in the new, revamped Grant Publishing Company which now goes by the name of 'Olsen Vanders

Publications'.'" He turns toward them and begins the grueling questions. To her surprise, he knew she was a graduate of Yale and even brought up her age, asking if her experience qualifies her for such a massive undertaking. He points out to her how publishing is not as it used to be with self-publishing options. She replies, "Mr. Fargos, anyone who graduates from Yale knows the University has extremely high expectations. Graduating top of my class was not a minor feat. I am more than capable of taking on this challenge."

He then asks a question that floors her. Looking back and forth between the two of them, he asks, "The two of you are extremely attractive. I'd say you make a nice couple. Did this partnership occur because of that personal relationship? Are you benefiting from this relationship, Miss Olsen?"

Ready to pounce on his chauvinistic remark, Grayson moves his hand over hers. He replies, "Actually, Mrs. Vanders selected Beth as the owner of the business. She has all the credentials needed to be a successful entrepreneur. In fact, I'm in charge of the magazine portion of the business. I often find myself seeking her expert guidance. They brought me in at the last minute due to my financial stabilization history with other investments."

Mr. Fargos responds, "I only ask because I see some affection between you. More than once I have seen you lay your hand over hers. Is there something between you two?"

Beth replies, "No, there is not. This is my first live interview." She looks at Grayson with appreciation. "He was trying to calm my nerves."

Mr. Fargo says, "If I were a betting man, I'd venture this relationship will be more than 'business partners' in the future." Before a reply is made, he moves on to discuss what they were there for, the new business.

After the interview was over, Beth rides back to work in silence. Grayson says nothing. Beth is the one to break the silence. "I wanted to tell him about your interest in my best friend, but felt it was none of his business."

Grayson replies, "Beth, I have no relationship with Rachel. In fact, I haven't even seen her at the house for over a month. I thought she had moved in."

"She had, but her life went in another direction."

"What does that mean?"

"I can't speak for Rachel. Ask Mrs. Vanders if you want details. It was all decided between the two of them."

"I'm not asking anyone. It's not that important to me. I barely got to know her."

"You acted smitten to me."

He looks at Beth, "Smitten? That sounds like a child's label. Was I attracted to her? Hell, yes. She's beautiful. Was I in love with her? Hell, no. I barely know her."

Beth replies, "Anyway, how you feel or do not feel about Rachel is none of my business."

He replies cynically, "Exactly."

Taking that as a cue for the conversation between them to end, the rest of the ride is in silence.

CHAPTER 12

FALLING IN THE FALL

Leaving to ride into the city on a brisk fall morning, Beth breaks out a heavier jacket. Breathing in the morning air, she sprints to the parking lot. Ten vehicles are aligned in a long row. Needless to say, hers looks out of place with the other expensive rides. Getting in the car, she turns the key in the ignition. Feeling the car sputtering to life, she's relieved when it eventually turns over. She makes a mental note to stop by a shop to purchase a new battery. Backing out of the space, she sees Grayson getting into his Bentley. She drives past him as his vehicle starts up with no problem. She comments out loud, "Show off." She flings up her hand for a slight wave. Laughing, she taps on her steering wheel, calling it old faithful as it trudges on down the road.

As customary, she's the first to reach the office. She plunges in to examine the sales totals. Grayson had earlier mentioned he would post the figures today. She's eager to get the results for all their arduous work. She's flabbergasted when she sees the numbers of online transactions, and the sales rate at the stores.

They have skyrocketed!

In the last few months, they have worked on getting some old books back out with appropriate marketing, adding audio for many. She can't believe the amazing sales figures. Moving to the next page, she sees the demands of her own book. It's taken off!

"Oh, my God! I can't believe it," she says out loud. Getting up from her seat, she performs a happy dance. Unfortunately, Grayson walks in at that time to witness her dramatic reactions.

He laughs! "You must have received the sales summaries."

Embarrassed, she sits back down. But she decides what the heck. Giggling, she replies, "Yes! I did!"

His chuckle is deep. His dimples and sparkling eyes bring out his most handsome features. She studies him for a moment, appreciating the pleasant expression on his face. Feeling sheepish, she looks away.

He catches her admiration. For the first time, she softens for a moment as Grayson remarks, "Those stats are from your hard work."

She counters, "Yours, too! Did you catch the magazine sales? Adding the new categories made your sales soar."

"I think so, too. Did you notice the marketing report of the demographics that are buying the magazine now? I can't believe we could shift it around so quickly. Thanks for the recommendations." He watches as her exuberance is written all over her face.

"This woman is gorgeous," he considers to himself. Shaking that thought, he shifts to leave but swings back to ask one last question. "Will you be around later today, say around five?"

She hits her computer to go live and views her calendar. "Yes, I have my last meeting at four."

"Okay. I'll catch you then." He leaves the room with a full grin on his face.

The rest of the day is busy. She calls an abrupt meeting to acknowledge her staff for their hard work. Sharing the success, she posts the numbers. It amazes everyone that they could turn it around so swiftly. The routine phrase, "If this book doesn't sell, we could all be looking for a job," had gotten old. Now, they work in a successful business that is run by people who know what they're doing. It doesn't hurt to have the Vanders backing either. Their name behind anything makes it an automatic success. You can't beat those Vanders.

At the end of the day, Beth's exhausted. Putting her fingers on her temples, she feels a headache coming on. Just as she combs through her purse for some meds, Grayson pecks on the door.

Seeing her in her handbag, he presumes she's searching for her keys. "Are you getting ready to leave?"

"I plan to, after our meeting. I was waiting for you. Throwing her things back down inside the purse, she stuffs it back in the drawer. She snatches a notepad and heads toward the conference table, expecting this to be an office meeting.

"I'm ready to go, too. We can chat while we head toward our cars."

She looks surprised. "Oh, it sounded like this would be a pretty important meeting when you asked this morning."

He grins, "It is, but we can talk about it as we go. Grab your stuff."

Pulling the drawer back open, she grabs her handbag and laptop. "I'm glad this will be brief. I feel a headache coming on."

They step into the elevator, and he stands in silence. Confused, she asserts, "And?"

He looks at her questioning what she means, then it dawns on him that they were supposed to be talking all the way to the garage. "I just wanted to hear what the staff thought of the numbers."

"They were thrilled. You know, with that in mind, I realize you're over finances, but do you perceive us to be in a position to offer bonuses to the employees at Christmas?"

Thinking over the idea, he responds, "If things proceed on the same path, I don't see why not."

Stepping out of the elevator, she turns toward her car. To her dismay, it's not there. "Oh no. My car's been towed."

Grayson says, "Yes, it looks that way."

"I don't understand. That's my designated spot. Why would anyone tow it away?" She feels her headache coming on stronger.

Grayson can't hold it in anymore. "Why don't you just drive the one that's there?"

She stares at him incredulously. "Ugh. Well, for one reason, it's not mine."

As he hands her a remote, he clicks the unlock door button. "Yes, it is." The car beeps and the tail lights flash.

Starting to say, "No, it isn't," she pauses and faces him.

"Grayson, what are you trying to convey?"

"We just purchased your first company car."

Excited beyond belief, she runs to the car. Of course, it's a Bentley.

He states, "It's a Bentley 2020 Flying Spur."

"Oh, my!" She runs around the car checking it out.

Grayson says, "Get in!"

She pulls the driver's door open and jumps in. Grayson goes around to the passenger side and slides in.

"Grayson, I know what these cars cost. Our company can't afford this."

Grayson smiles. "Beth, I'm the finance guy. I'm the one that makes that determination." He laughs when she squeals and pounds on the steering wheel. "Hey be careful there. You don't want the airbags to go off." He tells her to put her foot on the break.

He then reaches over and presses the start button. He provides a quick overview of the features. Reaching in front of her to the other side, he turns his head to tell her what a button does. He finds they're face to face. Her closeness draws him in. His eyes trail down to look at her full luscious lips, then up to her beautiful blue eyes. She stares back for an instant as if in a trance. He draws himself back from the threshold of kissing her. Leaning back in his seat, he takes a deep breath. Suddenly feeling nervous, he opens the glove compartment to show her the user manual. "Go through this. It will show you everything you need to know." He opens the door to get out.

"Grayson, where's my car?"

"I had a new parking spot added for you. It's in A19."

She peers down through the garage, then back at him. "Grayson, thank you. You'll never know what this means to me."

Shrugging, he says, "No problem, Beth. You deserve it. You've worked hard and earned it. We couldn't have our owner and CEO call in one day, saying her car won't start, could we?"

At that moment, she remembers her sputtering car this morning and how it would barely turn over. "Oh, that's right. You heard me this morning."

Finding him to be a thoughtful person after this, she's discovering it harder and harder to hate him. Or was he just embarrassed that she drove that piece of junk?

He smiles at the comment. Without responding, he walks into the darkness of the garage, leaving her with her new toy.

Beth pulls out slowly, stopping by her old car to retrieve some items out of the glove compartment. On her way home, she takes a detour by the neighborhood she grew up in. Driving down the small street lined with vehicles, she stops in front of her childhood home. She has fond memories of those times. Remembering the family in the yard, she could see and hear the laughter as if it were yesterday. Her parents gave so much for her to go to Yale. Not so much in financial support since she had gone on a scholarship, but in the devotion to her upbringing and her education. They encouraged her to be the best she could be.

She wishes they could see her now, owning a successful business, and driving a car that cost more than her parent's first house. Her parents died not so long ago in a similar way as Rachel's. It was a tragic accident, losing control of their car on a snowy night in November. Suddenly, she couldn't control the tears. She lays her head on the steering wheel and weeps. Letting go of who she was will be difficult. She came from meager beginnings. She'll carry the love her parents doted on her forever, but now she needs to stand up and put on her big girl pants. Mrs. Vanders has granted her a gift. A stranger who saw her value, just like her parents did. She can never repay her kindness.

Turning on the dash light, she looks in the rearview mirror to wipe her tears. Using a tissue, she removes the smeared mascara from under her eyes. Pulling out slowly, she heads for the mansion on the other side of New York. She takes deep breaths to exhale the tension from her body. By the time she reaches the Vanders' estate, she's exhausted and ready for bed. Going directly to bed with no dinner, she falls asleep the minute her head hits the pillow.

However, her fitful dreams are disconcerting. She dreams of Grayson Vanders taking her in his arms. The incident in the car was just the precursor of the passion they have for each other, a passion that erupts in her dream. She wakes in the middle of the night, shaken by the reality that she's attracted to Grayson. Closing her eyes again, she tries to squeeze his face out of her memory. She goes back to sleep with little effort. Tired and spent, rest is all she needs. She will worry about Grayson Vanders another day.

CHAPTER 13

THE HOLIDAYS BEGIN

Hard work and lengthy hours turn days into weeks. Two months pass by rapidly. Thanksgiving is next week. Deciding not to work that week, she determines an enjoyable trip is in order. She has no one to go with, so it would require a location for singles. Glancing at the clock, she decides it's not that late. She'll stay to clear up some things that need her attention. A peck on the door brings her head up from the computer. It's Grayson.

He asks, "Hey, why are you still here?"

She reads the clock on the wall. "It's only six. I frequently stay late. Why do you ask?"

"We have the ball tonight. Aunt Andrea will expect both of us to be there."

Recalling the invitation, she answers, "Oh gosh, I forgot all about that. You're right. She would want us there." Shutting down her laptop, she places it in the carrying case. Getting her purse from the drawer and grabbing her coat on the way out, they leave her office, shutting off the light.

Walking to the elevator, he asks, "Do you have an issue with us sitting together tonight at the same table?" He studies her to watch for a negative response. Not seeing a reaction, he continues. "I know she intends to speak to everyone at dinner about our successful venture. I think it may be significant for her to see us getting along, united in our efforts."

Putting it that way, he's right. Beth had made such a big deal about them not getting along. It may comfort Mrs. Vanders to perceive they are acting like adults. "Certainly. I think you're right. I didn't act thrilled when she announced you would be my business partner. I think keeping our distance has been beneficial. You doing your thing, and me doing mine."

He hesitates. "You've been keeping your distance?"

She sharply turns to peer at him. As if surprised that he wasn't doing the same. "Haven't you?"

"I confess, I've been busy. No, I haven't consciously been keeping my distance."

She laughs. "Okay, keeping your distance may be a stretch. Grayson, you know we have never gotten along. I certainly don't pursue your company."

He grins. "Okay, I'll give you that. We definitely have bristled personalities toward each other."

She giggles. "Bristled?"

"Well, you know what I mean."

Conceding to his description, she says, "I'll take it."

Stepping out of the elevator, the chilly night air hits her in the face. She's still carrying her coat, so she hands Grayson her purse and laptop to hold, while she dons the coat. Taking them back, she says, "Thanks, see you later tonight."

Smiling. he nods and they both head to their cars.

On the trip home, she decides she doesn't want to go to the ball. Running excuses through her mind, she eventually comes up with a suitable one. Sneaking in, she avoids all activities in preparation for tonight. Happy she has made it to her suite without issue, she walks in and dumps her belongings on the chair. Hanging up her coat, she kicks her heels off and plops on the couch. The oversized pillows allow her to settle back in comfort.

Glancing toward the chair, she sees the envelope she has plucked from her box at the door. Her mail comes to the central address, then the staff brings it to the box outside her door. Dragging herself up to get it, she opens the envelope. Seeing no stamp, she knows it's not external. It's from inside the complex. She opens it.

"Beth, I'm looking forward to tonight. We have been so busy. We haven't seen each other in a while. I understand things are progressing well at the publishing company. I want to hear from you that you are good. All work and no play, is not good for you. I took the liberty of ordering some dresses for you to select from for tonight. See you at dinner." Signed, Mrs. Vanders.

A tap on the door breaks her focus. The smile on her face disappears. Walking to the door, she lays the letter on the end table. Pulling the door open, she finds, as mentioned in the note, a rack full of clothes. Stacy peaks around the rack. "Hello Beth, Mrs. Vanders ordered these for you."

Grabbing the other end, Beth helps drag it into her suite. The gowns are beautiful. Of course, matching shoes and jewelry comes with each dress. Glancing at the hour, she asks, "How much time do I have, Stacy?"

Stacy replies. "About an hour, Miss."

"Okay, just leave these here. I'm going to jump in the shower." Looking at her, she admits, "To be honest, I wasn't planning to go."

Stacy raises her eyebrows. "Oh, that would not be a good idea. This ball is the beginning of the holiday season. From now until New Year, there are many gala events to attend. Next week, the huge Thanksgiving celebration happens."

She and Beth have become semi-friends, so she knows she can say these things to her that she would never say to another. "You need to accept your lot in life. We now regard you as a member of the Vanders. It's your accepted membership that commits you to a particular lifestyle."

Beth laughs. "Okay, I hear you loud and clear." Stopping to get serious for a moment, she says, "Stacy, I'm blessed to have you. I'm so grateful to this family. Mrs. Vanders has brought me in like I'm a daughter. It means so much to me." Getting very sentimental about all of it, she's interrupted by Stacy.

"You can be thankful in the shower."

Laughing, Beth throws her hands in the air as she scurries away. She loves Stacy's straight forwardness.

She selects a deep blue dress that has three quarter length sleeves. It has a low round neckline and a bodice that fans out halfway between the hip and the knee. There's a modest train. The front lands on the top of her shoes. It's comfortable to walk in. A small diamond necklace lays at the base of her neck, falling all the way down to a tee between her breasts. Matching dangling diamond earrings complete the ensemble. The makeup artist arrives just as she zips up the dress.

The wonderful thing about her stylist is that she knows her craft. One glance at the apparel, and she knows the makeup and hairstyle that will work. She gets to work immediately. Once satisfied with the makeup, she signals that she has completed the application.

Beth turns to view the mirror. She's stunned by the intensity of it all. Never giving her looks this much attention, it's such a contrast to her everyday existence. After observing how her makeup is applied on various occasions, she's gotten better about applying it herself. Gradually, she's been creating a moderate daytime version for work.

Tonight, they sweep her hair up, with long curled strands falling on the sides and in the back. She recalls the movie, *Somewhere in Time*. This hairstyle is similar. Remembering the time travel movie makes her think of Rachel. She misses her so much.

Arriving for dinner, she pauses in the doorway to allow the escort to seat her. As suggested, Grayson is seated in the chair next to hers. He stands as she approaches.

He says, "Beth, you look lovely."

"Thank you, Grayson. You look very nice as well." He's wearing a dark blue suit. If she hadn't known better, he planned it this way to make sure they both wear the same shade of blue.

He pulls out her chair. Sitting, she scans the table for those attending. The usual crowd is there, plus some unknown faces. The tables are full.

Mrs. Vanders walks in, accompanied by Frederick. They circle around her table, taking the seat near Beth and Grayson. Mrs. Vanders takes a slight sip of her red wine, then scans the room. She first views around her large table, then to others. The scattered seating has just the right amount of distance between them to make your way to the dance floor. When her eyes move to Grayson and Beth, a smile beams across her face. She's delighted to see Grayson and Beth together.

She hopes this business relationship will spark a flame and become intimate as well. Looking at Beth and her beauty, Mrs.

Vanders longs for her youth again. Clinking her glass, she rises to face the group. "Good evening, everyone. Thank you all for coming. As most of you know, today is the beginning of the year end merriments. It starts tonight and ends on New Year's Day. This is a special time of year for me. I love the happy festivities this time of year brings. Next week is Thanksgiving. We invite all of you to spend the day here. You are welcome to stay overnight as well. Just let the staff know, so they can make preparations."

During these celebrations, drinks are indulged heavily, so she always makes the offer. "If you decide not to stay, I will have drivers available to transport you home. Please, don't drink and drive." She gives a jubilant, "Eat, drink and be merry!" She clinks her glass against those that are near her before resuming her address with topics of business and updates on all the family holdings.

"We are going into the end of the year looking to have a prosperous year." She expands on each division. "I would also like to congratulate my nephew Grayson and my dear Beth on their successful business venture. Grayson was kind enough to update me this afternoon on the figures. I must say they're impressive." She holds her glass toward them. "I couldn't have picked a better pair if I tried. Congratulations!"

The room claps, and a few whistles are added for good measure. Beth looks around the tables and everyone is beaming. She sees pure elation supporting their success. Smiling at everyone, she ultimately gets the family dynamics. They are genuinely happy when a family member succeeds. She lifts her glass toward everyone and nods her head in acknowledgment.

Dinner is divine. The meat is tender. The salad is crisp and flavorful. Everyone is talking while music plays low in the background. The orchestra is performing a soft medley that makes Beth sway. Once dinner is over, they remove the dinnerware, leaving only their drinks on the table. Beth takes a sip. The warmth from the brandy allows her to relax as she enjoys the atmosphere. Couples are moving onto the floor to dance. Beth watches the couples, to see if she can detect who's in love. Some are dancing with no conversation. Men are peering over the head of their partners, watching everyone else. Others have their eyes closed, like they're falling asleep. Yet, some are gazing into their partner's eyes. When she sees that, she smiles. "There it is, love."

Grayson interrupts her gaze with a question. "Would you care to dance, Beth?"

Not prepared for this aspect of the night, she's taken back by the question. Trying to mask her discomfort, she replies, "Of course." While they've come a long way, there's still a sense of uneasiness with him. She can't let go of their initial encounter, and his condescending remarks.

He stands, extending his hand to help her out of the seat. Placing her hand in his, she rises. They walk silently to the floor. Grayson puts his right arm around her waist as she assumes a position that keeps a certain distance between them. She's leaning more into his arm than his body, leaving awkward space between them. Never having been this close to him, (excluding the incident in the new car), the proximity is unsettling to her. Trying not to think of their earlier interactions of friction, she decides to focus on the thoughtful Grayson that gave her the car.

He interrupts the silence. "I must say it again Beth, you look stunning tonight."

"Thank you, Grayson."

For the life of him, he doesn't know what to say next. He doesn't want to discuss work tonight, so he fumbles for the next statement. Finally, a topic comes to mind. "Do you have any major plans for the holidays?"

Grateful for a question she could respond to, she says, "I decided today that I may take a trip. Maybe to a ski resort, or something like that. No final plans yet. What are your plans?"

"Like you, I have finalized nothing. To be honest, I appreciate the downtime that the holiday offers. There are enough events to keep me busy, yet there's time to relax as well."

Actually, that's an excellent thought, she thinks to herself. "I hadn't thought of that. My concern is that if I'm close enough to run into the office, it may tempt me to do so."

He looks at her, then chuckles. "You took the words right out of my mouth. Before now, I never owned the businesses, but was invariably a significant player in the executive branch. This is my business." He halts mid statement, then corrects. "Our business." He grins. "I am more motivated than ever to check on things."

Letting out a giggle, she echoes his remarks. "Our business." Smiling, she has to admit he has changed since she met him. She looks into his eyes as he gazes deeply into hers. It seems the entire party has left the room, and it's just the two of them. Just as they lean in for a kiss, the music ends, and the crowd begins clapping. Looking around, they both see Mrs. Vanders coming onto the floor with a partner. In awe of the respect this family gives her, she claps as well.

Going back to the table, she grabs her small handbag, excusing herself for the powder room. Grayson acknowledges and smiles.

Laying her purse on the counter, she studies herself in the mirror and asks herself, "What are you doing, Beth? Grayson Vanders for gosh sakes!" Reapplying lipstick, she powders her nose lightly. Thinking about it again, she says to herself, "He'll break your heart!" Shaking her head and shrugging, she exits to return to the eventful night.

Returning, she notices Grayson standing with a few guests in deep conversation. As she passes, she hears they are congratulating him on the business success. To her astonishment, he says, "I couldn't have done it without Beth. She's been a phenomenal resource with her publishing acumen. I knew nothing about it." She knows he didn't see her return. His remarks chip away at the stone in her heart. She puts her purse on the table, pulling out the chair. A very handsome gentleman makes an approach.

"May I have this dance?"

"Of course." She takes his hand as he leads her to the floor.

Unlike Grayson, who maintained his distance, this gentleman holds her very close. She admits his cologne is divine. As soon as they get in rhythm with the steps, he whispers in her ear. "It is very nice to meet you personally, Beth."

She looks up into his eyes to ask his name, but he interrupts.

"Oh sorry. My name is Derek Grayson."

Surprised by the last name, she inquires, "So you are from the Grayson side of the family. I don't recall finding your name in my research."

He smiles and with a little humor adds, "How could you miss me? I'm a direct descendant of Chad Grayson."

Intrigued, she declares, "But, I'm certain I covered all the Grayson's side of the family as well." She must go back to reexamine her notes. How could she have missed his name during her investigation? His name Derek Grayson alone should cause him to stand out.

"You must have missed some research, because I am who I am." He laughs, then smiles warmly, gazing into her eyes. Then, follows with a question that implies a subsequent time for them. "How are you planning to make this up to me? I've been neglected by your research. My feelings are hurt, my heart is broken, and it will undoubtedly require some mending."

Laughing, she responds. "Ah, the age-old question, "How can you mend a broken heart?"

He furrows his brow, stopping to look in the air as if pondering. "Isn't that a song?"

Definitely liking his sense of humor, she replies, "I think so."

He adds, "I can see why you would have missed me during your interviews. I've been out of the country for the last six months. The old, out of sight, out of mind may be the catalyst."

She smiles. "That may be the case."

The music ends. As she draws away, he grasps her hand, pulling her back into him for the next slow dance that's starting. She complies, stepping back into his embrace. It's wonderful to be held this close by a handsome man. But as she's settling into the warmth of his arms, a voice breaks the silence.

Tapping Derek on the shoulder, the voice asks, "May I break in?"

Recognizing his voice immediately, she shifts to see Grayson. Surprised by his bold move, she stands there waiting for Derek's response.

Derek backs away. Slightly bowing, he answers, "Of course."

Grayson steps in and takes her hand. This time, instead of his distance, he pulls her in close, placing both of his arms around her. She finds herself with her arms around his neck. Not wanting to see his face, she turns her head, moving her arm down to place her head on his shoulder. They dance, swaying back and forth to the romantic melody. His arms tighten. Eventually he moves his hand to her back. She senses his warmth next to her. Unlike Derek's grip, his hold seems more intimate. Or was she blowing this moment way out of proportion? When she detects his chin rest near the top of her head, she holds her breath with delight, cherishing the one moment they may never have again.

The song ends all too soon. As they separate, he smiles warmly. Taking her by the hand, he leads her back to the table. At least, that's where she assumes they're headed until he starts walking toward the exit. She twists to look backward as they leave the ballroom.

Opening the closed door to a small room, he pulls her inside. It's lit by a lone sconce hanging on the wall. Grayson pulls her in and swings her around. "Why were you so cozy with Derek?"

Reacting defensively from the manner of the question, she asks, "Cozy?"

"Yes, you were so close air couldn't get between you."

"So? What is this all about, Grayson? Why are you asking a senseless question like this? It's not like you and I are a couple." Pondering the thought, she then replies, "It's inappropriate for you to act this way. We're business partners."

"Business partners, my ass!" He grabs her. Bringing her mouth to his, he kisses her deeply, passionately.

Responsive heat explodes in her body. She matches his fervor in the kiss. She sucks on his lip, matching his passion. He pushes her up against the wall, kissing and biting her neck. She moans with pleasure.

Grayson moves his hand to her breast, using his thumb to pursue her nipples. The dress is made of thin, delicate material. A slight touch and her nipples harden. His groin swells with desire. Backing her to the sofa in the middle of the room, he lays with her. He continues exploring her body, kissing the mounds of her breast. She pushes against him for more.

He lingers in this explosive pursuit of gratification, grinding his hardness against her. Tugging the shoulder of her dress down, he pulls her breast out for further access. He puts her nipple in his mouth and suckles. Feeling her urgency increase, he bites the tip. She gasps and pulls him closer. He rocks his hardened manhood against her pelvis. She meets stroke for stroke, grazing and nibbling his neck. They are in a whirlwind of seek and find. Touching each other so privately, they escape the world outside of this room.

Her emotions are running everywhere. Deep down, she has always wanted this to happen. Her common sense knows he is her business partner. Doing this can make things complicated. The touch of his fevered hands drowns out all reason.

As he moves his hand to pull the skirt of her gown up, a commotion disturbs them. Both hear laughter in the hallway. Abruptly sitting up, they straighten their clothes. As they sit beside each other, the door opens, and a couple enters. The gentleman asserts, "Oh, pardon me, we were looking for a private room." They exit the room without waiting for a response, shutting the door behind them.

Grayson looks at Beth, seeking permission to continue.

Confused out of her mind, she jumps up, wiping her lips, and leaves the room without a word. Making her way back to the ballroom, she goes to the table with the intent to grab her purse and leave.

Mrs. Vanders turns to her and says, "Oh, there you are, Beth. Sit, I have something to tell you."

Unable to decline, she sits in the seat beside her.

"Beth, I have so much to tell you." Looking around to make certain their conversation is private, she continues. "I went back in time to see Rachel."

Beth lays her hand over Mrs. Vanders, and responds. "Oh, my goodness! Did you really? Tell me what transpired? How did that happen?"

Again, Mrs. Vanders looks around, scanning for observers first. She says, "Rachel wrote a note informing me of the plans for her wedding. Knowing this was supposed to be me getting married, I wanted to see how my parents were responding to our marriage. I was curious to see if they had accepted Chad Grayson. So, I went to the room, and put on some clothes from the past. Poof, I'm there."

"Mrs. Vanders, that could have been extremely dangerous with your current health!"

Mrs. Vanders smiles at Beth's concern. "Yes, it was quite challenging. I was bedridden for a bit at first." Acknowledging Beth's gasp of apprehension, she nods her head accepting that it was a risky decision. "I needed this, Beth. I haven't seen my parents for years." Closing her eyes to keep the tears from spilling out, she says, "It was wonderful seeing them."

Looking at Mrs. Vanders, she notices the fresh glow on her face. "You look happy. I'm glad you're okay and it worked out."

"It's better than okay, Beth. I don't know what happened, but when I returned, of course I was terribly weak, but a miracle occurred."

Beth waits in anticipation for more.

"Beth, my cancer has practically disappeared!"

Gasping in disbelief, she exclaims, "What? Are you kidding me?"

Mrs. Vanders laughs. "No Beth, I'm serious. I went to the doctor for my usual cancer checkup, and they did all the routine tests to determine how much my cancer has progressed. The tests reveal there is very little cancer! The treatments are working. Of course, there will be further tests in a couple of months to verify, but so far, it looks promising."

"That's incredible! How can that be? I mean, don't get me wrong, that's the best news in the world, but it sounds too good to be true."

"I don't know. It could be that when I broke into fragments, the unhealthy cancer cells weren't strong enough to withstand the process. Me dissolving into particles alone may have shattered them."

"Oh, my gosh, this is wonderful news!" Hesitating with the question she asks, "Are you confident the tests were accurate?"

Nodding yes, Mrs. Vanders replies. "I had them repeated, and the results were the same. The cancer is barely there, which means we caught it much earlier than before. I'm in remission, with an expected full recovery!"

"That's amazing." Getting up, she moves to hug her. "This is the best news you could have ever given me."

Talking for a while longer about Beth and the business, they are interrupted by a suitor. Mrs. Vanders gets up to dance. Taking that moment to escape, she exits the room, not looking back. On her way to her suite, curiosity about the mysterious room takes over. Going up the additional flight of stairs, she opens the door and turns on the light switch.

Walking around the area, she rubs her hand over the mirror, then walks in front of it to look at herself. Wondering if she could do what Rachel and Mrs. Vanders have done, she looks toward the bureau where all the old dresses hang. Walking slowly toward it, she opens the large doors. Looking through the gowns, one catches her eye. It's a turquoise dress with the design of that era. Pulling it out, she spreads it out on the antique chair. Unzipping her dress, she puts on the gown. The fit is perfect. Feeling fear in every step, yet unable to resist, she walks to the mirror. As viewed in the video taken of Rachel's departure, she holds out the skirt and twirls. Dizziness overtakes her. She blacks out.

CHAPTER 14

A PLACE IN TIME

Beth's vision is blurred as she opens her eyes. Turning her head back and forth to examine the room, she squints, struggling to clear her sight. Attempting to move, she feels like dead weights are on her arms and legs. Lying motionless for a while, she gradually works up the strength to get up. Looking around the place, she sees her clothes are on the chair. It's absurd that she thought she had traveled through time. Picking up her dress, she puts it back on, placing the old gown back in the bureau.

Checking and adjusting her appearance in the mirror, she's satisfied enough to get to her suite. Opening the door, she instantly realizes things are not as they were. The corridors have long runner rugs, instead of the thick carpet that's normally there. Running down the stairs, she learns nothing is the same on any floor. Panic filling her stomach, she gets nauseous. Going down to what she knows is the main floor, she halts when she meets strangers rambling about. One person after the other passes by with no acknowledgment. She realizes time travel is legitimate. Stopping one person who looks like they could be staff, she asks, "Can you tell me where Rachel, I mean Adrianna is?"

The person stops, giving Beth the once over.

Realizing she's dressed in the evening dress that is assuredly not the style of the era, she panics. Self-conscious and tense, her heart races as she proceeds down the stairs. What if she has landed on the wrong date, and there is no Rachel?

"Come this way, Miss." A voice stops her. A man leads her to a room with various seating areas. Pointing to a settee, he asserts, "Have a seat, I'll let her know you are here." Looking at her again, as if examining her, he inquires, "What is your name, please?"

"Please tell her my name is Beth. I'm an old friend."

Slightly nodding, he leaves the room.

Unable to sit still, Beth gets up and starts pacing the floor. When the door opens, she sees Rachel and relief overwhelms her. She exclaims, "Rachel, I'm so glad it's you."

Holding her hand up to silence her, she closes the door. Shock written all over her face, she exclaims, "Beth, is it actually you?"

Voice quivering, she responds. "In the flesh. Well at least, I think I am." She touches her arms checking to be certain.

Rachel grabs her, hugging her with exuberance. "I'm so pleased to see you." Noticing Beth is trembling, she moves her to the settee to sit. Remembering what time travel does to a person, she understands there is extreme instability. "Here, sit down." Going over to a stand, she grabs an empty glass, filling it with water from a pitcher. "Drink this. You're probably very depleted right now."

Gladly accepting it, Beth drinks like she's dying of thirst. Realizing what she has now achieved, Beth gets emotional. "Rachel, I'm so sorry to just drop in like this. I honestly didn't expect it to work." She looks at Rachel, then finishes the sentence. "You know, the time travel and all."

Rachel laughs. "You should have seen me the first time I woke up in the past. Mrs. Vanders had mentioned that the estate had a portal for time travel. Down deep, I thought it was nonsense. I didn't believe time travel existed. You had an advantage over me in accepting this incredible experience. Both of us had confirmed its existence for you."

"Thank God you're here, Rachel. What if I had traveled to a time where I knew no one?"

Rachel smiles in understanding. "I think it's the clothes that land us in the time period. That's why I constantly keep those specific dresses in that room."

Thinking like a journalist, and analyzing the logic, she agrees with the deduction. She studies Rachel and asks, "Is it okay that I'm here?"

Rachel smiles, "Of course! I'm delighted to see my new best friend." Noticing Beth is very pale, she suggests, "Let's get you set up for tonight. It's late, so a proper night's sleep will help you come out of the fog and regain your strength." Rachel walks to the door. Opening it, she motions for someone in the hall. "Alice, please prepare a room for my guest. I think the pink room will be perfect." Turning back to Beth, she asks, "Beth, are you hungry? Can I order you something to eat?"

"No, thank you," Recalling her name here, she finishes with "Adrianna. I just had dinner."

Releasing Alice to go prepare Beth's room, she closes the door.

Beth realizes the absurdity of the remark that she had just eaten. She continues, "Well, if you consider 100 years in the future as just eaten, I did."

Both burst into laughter. They fall on the settee. Rachel says, "Well, you could make a return trip, and it could be double that time. Just consider how hungry you'd be after 200 years." They laugh hysterically. Rachel looks at Beth and announces, "That's what I remember most about you, our laughter."

Alice returns, informing Rachel the room is ready. Rachel says, "Come on Beth, let's get you a good night's sleep. Walking Beth upstairs slowly, she escorts her to her quarters for the night.

Walking into the suite, she discovers the décor is feminine, pleasantly bright and cheerful. The 4-poster bed looks antique to Beth. It shines like its brand new, though. Assuming it's modern for this age, she remarks on its elegance. A beautiful white nightgown is draped over the edge of the bed. She thanks Alice as she exits the room. Beth looks at Rachel and inquires, "What time is it here?"

Rachel replies, "It's a little after midnight."

Beth realizes it's the same as when she left her time. "Things really do tie in together somehow, don't they?"

Yes, when I time traveled before, I would be gone for months. But, when I would return to the future, I'd discover it's hardly been an hour. I could never comprehend how time can proceed here, but not there or vice versa. Rachel walks around checking to make sure Beth has everything she'll need. She tells her, "I'll send some gowns up for you in the morning. I'm assigning Alice to you. She'll wake you in the morning in time for breakfast." She hugs her friend, "I can't wait for you to meet Chad! You'll love him as much as I do."

Beth adds some humor, "I hope not. Is bigamy legal in this time period?"

Rachel slaps Beth's arm and giggles. Thinking for just one moment, she comes up with a plan she puts out there for Beth. "Chad has a handsome partner who is single. In fact, you'll meet many of our associations while you're here. There are plenty eligible bachelors to select from."

Beth throws up her hands to stop. "No match making Rachel! I plan to return to the future very soon. I have a life there that I'm grateful for. Speaking of, I can't wait to catch you up on everything that has happened." Beth suddenly feels weak, and leans against the bedpost.

Rachel moves to her side to helps her rest on the bed. "Beth, are you okay?"

"Just feeling a little unsteady."

"Okay, let's get you to bed." She pulls Beth back to her feet, directing her to turn around. Beth leans on the bed post again while Rachel unzips her gown. The air hits her back as she pulls the dress down until she is only in her lingerie.

Rachel grabs the garment off the bed. Handing it to her, she asks, "Are you okay to handle it from here? Should I call Alice to assist?"

Holding the gown in front of her chills develop. She says, "Thank you, Rachel. I'll see you in the morning."

Rachel glances back before she opens the door and says, "Beth, don't forget to address me as Adrianna. If you call me Rachel, they'll assume you're daft, and how will I respond to that?" Laughing, she continues, "Seriously though, Beth, I'm so pleased you're here. I can't wait to share my wonderful life with you. I'm delighted that Chad will get to meet you." Smiling, she blows a kiss and says, "Good night."

As the door closes, Beth undresses quickly. She makes a hasty plunge into bed. The air is chilly, unlike the warm, cozy suite she's accustomed to. Crawling under the covers, she wastes no time and falls into a deep sleep within seconds.

The next morning, she wakes to light streaming in her eyes from the window. Alice is drawing back the drapes, causing the sun to shine brightly on her face. Covering her eyes with her arm, she moans. She must have slept too sound, because she has a pounding headache.

Alice looks back catching the wince from Beth, and the eye covering. "Oh, sorry, Miss."

Trying to be gracious, Beth replies, "No problem. You don't happen to have any aspirin on you, do you? I have a pounding headache."

Alice understands the situation, and explains she'll be right back.

Beth props her pillow up, glancing around the bed chamber. In the daylight, the room is even more cheerful and bright than she recalled last night. There's a blazing fire in the fireplace. "Boy, I could have used that last night." Glancing at a chair, she sees clothing draped across it. Coordinating shoes are on the floor.

The door opens. Alice approaches her bed with some pills and water. Beth gratefully swallows both at the same time, handing the glass back to her. She settles back on the bed for a minute, closing her eyes. "Thank you for the fire, Alice. I needed that last night. It was chilly in here."

"I started the fire last night. You were fast asleep when I returned to light it." Changing the subject, she informs her, "Breakfast will be served in 45 minutes, Miss. I will escort you when you are ready. Do you require anything else, madam?"

"No, I'm good, thank you Alice." Beth closes her eyes as she hears Alice close the door. After resting for another ten minutes, she drags herself up to freshen up for breakfast. The dress Rachel provides fits perfectly. The shoes do, too.

A peek on the door occurs as she pushes the brush through her hair with one last stroke. Having long straight blonde hair is beneficial when you have no stylist available. Laying the brush down, she takes one last glimpse in the mirror, giving herself a thumbs up.

"Okay Chad Grayson, I'm here to make sure you are good enough for my Rachel." Turning, she goes to the door and follows Alice to breakfast.

Entering the dining room, she sees many people seated at a long dining table. Spotting Rachel, she smiles, raising her brows in a positive gesture of Chad.

Rachel gets up and comes to greet her. Smiling, she turns to those assembled and speaks. "Everyone, this is my best friend, Beth. She has come to visit me for a while." She looks at Beth and takes her by the arm moving down the table introducing her to each person. The men stand, bowing in a welcoming gesture. The ladies offer welcoming remarks of acceptance. When they arrive at the end of the table, she's introduced to the infamous Chad Grayson.

He responds, "Welcome Beth. It is so wonderful to meet you. My wife kept me up half the night telling me all about you."

Beth smiles at Rachel. Looking back to Chad, she replies, "It's nice to finally meet you, Chad. I've heard so much about you as well." In a million years, she has never seen anyone so handsome. The dilemma is that he is the spitting image of Grayson Vanders! As he gestures her to take a seat, Beth realizes that Chad is the perfect gentleman.

He is seated at the head of the table, while Rachel is to his left. They place Beth to his right. She's facing Rachel, who's directly across from her. Rachel's reassuring looks, help in the moments of oddness. A thought enters her mind, so she asks, "Adrianna, where are your parents?"

Smiling, as she motions for the server to bring a dish over for Beth, she replies, "They're in Europe. They've been traveling quite a bit lately. I'm delighted for them. They deserve this time after retiring."

The large plate in front of her has pancakes, eggs, ham, and bread. It's far more than she would usually eat. Rachel sees Beth's eyes widen, so she whispers, "You don't have to eat it all. Just pick what you want. I didn't know what to get you, so I instructed them to bring you one of everything." A small dish of fruit is placed beside Beth as well.

Understanding Rachel's dilemma, Beth thanks her. Picking up the fork, she attacks the scrambled eggs. She realizes after the first bite that she's starving. She dives into the plate of food. Eating a bit of each item, she quickly finds herself full.

During breakfast, small talk occurs between those at the table. Chad asks, Beth, "How are you feeling this morning after your journey?"

Understanding the hidden significance of that question, she replies, "I had a severe headache when I woke up, but it has diminished a bit now."

"Good, I'm glad to hear it. Please, let Alice know if your head continues to hurt. We can request something stronger."

Thanking him, she watches as Rachel and Chad look back and forth at each other. They exchange comments about Adrianna's travels, and how they affect her as well. He gazes at Rachel intermittently, indicating clear love and commitment. He watches her adoringly, as she gets excited over Beth's presence.

A host enters the room, followed by a tall, handsomely dressed gentleman. Grayson stands, grasping his hand, as he slaps his back. "Good morning, Brad." Turning toward Beth, he says, "Beth, this is my law partner Brad Hastings."

Brad walks around the table, extending his hand out to hers.

Chad says, pointing to a chair that's empty beside Rachel, "Have a seat, Brad."

Rachel says, "No wait, let me come around to sit beside Beth. Brad, you sit here beside Chad. I don't want you to have to speak over me to converse." Before anyone could disagree, she's up and around the table.

The two men chat about business while the girls ramble on about what a routine day is for Rachel. Today is Saturday, so Rachel has some minor duties of approving menus for the formal gathering later tonight.

She's delighted that Beth will be here to observe an evening of her life in this time. She tries to coax Beth into staying with her the whole day. Beth readily agrees. As a reporter, she is all about details. She wants to get the complete picture of why Rachel has embraced this life instead of the future. Beth already perceives the answer is love. She's concerned that love may not be enough. It has to be more. She wants to witness Rachel in her element, to be confident she's at peace with her decision.

Rachel takes Beth around the grounds for a tour. It's November, so the air has a brisk chill in it. They wrap up before venturing out. Walking outside, Beth breathes deeply into the crisp air lingering the familiar fragrance of fall foliage at its peak.

Beth and Rachel walk, arm and arm, chatting about everything. Beth tells her of Mrs. Vanders health improvements since the trip. Informing Rachel about the success of the publishing company is exciting. It's not until Rachel asks about Grayson Vanders that she feels uneasy. After all, Grayson was attracted to Rachel first. She's not even clear if he's genuinely interested in her.

Rachel senses Beth's discomfort. Trying to make her feel better, Rachel says, "Beth look, I recognize you have never gotten along with Grayson. You shouldn't let your dislike of him affect you in business. It sounds like you make a great team where it counts at work."

Beth looks at Rachel and grins sheepishly. "That's just it, Rachel, something happened last night before I arrived here. It has shaken me to my core."

Stopping to study Beth, Rachel asks, "What did that scoundrel do?"

Still unable to get the words out of her mouth completely, she answers, "It's not what he did to me, it's what we did to each other."

Anxiously waiting, Rachel says, "Okay, I'm listening." She twirls her hand in a circle, motioning Beth to get on with the story. "You're killing me!"

Beth sees a Gazebo. She grabs Rachel's sleeve, pulling her to sit. Sitting on the padded benches, she depicts the tale of her confusing night with Grayson.

Rachel's expressions do not give away her thoughts as Beth reveals the events of her encounter with Grayson. Rachel is silent when the narrative ends. Beth watches her, waiting for a response.

Suddenly, Rachel says, "Holy Shit Beth! I didn't know the guy had it in him. I mean, I knew he looked enough like Chad that there was potential, but to hear you describe it, he's HOT!"

Stunned by Rachel's response, she glares at her. "Are you kidding me? I declare how torn I am about what transpired last night, and you boil it all down to he's HOT?!"

Laughing, Rachel says in between her giggles, "I'm sorry Beth. I can appreciate how this must confuse you. I acknowledge the conflict between the two of you, but all I can think about is how I kept comparing him to Chad. He just never added up for me. It's fascinating that he is inching his way into your heart."

Beth spews a rebuttal. "No, I didn't express that he was in my heart. Rachel, in the beginning Grayson irritated me to no end. I labeled him as a spoiled, rich, cynical jerk. Then he buys me the new car."

Rachel lays her hand on Beth's arm. "Wait a minute, what about a new car?"

Beth tells Rachel how he surprised her with the new car, describing how hers barely started one morning. "He was explaining the features on the dash, when we came nose to nose close. That's the first time I felt an attraction to him. I don't know. Something changed that day. I saw him as a nice guy after that."

"Based on your explosive time together last night, I would maintain the word nice is understated." Laughing, Rachel says, "I'm back to HOT myself."

Rachel can take Beth's all too serious emotions and twist them into an all-out giggle session. "Oh my! Rachel, you're a sex fiend."

"Wait a minute here," Rachel says with gusto. "I'm not the one that almost got naked on a couch with a HOT guy."

Again, the laughter is uncontrollable.

They finally get serious enough to discuss Grayson without the word HOT. Rachel says, "Listen, I found Grayson to be an incredibly appealing man. He has demonstrated himself as a particularly savvy businessman. He's been a major player in the Vanders' successes. He's handsome, charming, and the ladies really like him. He's broken quite a few hearts, if the stories I have read about him are correct. He's almost 35, and hasn't settled down yet. If it hadn't been for my comparing him to Chad, to be honest, I would have been interested."

"That's the other thing. He chose you before me. I'm the second choice here."

Rachel replies, "Wait a minute, you were always unpleasant to him if you recall. I can't see him being interested in a viper."

"Oh, that stings!"

"Seriously, Beth. It wasn't until he got you the car that you saw him in a different light. Maybe he saw you the same way. He watched you help him turn a floundering company into a successful, prosperous business. He's the co-owner, that had to impress him. Maybe it caused him see you in a different light, too." She shrugs her shoulders.

"At least give him a chance. He got jealous for goodness' sake. His affections must be pretty deep for him to allow his jealousy to win over."

Beth ponders the thought. "Maybe, but if it doesn't pan out, it will ruin our business relationship. Not to mention, Mrs.

Vanders may not be pleased with us crossing the line as partners "

They get up to walk back inside. Rachel says, "Listen, if I know anything about Mrs. Vanders," she looks at Beth and whispers, "Adrianna…, I know she's a romantic. She gave up her life here to be there for love. She will understand before anyone else does. Also, you need to let him know, if you choose to take this further, if it doesn't work out, your business relationship is separate." Rachel pauses and grabs her arm. "We need to get back. Come on let's go inside."

Arriving in time for lunch, they relax in a delightful place where they can see out the window as they dine. It's a small, cozy setting with a small table for two. Rachel tells her more personal details about her life with Chad.

Beth witnesses a warm glow spread across Rachel's face as she speaks of him. After glancing around the area and, noticing a staff member close by, she asks the question that's been burning at the back of her mind. "Adrianna, are you genuinely happy here? I see the gleam in your eyes when you talk about Chad, but do you ever miss the future?"

Rachel takes a sip of her tea. Looking at Beth, she says, "I miss you. I miss my job a little, but that's it. Beth, I'm content here. Chad has offered to acquire a publishing company if I want it. Heck, he suggested buying the local newspaper for me to run. I'm not in a position to accept something like that right now. Beth, he wants to make me happy in every way. I think sometimes he worries that ultimately, I'll choose to go home. What he fails to understand is that I am home when I'm with him. I love him more than life itself." Rachel looks around the room then back at Beth. She whispers, "I haven't told him yet, but Adrianna is pregnant!"

Beth screams! "Oh my God!" She gets up and runs around the table to hug her. Still seeing the woman in the corner, "Adrianna, I'm so thrilled for you."

Still whispering, "I plan to tell him tonight."

"I can't believe I came here right now. I'm so glad I could be a part of this. How do you think he'll take it?"

"He'll be ecstatic. He's made it abundantly clear he wants children."

"This is wonderful news," she whispers, "Rachel."

The announcement is making Beth's visit all the more special. While she is delighted for Rachel, it saddens her to realize she will not be here for the birth or to see the happy family grow. It's bittersweet. However, watching Rachel be Adrianna all day, she celebrates her friend's new-found existence.

Beth readies herself for the evening festivities. Rachel brings her several garments to select from. She goes with the black gown that has sheer lace on the chest and arms. It bears a round neckline that circles the base of the neck. Inspecting herself in the mirror, Beth thinks it's a glamorous look. The black heels match the dress perfectly. Her blonde hair falls gracefully down her back and over her arms. Very pleased with the ensemble, she leaves her room to attend the party.

Following the other guests, she finds her way to the same ball room she has been to in the future. The décor is different now. In the future, there are bright shiny tables. Tonight, there are black clothes on the tables with flickering white candles in the center. White dinnerware, and the finest silverware are set before each seat. The venue has a glimmer of romance, and the soft music in the air makes it better. An orchestra sits behind the dance floor that shines like glass. The room is stunning.

The host requests her name. Checking the registry, he states, "Right this way, madam." As she moves to follow, she sees Chad and Rachel greeting guests. Rachel grabs her hand, telling her she will be at the table soon. "You look beautiful, Beth!"

Chad is immersed in conversation with guests. Looking back at Rachel, she says with a smile, "You do, too. You're glowing." Rachel gets teary-eyed.

Following her guide to the table, Beth discovers it's already full, except for the three seats reserved for Chad, Rachel and Beth. Chad's partner, Brad, is seated next to her. Coincidence? I think not

"Good evening, Beth. You look stunning tonight." He stands.

"Thank you, Brad. Adrianna was nice enough to provide me this lovely gown."

"Her taste is exquisite."

"You look dashing tonight yourself." She acknowledges to herself, he's good looking. He's not as handsome as Grayson, but there's something about those green eyes and dark brown hair that's hard to turn away from.

Brad pulls out her chair. A glass of red wine is already there. She takes a sip. She looks at Brad and inquires, "Did you order this for me? It's my favorite."

"No. I'm sure Adrianna let the staff know. She is amazing at organizing these events. She learns what each guest drinks, and how they like their food cooked. She has the finest chefs in New York."

She looks at Rachel heading her way and smiles. "She's a keeper, that's for sure."

Brad laughs. "I think Chad knows that." He clicks his glass against Beth's.

Chad grabs the glass while Rachel places her clutch down on the table. Rachel touches Beth's shoulders, and says, "I'll be back in a minute." Beth nods.

Chad and Adrianna go to the stage where the orchestra is set. He taps the microphone. Finding the noise levels desirable, he says, "Good evening, ladies and gentlemen. Adrianna and I welcome you. Thank you all for coming tonight. We begin our holiday traditions this evening. We look forward to seeing all of you throughout this joyous time of year. May the season bring peace and happiness. This coming Thursday, is Thanksgiving. Let us all be thankful for the blessings in our lives, and our good fortunes." He looks at Rachel, then kisses her on the cheek. Taking her hand, he yells to the crowd, "A toast to you all." He holds up the glass in his hand, then takes a drink.

Beth holds her glass up, drinking to the moment as well. This being her third serving, she's settling in, reveling in the celebrations. What she finds intriguing is that she had heard a similar speech the night before from Mrs. Vanders. Not wishing to mix up her fogging mind, she decides to focus on the present.

Chad and Rachel get off the stage and arrive at the table to take their seats. Instead, Chad sets his glass down, and pulls Rachel to the dance floor. They are cuddled close, whispering to each other. Beth watches them. They make a striking couple. Rachel looks stunning, and Chad is extremely handsome. He looks like a Greek God.

Beth has always felt that she could hold her own in the looks department, but she doesn't hold a candle to Rachel. Watching them tonight, she feels a little envious of the tenderness they have found. She has everything! She's found love that time couldn't keep apart. Feeling wistful, she hopes someday she discovers something nearly as special as what they have. Continuing to observe them, she sees Rachel's hand go up to Chad's cheek. She lays her cheek to his other cheek. It looks like an intimate moment. He breaks away and looks her dead in the face. He responds, "Really?! You are not toying with me, are you?"

When Beth sees her touch her stomach, she knows what has just transpired. She stands up just as Chad grabs Rachel. He swings her around, laughing. He puts her down, then yells, "I'm going to be a father!"

The entire room erupts into applause. Tears roll from Beth's eyes as she witnesses her best friend have the moment of her life. If she had any qualms about Rachel's happiness, it dissolved in this moment of jubilance and adoration. Rachel turns toward Beth with a smile that could light up a room.

The orchestra plays slow romantic music. Chad takes his wife in his arms, and they close out the world except to each other.

Brad asks Beth to dance. They move to the floor, embracing the melody of a love song. Beth is indulging in the happiness of the occasion. Brad whispers in her ear, "That is delightful news for Chad and Adrianna."

"It's wonderful news. I'm so happy for them."

He glances over at the couple. "He's a transformed man since he found her."

"Really? How did he change?"

"If you had asked me a year ago whether Chad Grayson would ever marry, I'd tell you no, absolutely not. He broke so many hearts. I thought the only way he would marry, is if it was a shotgun wedding."

Laughing, Beth glances at the couple, and replies, "You'd never guess that now." The two are entangled in love. As they dance, she wishes she were in the arms of someone she loved.

The night gets lively as the clock ticks on. Drinks are being downed like water. Beth's feeling no pain herself. Trying to grasp the dance of the period is more entertaining when you're lit.

Rachel watches her friend having a good time and grins. However, she makes a mental note not to push Beth too much to stay. She watches Brad and Beth laughing, as they tear up the floor.

Before Beth gets too far gone, Rachel and Beth go off into another quiet place to chat. Rachel says, "You look like you're having a good time out there. You and Brad seem to be hitting it off nicely."

Beth looks at her, then shakes a finger at her. "No, no, no! No matchmaking."

Rachel laughs. "I can't help myself. I cherish having you here. You're someone who knows all of me. I'm enjoying this."

Beth takes Rachel's hand. "I know you are. It must be so hard to be where you have no one."

Rachel corrects her. "I have Chad. That's all I need. Beth, don't forget I was extremely unhappy in the future." She glances around the room. "This is where I belong. This is my destiny in life. It's just that it's been great having you here today."

"It's been wonderful, but you know I can't stay, right?"

Rachel puts on a pout. "I was hoping, but I know you can't."

Beth states, "To be honest, if the business had failed, I might have considered this. Of course, I didn't know whether it was indeed possible for me to travel here. But if it had failed, I think I would have tried, just like I did this time."

Rachel replies, "It has been a joy having you here to share the good news." She lays her palm on her abdomen.

"It's wonderful news. I can't wait to tell Mrs. Vanders."

Rachel looks at her, then asks the dreaded question. "When are you returning?"

"I'll be returning tonight, Rachel. Watching you and Chad has made me crave more. I want what you have. While you discovered your place here, I know mine is in the future."

"With Grayson?"

Beth ponders the question. "Honestly, I don't know, but I will never find out if I don't go back. I need to see where it leads."

Tears welling in Rachel's eyes, she cries, "I will miss you."

Seeing the tears, Beth goes, "Oh Rachel, I'm sorry I upset you."

Crying and giggling, she responds, "It's not you. It's the hormones."

They laugh until it hurts.

Returning to the ballroom, Brad orders another round of drinks for the group, and a glass of water for Adrianna. Tasting hers, Beth squinches from the strength of the alcohol. Taking a swig, she thinks, what the heck. I'll enjoy myself while I'm here. They dance and party half the night away until one o'clock.

Beth needs to pull herself together before she attempts the trip home. She realizes she's tipsy, as she is about to go to the powder room. She plans to make her exit now, but Brad pulls her to the floor for one more dance. Deciding one more dance couldn't hurt, she follows him.

The music is slow, thank heavens. Brad pulls her in close. They dance, swaying back and forth. They are wrapped up together, melting into the moment. His cologne has made its way to her muddled mind. She enjoys the moment and his touch. Alcohol tends to make her more comfortable than she should be. Time slips by, as they cling to each other. The music ends. When they pull apart, she's burning up. There's no air conditioning, so she makes her way to the balcony. Brad follows her to make certain she's okay.

She steps out into the cool night air, taking in a deep breath, feeling cooler instantly. He asks if she's okay. She assures him she's fine. He pushes her hair behind her shoulder to help her cool down. Their eyes lock. Whether it's the alcohol or the fresh air going to her brain, when he leans in to kiss her, she meets him with eagerness. Her brain is foggy, but her body is reacting to his kiss. He places his hands around her neck and pulls her to him, deepening the pressure. Their tongues find each other's, turning the kiss passionate. Throwing her arms around his neck, he pulls her body next to his.

They have backed into a corner into the shadows. He kisses her neck, saying, "I want you."

Pulling herself out of the confusion, she tries to clear her mind. Moving away from him, she wipes her lips. "Brad, I'm so sorry. I can't do this."

She runs from the balcony, stopping by the table to pick up her clutch. She kisses Rachel on the cheek and says, "I'm going home."

Seeing the desperation in Beth's face, Rachel follows her to her room

Beth tears off the gown quickly, grabbing the gown she arrived in Putting it on, Rachel zips the back for her.

"Beth, can't you wait until tomorrow? You've been drinking. I don't think now is the best time to do this."

Sitting on the bed feeling somewhat dizzy, Beth agrees this may not be the best idea she's ever had. Agreeing to wait until morning, she lies back on the bed. "I've had too much to drink."

Rachel goes to get Beth some medicine for her future headache. When she returns, Beth is sound asleep. Laying the pills on the nightstand, Rachel takes Beth's hand. Knowing she will not see Beth again, she says, "It has been so special having you here today. I will always remember you here on my special night. You are the first person I told I was pregnant. Safe travels, my dear friend." She leaves the room with only the flicker of the fire in the hearth, softly closes the door behind her.

Beth wakes in the early morning dawn. The sun is just rising. Looking down at herself, she remembers changing into the gown. Looking at the nightstand, she sees the glass of water and two pills. Downing both, she finishes the entire glass. Not feeling too bad, considering the amount of alcohol she consumed, she heads up to the top floor to the secret chamber.

She remembers having the conversation with Rachel last night, when she revealed she doesn't want a sad goodbye. She prefers to remember Rachel as she was at the ball, full of love and happiness. They had said their sad goodbyes last night and agreed she should do this alone. Promising to leave a note of her safe return once home, she opens the door to the travel room and enters. As the morning rays shine through the window, she walks to the mirror. Slowly she holds out her skirt and makes the turn, falling into darkness.

CHAPTER 15

AN AWAKENING

Going to her floor in the wee hours of the morning, she's glad to see the thick carpets in the hallway validating her safe return. It's a true sign she's back. Entering her suite, she looks at all of her lovely possessions. She's never been more grateful for her existence at the Vanders' estate than now. She has always considered this place belonging to the Vanders. She hasn't surrendered that awareness of being a guest. Now, she realizes just how much this place feels like home. Taking the gown off, she slides into her own bed to get a few more hours of shuteye.

Waking at noon, she gapes at the clock on the wall. Shocked at how late she has slept, she double checks the time on her phone. Getting up, she jumps in for a brief shower, throwing on a pair of jeans and a tee-shirt. With hair still wet, she turns her head over, lifting the hair dryer to blow it out. Putting on some lip balm, she heads downstairs for lunch.

The place is full of people. Forgetting that the party was last night here, she's surprised at the number of guests. Noticing most are in poor shape with hangovers, she snickers. She's been through two nights of partying. There's a vast buffet set up for the crowd. She grabs a plate, fills it, then takes it out to the veranda. The sliders that are usually left open in warm weather are now closed for the fall chill.

The sunlight shining through the glass warms her. There's a fire blazing in the gas fireplace, adding to the coziness of the environment.

Selecting a small table in the corner, she dives in. She eats hoping to get her strength built back up. Time travel makes you weak in every sense of the word. She even feels slow at thinking right now. Before she could taste the first morsel of egg, she's interrupted.

"May I have a word with you, Beth?"

Looking up, it's Grayson throwing a shadow over her.

With an indifferent attitude, she asks, "What's on your mind?" She knew she was being coy.

He sits. "What do you mean, what's on my mind? What do you think is on my mind?"

Stopping to study him, she recognizes that spoiled, cynical tone he used on her when they first met. "I think the question speaks for itself." She takes a bite of her egg.

He just sits there, not responding, glaring at her. The lack of interest in what transpired last night is perplexing.

She stops chewing. Seeing his frustration, she states, "Look, if you're concerned about what happened," she pauses. Almost saying the other night, she corrects herself with, "last night. It's no big deal. We had a few drinks and got carried away."

He fumes. "No big deal?"

She stares at him. "What is wrong with you, Grayson? I hear you've broken hearts everywhere. Why are you making such a huge deal out of this? I'm not urging you to apologize, marry me or anything foolish. I'd think you would be pretty relieved. Our relationship is still intact."

He's dumbfounded. He acknowledges to himself that she's right, though. Why is he making such a big deal of it? He seizes her lead. Standing up he replies, "Okay, just wanted to clear that up." He strides off.

Suddenly regretting her meaningless charade, she takes a bite of her eggs again and discovers she can't stomach another bite. Throwing her napkin on her plate, she pushes back her seat. It makes a loud screeching noise on the floor. Glancing around, she notices everyone is looking her way. She walks out and heads back to her suite, hibernating there for the remainder of the weekend.

It's Thanksgiving week. Grayson and Beth have shut down the business so everyone could enjoy the holiday. Opening her laptop, out of curiosity, she looks up Brad Hastings on the internet. Many men pop up with that name, but all were of this generation. Finally, an article shows up about Chad Grayson and his partner, Brad Hastings. She reads, "The successful duo has turned a modest practice into a top law firm of the ages." They offer family backgrounds of each, stating they are from influential families. The article doesn't get personal enough. Did he ever marry? She's a little disappointed not to find any juice about his personal life. Not understanding her sudden interest in him, she pushes away the recollections of their explosive kisses.

A tap on the door startles her back to the reality of today, not the past. She opens the door to find Mrs. Vanders. Shocked by this impromptu visit, she gladly opens the door wide for her to come in. Mrs. Vanders has never come to her. She always schedules a meeting at the venue of her choice.

Mrs. Vanders walks in, surveying the room. "Hello, Beth. This suite is charming. Is there adequate space for you?"

"Yes, I love it, in fact."

"Good, I'm glad to hear it."

Beth motions for her to sit in the chair near the fireplace. She says, "This is a surprise, Mrs. Vanders. You've never visited me before. Normally, I come to you."

"Well, I thought it was due time." Looking around the room again, she inquires, "Are you content here, Beth? I don't mean just in this suite, but at the estate and with the business, of course."

Wondering if she knows about what transpired with Grayson last night, she becomes concerned about the intended question. "I love it all, Mrs. Vanders. I've never been so fulfilled in my life. You have been so good to me in every aspect. I have no one who thinks enough of me to do what you've done. I don't know if I'll ever be able to repay you."

"I can think of one way."

"Ask anything of me, I'll do it."

"I told you about attending Rachel's wedding. I've found myself eager for the book to be written regarding time travel. As you recall, it was to be a fictional piece, but only we know the truth."

"Yes, Mrs. Vanders, I knew you had mentioned it. Are you ready to begin?"

She smiles. "Yes, I think so, Beth."

"Okay." Beth gets up and goes to fetch a notepad. "Let's get some plans down to get started. It will take a considerable amount of time. Let's launch with the beginning of your life as Adrianna. We need to establish the fundamental basis of why you chose this life, instead of returning to the past."

"That's definitely what we need to do. I'll get Mrs. Carlyle to set up weekly sessions for us. I will also take some time on my own to write about things. I want to include things I remember that were significant to me, like my best friend Celeste and the events in my story that make me who I am."

Beth smiles at her. "That is a wonderful idea. I can't wait to hear about your life back then." She gazes at Mrs. Vanders. "You're such a powerful woman."

"It may be hard for you to understand the whole-time travel aspect. I know you saw Rachel on video, but that's much different from experiencing the actual travel yourself. You can never perceive what it does to your body. We'll need to get very detailed in the effects of that experience, so the readers comprehend the toll it takes."

Beth smiles, then replies, "Oh, I think I know as well as anyone does."

Mrs. Vanders looks at Beth, questioning what that remark means.

"Yes, Mrs. Vanders, I have time traveled as well."

Shocked, Mrs. Vanders asks, "You did? When?"

"Last night, after the ball."

"Oh my, Beth! Why didn't you tell me?" Mrs. Vanders reaches across to the other chair and lays her hand on Beth's arm. "Are you okay? A trip that soon, I'm astonished you're out of bed."

"I'm fine. Yes, a little fatigued, but I slept away half the day this morning. I didn't get up until noon. I arrived at sunrise." She can't wait to share her adventure with Mrs. Vanders. Sharing the news of Rachel's pregnancy made Mrs. Vanders lay her hand over her mouth. She becomes emotional when it's specific news about Rachel's life as Adrianna. After all, Rachel is carrying on her legacy. Rachel is giving her parents their first grandchild. Sharing everything except the personal kiss with Brad Hastings, she finishes with her own perceptions of time travel.

Mrs. Vanders is pleased that Beth now understands everything there is to know about time travel and the concept for the book. She looks at Beth and says, "Beth, you've been such a blessing in my life. The moment you and Rachel walked through our doors my life has finally found peace. All of those years of not understanding the portraits of myself and Chad Grayson, haunted me. Everything has come full circle."

"Mrs. Vanders, you've changed my life in so many ways. I can't keep up." Tears well up in Beth's eyes. "You have no idea the magnitude of how meeting you, turned me into someone else. I had no direction. Meeting you gave me purpose." Wiping a tear falling down her cheek, Beth jumps up and hugs her.

Mrs. Vanders wipes away a tear as well. Pressing on with other matters, she asks, "How are you and Grayson getting along? Have you managed to get past your dislike of him? I see it hasn't affected your business relationship. That is a success story in itself."

Thinking beyond what occurred at the ball, she focuses on work information. She shares his thoughtfulness of buying her the new car. She confesses that she sees him in a different light now.

"Good, I'm overjoyed to hear that. Beth, I should never say this to you, but I think Grayson has fallen in love with you."

Shocked out of her boots, Beth asks, "Mrs. Vanders, why would you say something like that?"

"He praises you nonstop. It's Beth did this, and Beth did that." She smiles at Beth. "He isn't just taking credit for the business successes. He glows when he compliments you. To be honest, I've been quite concerned that you're going to break his unbroken heart."

Guilt and redness fill her face. Remembering their interaction this morning, makes her feel like a heal. "I don't know what to say. To be honest, I've been protecting my heart from him. I've heard about his womanizing and the hearts he's broken."

"I understand your caution, but remember, everyone meets their match. I expect because you have matched him in business, you've gained his respect. I think his heart became involved somewhere along the way."

"Mrs. Vanders, did he share this with you, or are you just assuming he possesses these feelings for me?"

Laughing, she replies, "You young people, always playing games." She looks her dead in the face and says, "He doesn't have to say the words. He loves you. He dances all around it. I've never seen Grayson this taken by any woman."

Not knowing how to process this new information, she just smiles.

Mrs. Vanders stands to leave. She turns saying, "I suspect the feeling is mutual if you ask me."

Choosing not to react to that last comment, Beth walks her to the door. "Mrs. Vanders, I've enjoyed our visit. I'll get started right away on outlining the book. If you would ask Mrs. Carlyle to set up our appointments, and begin composing your memoirs, that would be a good start."

Turning back to face Beth as she steps into the hallway, Mrs. Vanders says, "Be good to my Grayson. He's special to me. I'm not saying be with him if your affections aren't mutual. I'm saying, let him down easy or go the distance." Adding a last-minute declaration, she says, "I love you both."

Beth lays her hand over her heart. Voice quivering, she replies, "I love you too, Mrs. Vanders." She closes the door and weeps. It makes her miss her parents so much. She hasn't heard the words 'I love you' from anyone in years.

Deciding to plunge into the novels concept, she takes the next three days to lay out an outline of all she knows, and to establishes a timeline. She gets so engaged that time vanishes. She starts taking her meals in her room, committed to have a draft to show Mrs. Vanders on their next meeting.

On Thanksgiving Day, she finally pulls her head out of work. The major feast is happening at six. She selects a nice fall outfit. Moistening her lips, she takes one last look in the mirror. Locking the door behind her, she heads downstairs. As she arrives, she finds the festivities are in full swing. Children and their families are everywhere. The running and screaming, echoes off the walls in the immense room. It's an appealing sound for Beth. All she has experienced since her arrival at the estate, is adult parties. Seeing children's faces, and the adults they belong to are fascinating.

Perusing the room with a drink in her hand, she suddenly stops dead cold. Grayson is standing with a woman. They're at the bar getting drinks. Beth backs away hastily, spinning in another direction. Hiding behind guests, she watches them. As people join them, he introduces the stranger. It's undeniably a date. Horrified, she doesn't know what to do. She finds Mrs. Vanders and initiates a conversation so she's not alone. Unfortunately, Grayson and his date find their way to them.

Grayson leans in, kissing Mrs. Vanders on the cheek. "Hello. Aunt Andrea, I would like you to meet a friend of mine. Caroline, this is my aunt, Andrea Vanders."

Looking at Beth, then back to him, Mrs. Vanders replies, "Hello Grayson." Not the one for beating around the bush, she looks at the woman and says, "It's a pleasure to meet you, Caroline." Touching Beth's arm, she says, "This is Grayson's business partner Beth Olsen." She sneers at Grayson when she sees Caroline look elsewhere. With eye contact, she glares at him. Without a word she sends a message. "What the hell are you doing? You are being irresponsible with any chance you have with Beth."

Grayson is stunned by his aunt's response. He has never brought a date before. He assumed she'd be pleased. Suddenly he understands the aspirations she has for him and Beth. Looking at Beth, he could see her discomfort in the situation. Did he read her wrong? Her message, "I don't want you," sounded authentic to him. He had to admit to himself, her kisses told another version. Instantly, he regretted his actions tonight. Obviously, his aunt knew more about her affections than he did. Or, was this dreaming on his aunt's part and trying to play matchmaker? Standing awkwardly, the four try to small talk their way out of the discomfort. When Derek Grayson walks up, Grayson doesn't think it could get any worse.

Derek kisses Mrs. Vanders on the cheek. He looks at Grayson, who introduces him to Caroline. He moves to kiss Beth on the cheek as well. "Hello Beth. It's good to see you again."

Smile widening for this saving grace moment, Beth counters, "It's good to see you too." She shifts to look directly at Grayson with cold eyes. As luck would have it, Derek asks, "Beth, do you have a moment? There's someone I'd like you to meet."

Looking at Derek's handsome face, she answers, "Of course." They excuse themselves, and Derek takes her to another couple. She thanks God for small favors. She didn't think she could stand there a minute longer.

Derek and Beth sit together during dinner. The events of tonight are nothing like they have been in the past. There were no guests, just family. Including the entire family in the festivities was a refreshing change. The children had their own small table to sit at. The nannies took the infants and toddlers away for their feedings. They would return later.

After dinner, Beth excuses herself, feigning exhaustion. Throwing on a coat, she decides to take a walk before she turns in. The night air is cool. The path is lit by lights that lead to the Gazebo. She walks using a moderate pace, enjoying herself, stopping to sit on the cushioned seat. Looking at the sky and the moon, it couldn't be a more beautiful night. Closing her eyes, she lays her head back and rests.

A familiar voice comes out of the darkness. "It's too cold to sleep."

Not possessing the energy to argue with Grayson right now, she states, "Go away, Grayson."

He retorts, "Tsk, tsk. Please mind your manners, Beth."

She opens her eyes as he steps onto the Gazebo. "Okay, what is it I can do for you, Grayson?"

"Oh, nothing, I'm just appreciating the night air. Isn't there sufficient air for the both of us?"

"I guess." Still suffering the disappointment of him bringing the date, she asks, "Where's your date?"

"I took her home after dinner."

Rubbing her forehead like she's getting a headache from the stress, she comes back, "Oh, that's too bad."

"Where's your date?" He asks with sarcasm in his voice.

She quips. "I didn't have a date. You're the one with the date tonight."

Smiling, slightly, he asserts, "HMMM, do I hear jealousy in the tone of your voice?"

"No, you do not!"

He snickers. "I don't know, it sounds like it to me."

"Think what you want." She rises to leave.

He stares at her with her furred hat and realizes she's the most beautiful woman he has ever seen. Even in the moonlit night, he can see her blue eyes and plump luscious lips. The long dark lashes are just one of the many details that make her so appealing. As she walks past him, he grabs her hand. "Don't leave, Beth."

She stops without turning back to look at him. If she does, she'll melt. He hurt her too much tonight to let out her raw emotions. She would rather he assume she doesn't give a damn.

Walking around in front of her, he places his finger under her chin, lifting her face to his. "Don't fight me, Beth. We need to face this."

She remains still, peering into his eyes. Hoping her knees don't buckle, she doesn't move.

He leans down, and gently kisses her lips. With the first kiss, she just stands there and allows it. The second, her lips betray her and respond. He backs her up against the frame of the gazebo, placing one hand on her jawline and throat. He kisses her intensely. Back and forth it turns into a hot passionate kiss. There's no alcohol pushing their lack of restraint. It's pure attraction. Her arms go around his neck. He opens his coat and wraps her inside. Moaning when he moves to her neck, she yearns for him to touch her in every way. Getting so heated their breathing becomes labored, she pulls back.

"Don't pull away, Beth. I want you more than I have ever wanted anyone."

"More than Rachel?" Immediately scolding herself for bringing this up, she closes her eyes.

He stops. "Rachel? Where did that come from?"

It's out there now, so she may as well ask him all about it. Pulling away from his hold, she declares, "Grayson, you were extremely interested in Rachel if you recall. Now that she's not here, you think you can move in on me."

"Ugh, recall it accurately Beth. You were cynical and rude. I'm not in the habit of fawning over women who can't stand me." Reasoning further, he adds, "Do you know what attracted me to Rachel?"

Giving no response, she waits.

"I couldn't get over how much she looked like the portrait of our ancestor Adrianna. I was intrigued, I guess."

"So, you have fantasies about your great, great grandmother?"

Bursting into laughter, he maintains, "Well, I hadn't thought of it quite in that format."

She had to laugh, too.

"Beth, in case you haven't noticed, I'm beginning to have feelings for you."

She replies, "No, I didn't notice. Seeing you with a date tonight didn't send that message."

He chuckles. "Well, I'm a man. It's chronically noted that men make poor decisions a lot."

She smiles. "Well, I can't argue those facts." Suddenly getting a chill, she shivers.

"You're cold. Let's get back into the house." He grabs her by the hand and they head back down the path.

Entering, they head toward her end of the estate. His flat is where the immediate family dwells.

Getting to her door, he leans her up against the door frame and kisses her again. "I'm glad we finally worked out the details of my obsession with my great, great grandmother."

She giggles and pushes him back. Not wanting the night to end, she shifts to unlock the door.

He doesn't get that message, so he backs away saying, "Well, good night, then."

She grabs him by the coat collar and drags him in. Throwing their coats to the floor, he pushes her into the bedroom. His mouth finds her succulent lips. Pulling her sweater over her head, he stares at her heaving chest and declares, "Damn, I've had those on my mind since the night of the ball."

She reaches up and helps him remove his sweater, then he unbuttons his shirt. Helping him pull it off, she looks at his masculine chest and smiles. While unzipping his trousers, he kicks his shoes and socks off. She discards her slacks.

All of the longing that both have been denying from the beginning has now exploded into this moment. The lust of course, is at the forefront, but it is prefaced with the love that has been growing between them for months. The pent-up raw emotions of denying their feelings are raging as the built-up walls crumble.

He has never wanted a woman so much. His every effort, since the day he met her, has been to push her beautiful face out of his mind. No matter how hard he tried, his mind, body, and soul denied him, giving him no choice but to fall unwillingly.

Falling back onto the bed, their bare legs tangle together. Reaching behind her back, he skillfully unsnaps her bra. Looking at her, his groin swells. He softly slides a finger over the mound of her breast, causing her to writhe with want. Her breathing quickens. Finally reaching her nipples, he squeezes the tips while kissing her passionately. She moves against him, wanting him desperately. She moans when he licks her nipple to peak attention. She reaches for his manhood and begins to massage. His breath catches as she lightly caresses the tip. They take pleasure in exploring each other. Kissing and touching with tenderness. They move toward the moment of consent that can never be taken back. Both are too far gone to stop. He discards her panties and his own, and enters her.

"Ahhh," he groans as he penetrates. He slowly moves back and forth in her savoring the moment. Kissing her passionately, he again makes his way to her breasts. It excites her, and her strokes increase with his. Both gives in to the insatiable lust. Their bodies are hot and ready to consummate their feelings once and for all. They go on and on, not able to get enough of each other. She bites his neck, compelling him to quicken his rhythm. Both lose all reality, plunging into blissful orgasms. The pulsing climax sends ripples of pleasure to her core. Together their release is filled with heightened pleasure and satisfaction.

He falls on her, breathing heavily. Their bodies are saturated with perspiration. He looks at her and asks, "Good grief, woman, are you trying to kill me?"

Laughing, she nuzzles up against him to be closer. "Yes, that was my intent." She kisses his shoulder as he adjusts to lie beside her.

"Well, you did a darned good job. I thought I would lose it at one point. I was lost in you and couldn't get enough."

Smiling, she runs her fingers across his chest. He has never been more handsome to her than now. His dark eyes and dimples are mesmerizing. She takes his hand in hers. She has always loved a man's hands. When his palms caressed her body, it drove her to explode with want. Kissing his fingers, she puts one finger in her mouth.

He watches her and replies, "You'd better stop, you'll wake up the dragon again."

Cuddling in his arms, she finds warmth and the perfect fit. Their bodies interlace as if they have known each other before.

She's quiet as she reflects on what just happened. Never in a million years after their initial encounter, did she consider that this could happen. As she lay with her head on his shoulder, she soon hears steady breathing. The sound lulls her to sleep in peaceful contentment.

Waking for just a moment as light is barely visible, she looks up to discover he's still sound asleep. Enjoying his presence, she closes her eyes. Waking later in the morning, she feels Grayson, sucking on her nipple. She moans. He sticks his finger on her spot and moves it back and forth, building the tension in her body to explosion. She rocks as he continues, matching his strokes. She begs, "I want you." He continues instead of entering her, she realizes he's bringing her to a climax. She thrives under his fingers, moaning and biting and sucking his lips until she succumbs to an orgasm that sends quivers throughout her entire body.

He moves over her and enters her afterward. Pushing in, his breathe catches. He claims her for the second time, as he ravishes her yielding body to his. The veins on his neck are bulging as he moans. Their wet bodies drop with satiated fulfillment.

He moves off her to lie on his back. She lay, breathing hard as her chest rises and falls. Not speaking, she closes her eyes, savoring the memories of this night.

Getting his senses back, he looks over at her and sees she's closed her eyes. Moving to his side and leaning on his elbow, he asks, "Are you alright?"

Turning to gaze at him, she responds, "Content."

Smiling, he leans over her to kiss her. "HMM, that's precisely what I feel."

Looking into his dark eyes and long lashes, she lifts her head to kiss him.

He pulls back after the kiss and inquires, "Where do we go from here?"

Laughing, she asks, "Breakfast?" Seeing his expression as serious, she asks, "Where do you want to go, Grayson?"

"I mean us. What happens now?"

Looking deep into his eyes she asks, "Grayson, what do you see happening?"

Rubbing his fingers through his jet-black hair, he replies, "Beth, I've been falling for you for some time now. It's no secret after tonight that I'm in to you." He laughs, "Poor choice of words I know, but I'm falling in love." He shrugs his shoulders. "Honestly, I don't know what to do with that."

"You've never been in love?"

"No, I haven't." He shrugs, again unapologetic for his affections. He asks, "What do people do when they're in love?"

She chuckles. "Well, I don't think there is an exact script on how to do this."

"Answer me this. Am I in this alone?"

She's uncertain what he's asking. "Are you alone?"

"Do I need to spell it out? Okay, what are your feelings?"

She's not used to this at all. She fumbles for words. Finally, she answers, "Grayson, I fell for you the night you gave me the new car."

Confused, he asks, "You like me because of the car?"

"No, silly. I can buy my own car, but it was the first time I experienced a tender side to you. Until that point, we had been sometimes hostile with each other, or strictly business. When you leaned across me to show me the controls, my heart skipped a beat."

Surprised, he says, "Damn, if I had known that, I would have made this move a lot sooner."

She slaps his arm. "I wasn't ready then. I am now. It's time for love in my life."

He leans in to kiss her. "I'm ready too."

He kisses her intensely. Pulling back, he looks into those beautiful blue eyes, "I think I'm in love."

She kisses him again, "I think I'm in love too." Popping into her mind she asks him, "What do you think Mrs. Vanders will say about this?"

"Are you kidding me? I thought she would kill me for bringing Caroline last night. She is dead set that you and I end up together."

"I'm glad." She pecks his lips.

He sits up and asks, "What do you say we walk in for breakfast together, holding hands and watch everyone's expression?"

She grins mischievously, "I'm game if you are."

CHAPTER 16

THE NEW NORMAL

Walking into breakfast, Grayson grabs Beth's hand possessively. Elbows nudging each other, Beth could see expressions of "I knew it" or utter confusion and shock. The one person who displays neither of these reactions is Mrs. Vanders. A mile-wide grin crosses her face. Beth is holding her breath until she catches the grin. Relief sweeps over her. The one person most important to her is pleased. That's all that matters to Beth.

Grayson sits in the seat next to Mrs. Vanders. Beth notices her lay her hand on Grayson's arm. With the noise in the room, she can't hear what she is saying.

Mrs. Vanders says, "It's about time."

Grayson leans over and places a peck on the cheek. "I knew you'd be happy."

"The question, my young man, is, are you?"

He twists to glance at Beth, then back at Mrs. Vanders. "I am. To be honest, I'm amazed at just how thrilled I am about it."

Beth hates that Sally won't quit talking. She's in the seat beside her just rambling. She tries with all her might to hear the conversation between Grayson and Mrs. Vanders, instead, she's disturbed by the crying baby on Sally's lap. Any chance of overhearing is not in the cards. Sensing the conversation is positive between Grayson and Mrs. Vanders, she focuses on breakfast. She's famished after her night of passionate lovemaking. Smiling, she takes a sip of her coffee, then leans back in peaceful contentment. The baby cries louder, and even that cannot break Beth's peaceful glow. It's the happiest she's been in a long time. Also, the fact that she just made passionate love is the icing on the cake. She admits it's been a while. Beaming she glances at Grayson, content in the moment.

To her delight, he's watching her. He grins. "If I didn't know better, I'd think you're happy. You have a big grin all over your face."

Slapping his arm, she giggles. Looking at his expression and the dimples, she retorts, "I see a grin on your face as well." She clutches his chin with her fingers and shakes his jaw back and forth.

He leans in close to her face. "I dare you to kiss me, right here, right now."

Beth looks around the table and notices that many are looking their way, including Mrs. Vanders. She accepts the dare and leans in.

Just as he's about to kiss her, she shifts her cheek for his kiss.

He opens his eyes, backing up in surprise. "You little devil, you! I'll get you for that."

Leaning her head on his shoulder, she counters, "I hope so." Looking up into his eyes, he grasps the insinuation and says, "Let's get out of here." Grabbing her hand, he gets up, pulling her to her feet. Leaning over, he kisses Mrs. Vanders on the cheek. "We'll see you later."

Mrs. Vanders smiles. "You two kids have fun."

Beth walks over and gives her a hug. She whispers, "Big shock, huh?"

Mrs. Vanders chuckles, "Indeed."

Getting back to her suite, they grab their coats. Grayson tells her they're going on an adventure. Getting into one of the four-wheel drive vehicles, they head out of town. The drive is beautiful. She continues to ask where they're going, but he just repeats, "You'll see." Finally, after an hour and a half, they pull up to Mountain High Lodge. Giving the attendee his keys, Grayson takes her inside of a beautiful lodge with an enormous fireplace blazing. Pulling her to the check-in counter, he books a room. As soon as he gets the card to the room, he drags her toward the shop.

Inside there are skis, snowboards, and weather gear. He instructs her to pick out a ski outfit and anything else she will require for a brief stay. He chooses what he will need as well. He completes their purchases with hot chocolate and snacks for later.

Opening the door to their room, Beth says, "It's gorgeous!" A huge window overlooks a mountain peak capped with snow. Amazed, she gushes over the view. "I didn't know this place existed." Turning to look at him as he walks up, she asks, "Do you come here often?"

He peers out the window and replies, "No." Looking at him, she can see he has a solemn expression on his face. Nodding his head to imply I'll tell you, he says, "We used to come here all the time when my brother and I were kids." A smile curls his lips. "Alex and I made everything a competition. Who could ski the fastest, or who could snow board better?" Regret written on his face he looks at her. Shrugging, he adds, "Now, we're both so busy with separate lives, we haven't been back as adults."

Kissing him tenderly, she wraps her arms around his neck. "I'm so sorry. It sounds as if it's a wonderful memory. Maybe you should invite him during the holidays."

Looking at her, he places a delicate peck on her cheek. He surprises her by picking her up, twirling her around. "You, my dear woman, are going to help me create new memories."

She squeals as he whirls her around, reveling in the moment of silliness.

Setting her down, he pulls off her hat and scarf and unbuttons her coat. Throwing everything on the floor, he lifts her sweater over her head. He says slyly, "I think we should begin by turning the heat up in the room."

Giggling, she pushes his coat off, tossing it on the floor as well. He doesn't give her time to help with his sweater. He has it off before his coat hits the floor. She states a fact, "Aren't you eager?"

"Oh yes. It's been too long. We must make up for the lost time."

Looking at the clock on the wall she claims, "It's only been four hours."

Pushing her back on to the bed, he asserts, "Yes, way too long." He smiles as he reaches around her back and unhooks her bra. Kissing her passionately, the heat between them escalates. He unzips her slacks and moves his hand in to find her hot spot.

She stops him. Reaching down to his zipper, she unzips his jeans. Both decide what the heck, purging themselves of shoes and slacks at the same time. They settle back on the bed, eager to begin again. She kisses his neck then makes her way down his chest. Reaching his nipples, she takes the tip in her mouth. It hardens where she can brush her tongue back and forth across it. He moans in pleasure. She runs her hand down his abdomen, reaching the hair that surrounds his manhood. She runs her fingers on the inside of his thigh, then works her way up to find him hard and erect. Fingers surrounding it, she begins softly caressing. His moan is deep and husky as his hips match her strokes. Unable to take it anymore, he reaches up and pushes her on her back. Grabbing her nipple in his mouth, he quickly flicks it back and forth, driving her to peaked frustration.

She sighs, "I need you."

He whispers, "I know you do, but in time, my love." He moves his hand between her legs as he continues suckling her breasts. Finding her hot spot, massaging it with two fingers She gasps and quivers in anguish. Feeling her moist, he moves on top of her, spreading her legs to enter. She's hot and ready for him. As he enters her, he groans in pleasure.

She wraps her arms around his back, receiving his full penetration. Starting slowly, they enjoy the pleasure of one another. Their lovemaking is passionate, yearning for more and more of the give and take. They explore each other, kissing, fondling, building the pleasures of their newfound relationship.

As he ramps up momentum in his strokes, they both moan with pleasure and hold on to each other, peaking to the moment of rapturous release. His neck veins are pulsing as he surrenders. Quivers are running through her. She breathes sharply while her orgasm consumes her body.

Falling on top of her, he hides his face in her neck. She drapes her arms around him, touching his damp hair from the exertion. Looking at her, he says nothing. Reaching up, she pushes the dark strands of hair away from his face. Giving him a delicate kiss, he continues to gaze into her eyes. Getting concerned, she asks, "What is it, Grayson? What's wrong?"

Shaking his head, he replies, "Nothing is wrong. In fact, it's too right."

"What does that mean?"

Still gazing into her eyes, he asks, "Aren't you a little freaked out about what has happened to us?"

"Freaked out? No. A little scared, yes."

He kisses the tip of her nose. "Don't be scared, baby, I've got you."

Looking into his eyes, she can see sincerity mixed with a matter-of-fact attitude.

Rolling onto his back, he tells her all about his escapades as a bachelor.

Cuddling under his arm, she lays her head on his chest and silently listens while he unloads his past. She understands the need for him to share and appreciates his honesty. Some things he mentions are not always complimentary. He has used women and left many broken hearts in his wake. Laying all of his not so pretty details out there, he is compelled to share his unsavory past. Admitting to himself and her that at the time, he couldn't have cared less. He looks at her finally. She's been silent, so he lifts her chin to look into her eyes. When she grins at him, his anxiety dissipates. He asks, "Doesn't everything I just shared make you hate me?"

"No Grayson, it doesn't." She looks directly into his eyes. "If you had been trying to withhold these things from me, I would expect to be your next victim. Instead, you're baring your soul." She raises an eyebrow. "Some not-so-great moments of your past are just how I see them, in your past."

Leaning on her elbow she says, "To be truthful, my past hasn't been so perfect either. Mine may have been for different reasons, but I haven't always treated men fairly either. My beginnings are humble. We had to struggle for what we wanted in life. My parents sacrificed a lot for me to go to Yale. Hell, I sacrificed a lot. I had to get top grades to get the scholarship. My high school years were spent in my bedroom studying. I missed proms, dances and boys, because I was dead set on my goal. Don't get me wrong, I have fond memories of my parents and our life together. They loved me so much. If I have had one honest thing in this life, it was the love of my parents. But my struggles made me a little resentful of life in general. I could see others enjoying life, while all I did was study. I had to convince myself on many tearful nights that it was worth it. When I arrived at college, I found the Yale rich boys to be spoiled and self-absorbed. It became my mission to knock them down a notch." She glances at him, "I was a bitch to be blunt."

"You a bitch? Nah…"

She laughs, "How quickly you forget my first interview with you. You were condescending to me, and I was undoubtedly not going to take it. I didn't care who your aunt was."

He snickers, "Oh that. You were a little confrontational. But to be honest, I deserved it. I was rude and trying to tell you how to do your job."

She giggles. "Yes, you were."

He kisses her cheek. "I'm really sorry you had to go through such a tough life. I admit, I was pampered, but not the way you think. As a boy, they definitely gave me all the things in life I wanted. But, when it was time to grow up and take on responsibilities, they threw me into the fire head first. No one gave me a gravy job. I had to start in the mailroom learning my way to the top. Because I was a relative, it appeared they were tougher on me than the employees. They handed me nothing. I got each promotion from hard work and by proving myself."

Squeezing his arms around her tighter, he says, "Kind of like you, I worked day and many late nights to outshine everyone else. I was ruthless in my endeavors. I probably created some enemies on the way up. Not intentionally, but nothing was acceptable to me except success."

"I've been so proud of your work at our publishing company. You are a top-rated business man Grayson. I don't know if we could have been successful without your business savvy."

He nods yes, but then finishes with, "Trust me, I knew nothing about publishing. It has been all of your decisions, that's taken us to the top. We are the best publishing company in New York right now. Hell, people are begging us to publish them, instead of us out searching for authors."

"Grayson, I do want to get back to the point of our conversation. I will tell you today, I trust you." With hesitation she adds, "And love you. I will have these feelings until you show me I can't. You have a past and so do I. Let's make this our new beginning. We can't let the business come between us. If something goes wrong with this." She points to his chest and hers. "We need to promise to put the business above our pain of a breakup. Deal?"

He seals it with a kiss. "Deal." He glances at the clock on the wall. It's already two. "What do you say we go out and play in the snow for a while, have a nice dinner, then come back here and repeat what we just did?"

She jumps up, practically tripping on the coats on the floor. She loves to ski, so she's game.

He runs after her, trying to beat her to the bathroom.

The weekend is beautiful. They stay overnight and have a candlelight dinner. Staying late for a few drinks in the lounge, they slow dance to a live band. She watches him, wanting to pinch herself. She's now in love with Grayson Vanders. During her college years, she would never have imagined this. She doesn't care about his wealthy family or his assets. As far as she's concerned, she has her business and is now wealthy in her own right. She feels like his equal. Looking around, she can see women checking him out, but he only has eyes for her.

Sitting at their table, Grayson leans into her and in an overly serious voice asks, "Do you see that guy at the bar?"

She searches. She sees a nice-looking man at the bar. "Yes."

"Do you think I should knock him off that stool? He continues to gape at you and I don't like it."

"Okay, I think that's an excellent strategy. While you're knocking him off the barstool, I'm going to the woman two tables over and push her face in her plate."

He looks around and laughs. "Oh no, what have we become?"

She laughs so hard she snorts. It makes him laugh even harder. Reaching over to kiss her, he pulls her chair closer to his. "I'm a fortunate man tonight, Beth."

Smiling, she replies, "I'm happy too, Grayson." Looking at him she asks, "Is this our new normal?"

Grinning, he replies, "I sure hope so."

CHAPTER 17

PRE-CHRISTMAS SURPRISE

Getting back to work on Monday feels strange. Usually, she's sharply focused on the business. Today, her mind wanders back to the fabulous weekend she and Grayson just had. Still feeling like it's all a dream, she turns on her laptop to start the day. The first thing she sees is the meeting invitation with Mrs. Vanders. Accepting the schedule, she pushes a few meetings around, to accommodate the time needed to get back to the estate.

Spending her day drafting the outline for the book, she dives into her vision. Not sure about how much Mrs. Vanders wants to reveal in this publication, she drafts two outlines. Feeling it needs to have anonymous characters, she develops fictional names. Mrs. Vanders will be the sole person who knows the truth. If Mrs. Vanders is composing her memoirs, she may be ready to embrace the original book Beth was initially interviewing for when she arrived at the estate. Taking both objectives and laying out her vision, she wraps up her day, leaving in time for their meeting.

Mrs. Vanders is in the library when she arrives. "Hello Mrs. Vanders." Laying her purse on the table, she unzips the case and drags out her laptop. Opening the lid, she initiates the startup.

Mrs. Vanders says, "Let's begin our session by establishing ground rules."

Surprised, Beth replies, "I love that idea."

"First ground rule is that you must call me Andrea."

Coming out of left field, she asks, "Are you sure? Am I showing you less respect by doing that? So many people call you Mrs. Vanders, even family members."

"I know they do, but you and I are about to dive into some pretty personal information. I'll be sharing things I've never shared with anyone, so I think Andrea would make me feel more comfortable."

"Sure, if that's what you want." She glances at the closed library door and asks, "What about Adrianna?"

Her smile widens. "I fear you would accidentally call me by that name in public. Let's just stick to Andrea. I've gotten so used to it now. I think it would be odd. Plus, I'm truly no longer Adrianna, Rachel is."

"That sounds good. I'll call you Andrea behind closed doors then."

"No, I would prefer you address me that way always." Looking at Beth, she adds, "Beth, you have become like a family member to me. And of course, if you and Grayson end up marrying, you will be."

Beth cuts in sharply. "Mrs. Vanders, I mean Andrea, you are reaching way out there for that to occur. Until this weekend, we were hardly speaking."

"Oh, shew! You two have been in love since the day you met. You just weren't ready to face it until now."

Laughing, Beth replies, "I can't argue with you there. I've been fighting my emotions for a while."

Mrs. Vanders lays her hand over Beth's, "I couldn't be happier. My two-favorite people in the world, coming together is perfect."

Beth lays her other hand on her own chest. "You will never know what that statement means to me. You are like family to me. Because you cared enough for me to include me in your life, I now have happiness I never dreamed possible."

Her eyes fill with tears. "Thank you."

Trying to hold back emotions she adds, "Speaking of love, I hope you don't mind my telling you I have a fondness for you as well. You have been like a mother to me. I consider you a mentor. If my life could be half as grand as yours, I would be extremely blessed. After doing the proposal for the script, I feel I know you personally, not to mention, I probably know more than anyone since I have experienced time travel. I will protect that secret until my dying day."

Mrs. Vanders is also overwhelmed. Fanning her eyes to keep the tears from falling, she says, "You are very special Beth."

Trying to regain her composure, she asks, "Okay, what do you have for me?"

Beth pulls the printed drafts out of her computer bag. Beginning, she introduces the two outlines. "Okay, so I didn't know which direction you wanted to go first, so I designed two drafts. One is for the initial angle of doing your biography. The second, prepares the fictional manuscript of time travel." She pitches the title 'Timeless', stating that it was up for discussion and subject to modification as they delve into the details.

"Do you have an inclination of what we undertake first?"

Mrs. Vanders reads through both drafts. "Prospectively, both are my biography. Let's concentrate on the one about time travel. I would prefer the biography be introduced as the Vanders history, coming from my perspective. I don't want that one to be just about me."

Beth nods in agreement. "So, we do the time travel fictional book first?"

Pondering for a moment, "Yes, that's what I prefer."

"Perfect, you'll need time to create some memoirs about you as Adrianna?"

She hands Beth a bundle of papers.

"Okay...." She stares at Mrs. Vanders. "There's no way you have had time to do this much since the last time we discussed this."

Mrs. Vanders smiles, "You would be correct in that supposition. I've been laboring over these for quite some time."

Laying the stack on the table, Beth asks Mrs. Vanders to provide her a brief rundown of her history back then and why she chose to remain in the future.

Mrs. Vanders begins the account of her previous existence. Part of it she had already shared with Beth when she first divulged her identity as Adrianna. Now she's sharing more in-depth details and behaviors contributing to her decisions. They ran through her childhood and the characteristics between today's youth and the children back then. She shares distinctions between the two lives and why she preferred one over the other. After three hours, they break to dress for dinner. Not wanting to stop, Beth asks one last question for the day. "Do you have any regrets?"

"Of course. I miss my parents all the time. Watching them glow over Rachel's wedding and wishing to scream, 'that's not me' is a heartache I will never get over. However, that's the past I had to let go of."

Sadness overwhelms Beth. The sorrow Mrs. Vanders must feel is indescribable. Just as she's about to end her inquiries, she asks one more question. "Mrs. Vanders, do you think you would ever consider returning to confess everything?"

"What would that solve? I'm a woman their age. They would never believe me."

"Okay, I understand your train of thought, but should you go back and share it all? The time travel, how you did it. Then," She hesitates, building the anticipation. "Then, urge them to travel to the future to see for themselves."

Mrs. Vanders looks at her in thoughtful silence. "I don't think they can."

Beth retorts, "I did. Why can't they? Let's go back together. You'll wear two sets of future clothes, and I'll wear a man's suit of the future under my dress. It could work, Mrs. Vanders. What do you think?"

Astonished at the suggestion, she slowly thinks it through. Then, declines with an excellent reason. "What about Rachel? They will think she's a fraud and have her prosecuted for being an imposter."

"No, we will go back to the time, right before you leave. Go to them and tell them. It will be you. The challenge I need to unravel is, how to get you back as the young Adrianna instead of the age you are here and now. Every time you've gone back, it's been at your current age, right?"

"Yes, it has. I don't think we can alter that."

Beth, being more analytical, reacts, "Don't be so sure." Enthusiastic, she shoves her laptop and documents back into the sack. Let me do some research on this. Maybe it has to do with the date of the clothes." Throwing that out, she says, "We went back to the date of the clothes and you weren't younger." She studies Mrs. Vanders, "Just remember, when you went back the last time, it did something to your cancer. It changed you back to where the cancer barely exists. What if we can transform you back in age as well?" Gasping, she dramatically asks, "What if we can take you back to when you first met your husband, and you relived your life with him, having children?"

Mrs. Vanders grabs her arm. "Beth, could that really happen?"

Looking at her with a hopeful expression, she responds, "I don't know, but shouldn't we at least contemplate the idea and investigate?"

Mrs. Vanders gets a glimmer of hope in her eyes. "Okay, let's do it. I'll hire a researcher to dig into details about time travel, convincing him it is for the fictional novel. I'll ask him to investigate any claimed persons who swear they've time traveled. You can explore the scientific side of it. What are the mathematical concepts of how it happens and is it conceivable?"

"Perfect!" Beth pauses, then says, "Mrs. Vanders, if we pull this off and somehow it alters our union, please remember that I have cherished our time. It may be that I won't exist in your life the second time around."

"No, Beth, I will still be me. This time when you come to my estate, it will be a purposeful request when I ask for you."

Both stand to leave. She looks at Mrs. Vanders and she can't help but be excited about this. "Okay, here's the game plan. We will meet once a week between two and four. Does this day of the week work for you?"

Mrs. Vanders contemplates her schedule, then replies, "Yes, that works. If something crops up and I need to modify the time of the meeting, I'll let you know in advance. Although, this is a priority to me. It would need to be a death or something that drastic to get me to change it. But, if you have commitments, you can't get out of, I'll understand. You need to put your business first."

"No, this is a priority as well. I have a quick question though."

"What is it, Beth?"

"Do we share any of this with Grayson?"

Understanding Beth's newfound commitment to Grayson, she's careful with the reply. "Let's wait until we have something concrete to share. At this point, everything is speculation or wishful thinking on our part."

"You're right." Walking out the door, she tells Mrs. Vanders she'll see her in an hour for dinner.

Getting dressed for dinner, Beth's eager to get started on her research. Wishing she had told Mrs. Vanders that she will take dinner in her room, she dresses with limited enthusiasm. Putting on her dress, she hears a tap on the door. Walking to open it, she sees Grayson with a huge grin on his face. "Hey, I tried to catch you at work this evening, but the receptionist said you left early. Everything okay?"

"Yeah, sure." Turning around, she asks him to zip up her dress. He kisses her bare shoulder, first, then zips it. "Mmmm, you smell great."

Not allowing him to take things further, she moves away from him "Are you ready to go down to dinner?"

He throws out his arms like, gesturing that he's ready.

Walking back up to him, she kisses him passionately. "Reserve this as a reminder of things to come later."

He laughs and waves his hand in the air as if catching something, then replies, "Got it, right here in the palm of my hand. I won't forget, nor will I let you forget."

She giggles and pushes him out the door to go downstairs.

Not able to concentrate on anything but her research, she doesn't attend the after dinner gathering. Telling Grayson to linger and enjoy, he tries to dismiss the notion. Kissing him, she says, "Grayson, I need a few hours alone. I have some research to do before I get to the office tomorrow. You can come up in an hour or so." She's pleased with his disappointed expression. She feels very appreciated by him. Not just for sex, but that her presence is desired.

Getting back to her suite, she pulls out her laptop and gets to work. Reading through everything she can about time travel, she dives into internet articles on the subject matter. She finally types in a search 'Traveling back in time to your youth.'

Bingo!

Every time Mrs. Vanders had returned home, it was after she traveled to the future to start with. What she needs to do is travel back to when it was truly her. You can't have the same soul in two different people. She traveled to the future right before Christmas. Getting the time here, and the time there to match is the key, or at least worth a shot. Beth gets excited. She never dreamed she would discover the answer so fast. It's fate! She gets up and dances around. Excitement running wild, she answers the door when she hears the peck. Of course, it's Grayson. She grabs him, placing a smoldering kiss that hardens him instantly. She unties his tie and unbuttons his shirt.

Between kisses he says, "Okay, promise kept!"

Pleased, she backs him into the bedroom.

Still mumbling between kisses, he adds, "I'm going to let you go up early every night if you miss me this much."

She replies, "You haven't seen anything yet, Mister."

"Okay, you win, show me."

That night, they climb to a whole new level of desire. Their lovemaking is urgent and wild. They both go to places neither has been before. She realizes the links that binds them is far greater than mere attraction. It travels beyond time as if this was meant to be. She wishes for a moment that she could share it all with him, but concludes it's not her story to tell. They lay in each other's arms and a restful peace settles over the two, as they sleep the night away full of wonderful visions to come.

The next few weeks are pivotal in calculating the appropriate moment for Mrs. Vanders to return to the past. During the time of putting all things together, they contact Rachel to ask her to put a specific dress in the bureau. It's a dress Mrs. Vanders remembers wearing before she departed for Virginia. They didn't want to get too close to Rachel's arrival and interfere with what she has found. They still wanted that to materialize exactly in the same manner. Also, they needed Mrs. Vanders to be there for the exchange. They know it was at the Christmas gala in Virginia that Rachel arrived. They must do everything prior to that point in time.

Christmas is only days away. Mrs. Vanders and Beth go up to the room to find the requested dress is there. Excitement is only one of many emotions both are feeling. The plan is to see if it works. They have rehearsed what Mrs. Vanders can and cannot say to her parents. She will need uninterrupted time with them to get the complete story out. Donning the dress, Mrs. Vanders hugs Beth. "I will put a note in the desk to tell you if this works."

Somewhat worried about what they are attempting, she feels herself shaking with nerves. Mrs. Vanders tells her not to worry. "It will be alright," she says.

Walking to the mirror, Mrs. Vanders twirls the skirt and before Beth's very eyes, she dissipates into thin air. Pieces of her scatter and disintegrate.

Waiting for an hour, she finally hears sounds from the desk. When the noise ceases, she trudges to the desk, heart pounding in her throat. She yanks open the drawer with anticipation and snatches the letter immediately. She reads, "I've made it. Beth, I'm me again, young and vibrant."

"Oh, my goodness! It worked!"

They hadn't discussed if she should remain and wait for Mrs. Vanders to return, or leave. Just to be certain, she remains for a while. When nothing develops, she leaves the room to return to her suite. Feeling exhausted from the day's events, she throws on some PJ's and crawls into bed. Fatigue taking over, she falls fast asleep.

The next morning, she gets up and dresses for breakfast. Not having an inkling of what she will say to everyone when Mrs.

Vanders doesn't show up, she tries to think of excuses to give. She could act as if she doesn't know where she is, or she could say she heard she's staying in her room for breakfast. That's one detail of planning they failed to do.

Walking into the breakfast hall, she sees Grayson sitting in their customary spot.

He says, "Good morning, sleepyhead. I didn't think you were coming down. It was getting so late."

"Oh, I went to bed very late last night. I'm so tired."

"No bother. You're here now." He reaches over and pecks her lips. He looks at her and asks, "Are you alright? You're acting like something's wrong."

Almost ready to answer, she turns when she sees everyone watching the entrance. She twists to look as well.

To her utter shock, Mrs. Vanders and her husband are walking in. "What the hell?!"

Mrs. Vanders seeks her out. Seeing the shock on Beth's face, she walks directly to her telling her husband to go ahead, she'll be right back. Grabbing Beth by the hand, she pulls her out into the hallway, then down the corridor. Finding an empty room, she closes the door. "Beth, I know you're shocked, but I need you to act naturally in there."

"Natural? I can't act normal. I don't know what the hell just transpired in there."

Sitting her down, Mrs. Vanders tells her everything that's occurred. She explains how she found her parents and talked to them for hours about what was going to happen to her with time travel. At first, her parents thought she was out of her mind.

However, she insisted they believe her. Knowing time was short, she took drastic measures to show them.

"I took them to the room and traveled back to the future. But instead of here, I landed back to when I first met my husband."

"It all began happening again, Beth, just as before. I knew the next words out of his mouth. I stayed with him as I did before. Then, on my first trip back, I returned to the exact point where I left my parents in the room. Beth, the shocked expression on their faces was disturbing, but even they couldn't deny what they had witnessed."

Beth says, "I can imagine. It was a lot to take in and believe. I remember when we first watched Rachel leave. The sight stayed with me for a long time." Thinking back to her husband, she adds, "I don't understand how your husband is here."

"I knew what he died of. I decided if we alter the circumstances, he could live, so we did."

Beth is still amazed, but recognizing everything she knows, she has to accept it. Dramatically, she says, "I'm so surprised to see him here."

"I know you are Beth. I'm sorry, but I have one more astonishing fact to share."

She looks at her with an expression that says, "What more could you tell me that would startle me worse than this? Go ahead. Tell me."

Mrs Vanders stops and holds her breath for a moment. "Grayson is not my nephew now. He is my son."

Beth jumps up and begins pacing the floor. "He's your son? How can that be?"

"Time is sequential. It was time for Grayson's soul to arrive. Since it was me who got pregnant first, I conceived him." Pondering the circumstances, she continues, "I always wondered why I felt so close to Grayson. I cherished him more than any of my nephews and nieces."

Sitting down on the chair across from her, Beth lays her hand over Mrs. Vanders. "So, you had children. I'm happy for you. I know that was a regret you had."

"Not children, child. Grayson is my only child."

Her mind still storming, she reiterates the fact that Mrs. Vanders is the mother of Grayson. "I'm dating your son." She looks at her dead in the eye and asks, "I know you were for us getting together when he was your nephew, but how do you feel about it now that he's your son?"

"Beth, I could not have handpicked a better match for Grayson."

Tearing up, she thanks her for the compliment. "Does Grayson know you are his mother?"

"Yes, everyone adjusted but you. I only had to see your face to know the same alteration didn't happen to you since you were involved in my travel. When we met, I continued everything that has occurred between us as normal. The only thing that transpired differently was last night. The time travel didn't happen last night as before. I knew it the minute I saw your face. I could see it had just caught up with you."

Standing and looking at the clock, Beth says, "Well, we had better get back." Right before they get to the door, Beth turns to ask, "Is there anything else that I need to know that has changed? Do Grayson and I still own the magazine?"

"Everything else is the same. Well, except Grayson's mother is now the mother of Alex and Brad."

Beth bursts out laughing. "Oh my God, no one will ever believe this happened."

Amused, Mrs. Vanders says, "No truer words were ever spoken."

CHAPTER 18

CHRISTMAS MAGIC

To say going forward was an adjustment is an understatement. Mrs. Vanders having a husband and Grayson being her son was quite a turn of events. The fact that Grayson is unaware of the events, makes it even more difficult. Understanding how confused she can get at times, Beth is cautious. She constantly has to adapt her thoughts to adjust to this new reality. However, eventually, they all settle into a peaceful harmony. It's especially exciting when the holidays bring special guests to visit.

The shopping and endless parties at the estate are exhausting. Christmas Eve arrives quickly. The big family gathering occurs tonight. Tables are placed all around the ballroom. Beth, Grayson, Mrs. Vanders (Andrea), and Mr. Vanders (Nathan) are seated at the main table. Beth feels so blessed to be a part of this family. Watching Mrs. Vanders and the happiness she lacked before is priceless. She never noticed the absence of a spark prior to now. Seeing her with Nathan, Beth can see a new energy in her. A smile breaks out across Beth's face.

Grayson sees Beth watching his parents. "What is enticing that beautiful smile on your face?"

Looking at Grayson, she leans over and kisses him. Turning back to watch his parents, she says, "They look so happy."

Grayson looks at them and replies. "They have always had this intense love between them." Thinking back to their lives, he continues, "I hope I have that kind of marriage one day."

Beth looks at him and responds. "You will, Grayson. This family is all about love and your parents have set a good example for you."

Smiling, he watches his parents get up to dance. He holds his hand out to his mother as she walks past him. Andrea squeezes his hand as she continues towards the floor. He turns back to Beth and leans in for a kiss.

Getting ready to go to the lady's room to freshen up, she stands but is halted by the shock of her life. Rachel and Chad Grayson are standing right in front of her! Almost passing out, Beth leans on Grayson for support.

Feeling Beth lose her balance, Grayson turns around to catch her. That's when he sees Rachel. He's just as surprised as Beth. Fumbling for words he says, "Hello, Rachel." Looking away from her to Chad, he extends his hand. Feeling as though he is looking at himself in the mirror is rather awkward, but he presents a welcoming smile.

Rachel says, "Chad, this is Grayson Vanders. He's from the Vanders side of the family, while you're from the Grayson's side." Finding herself explaining needlessly, she continues, "Grayson, do you remember your ancestors Chad Grayson and Adrianna Vanders? They're the portraits in the gallery."

Grayson thinks back to the gallery room then reacts, "Yes, I recall those portraits." Looking at Chad, he exclaims, "Man, you could be a reincarnation of him."

Chad laughs convincingly. "I've been told that all my life. You know, you have his looks too. I'm sure you have received the same responses."

Beth is still dumb founded, but walks over to hug Rachel, interrupting the conversation. She says, "It's so wonderful to see you, Rachel."

Rachel returns the hug and whispers, "Let's find a private room for a minute."

Beth walks back to her table, grabbing her clutch. Lightly kissing Grayson, she tells him to order Rachel and Grayson a drink. "Rachel and I will be back in a minute."

They locate a quiet room down the hall and slip in. Having gotten over the shock, they both embrace, ecstatic by the visit. Beth says, "Rachel, I can't believe you're here."

"I could see we surprised you. I left a note in the desk that I was coming. I was dying to see Mrs. Vanders and her husband together. You guys are like family to me, I wanted to be here for Christmas."

"Now that I'm over the shock, I'm so glad you're here. This couldn't be a better Christmas if I tried! Instantly popping into her mind, Beth asks, "Rachel, what about the baby? Was it a good idea to travel while you're pregnant?

Acknowledging her concern, she lays her hand on Beth's. If you recall, I would be back in the past for months, but only an hour would have passed here when I returned. I had my son three months ago. It's actually one year later there. We had to do some calculating to arrive in time for Christmas"

Beth squeals, "A son!" Hugging Rachel, she declares," I'm so delighted for you."

"Thank you, Beth. We couldn't be happier. I almost wished I could bring him, but he's too young yet. When he's older, we'll determine if he can travel, too. Grayson wanted to see if he could." She giggles, "You should see him gaping in shock at the transformations in the estate. He's like a kid in a candy store, scrutinizing and examining everything."

"I'll bet! It's just so fascinating to see the past or the future."

Rachel pokes Beth's arm. "Let's get back to you. You didn't see us when we walked in. You and Grayson look very happy together. How's that going?"

Beth smiles. "Rachel, he's not the ass I always thought he was." Remembering the change in history after Mrs. Vanders return, she adds, "Oh, he is Mrs. Vanders' son now, not her nephew."

Rachel shakes her head in acknowledgment. "I know. Since Mrs. Vanders told her parents about her time travel, she came back to let her parents know after she had Grayson. We knew all about it before you did, I suspect."

"You have that right. I found out about it only days ago. When she landed in the era when she met her husband, she stayed and relived her life. She reshaped history as we knew it. Grayson is one of those life-changing moments worth living. She also knew her husband's cause of death, so they took actions to prevent it."

"Beth, Mrs. Vanders did so much for me. I had to see her after the changes. I still don't understand how she has relived all these years again, and I haven't aged with her. It's like time moves differently in the past than it does in the present. Or your arrivals and departures dictate time manipulation." Shrugging, she adds, "I have given up trying to figure it out. All I see is happiness, so it works for me."

Beth looks at Rachel, who is still the most beautiful woman she has ever known. Her long black hair and beautiful gray-blue eyes are a compelling combination. Suddenly, she remembers how interested Grayson was in her. Getting a slight feeling of insecurity, she decides this will be the time she finds out how Grayson really feels about her. Grabbing Rachel's arm, she says, "Come on, I can't wait for Mrs. Vanders to see you. She will be ecstatic."

Entering the ballroom, she sees Mrs. Vanders has returned to the table. They are all standing in a circle. Rachel walks up to her, touching her arm gently. Mrs. Vanders turns to see Rachel. "Rachel, this is such a treat! I'm so pleased you're here!" They embrace.

"I'm so happy you think so. I was concerned when Beth was so surprised. I left a note in the desk that I was coming."

Mrs. Vanders laughs. "Did you really? I'm so sorry, I haven't been up there in a while. Holiday planning always takes a lot of my time," she says, reassuring Rachel that she's thrilled to see her. She nods toward Chad, "How are things with you and Chad?"

Rachel turns toward Chad just as he looks at her. He grins and raises his eyebrows to let her know he's enjoying himself. Longingly she replies while still gazing at him, "We are perfect, Mrs. Vanders, just perfect." Touching her arm, she says, "Oh, and there's a little Chad Grayson now. We had a boy."

Getting excited for Rachel, Mrs. Vanders exclaims, "That's wonderful news. At times, I worried that you might resent me for having to live my life."

Rachel looks at her in astonishment. "Are you kidding me? I constantly wonder if you regret giving up your life."

Mrs. Vanders smiles while watching Nathan. "No, Rachel, I have the most incredible life I could have ever lived. A husband I adore and the son I always longed for. I couldn't be happier.

Beth walks up as the two embraces. "This looks like a joyful reunion." She gets hauled into the embrace.

Grayson walks up and pulls Beth away from their grasp. "Come on Beth, we haven't danced yet."

Smiling, they go to the floor and indulge in an energetic dance. She turns, facing the group, and motions everyone to join them. She can see Rachel is having some issues convincing Chad, so she runs back to the table and grabs his other hand. Both pull him to the floor. Rachel yells over the music, "Just follow my lead. Don't forget I went through the same thing when I first came to the past."

His hesitation didn't last long. Being the adventurous type, he jumps in and falls into step like the rest. The six of them enjoy moving around to the music. Some, who knew the song, sang loud and harmonized with the lyrics. Chad, who knew none of it, just shook his head and dove into the steps.

When the music stops, Rachel moves into Chad's arms and kisses him again and again. There is so much tenderness between them. Watching the union, Beth feels jealous that they are married and so much in love. Grayson grabs her hand and pulls her into his arms when the slow music begins.

"Are you as astonished as I am about Rachel and Chad? Until now, I didn't know he existed. Where did she meet him? I have heard nothing about him in the family line before."

Leaning back, she studies Grayson's face. Not understanding his focus on them, she replies, "Why the scrutiny, Grayson? Are you jealous?"

Perfectly shocked at that accusation, he goes, "Whoa, whoa! Not in the least!" He studies Beth and asks, "Are you for real right now?"

Feeling a little ashamed, she quietly responds, "Don't forget she was your first choice."

"No, I hardly knew her. We met all of four times, maybe."

"Grayson, you don't have to deny your interest. She's married, so it certainly doesn't matter."

Getting frustrated, he reacts, "Beth, if I had been so interested, I would have called her. Have you forgotten she gave me her number?"

Feeling this is a lose, lose conversation, she replies, "Grayson, I don't want to talk about it anymore. She's my best friend. I'm happy to see her." She watches Chad and Rachel. They are preoccupied with each other.

"I couldn't agree more."

Mad at herself for initiating the trivial conversation, she lays her head on his chest. Why did she ruin this beautiful night? It's Christmas Eve, for goodness' sake.

Feeling his arms tighten around her, she wraps her arms around his neck, laying her face into the side of his neck.

Grayson asks, "You do realize I love you, right?"

She pulls her head back to face him. "I know I love you." Seeing him react, she puts her finger across his lips. "Grayson, I have never been in love. I constantly find myself wondering what genuine love is. I have spent my life judging men like you. I categorized you." Smiling, she continues, "Now you are breaking the mold, and I don't know how to handle it."

Grayson stays silent at first, then says, "Beth, I can't be in this alone. Either you trust in our love or you don't. You have no reason to mistrust me."

Laying her head back on his chest, she replies, "I know."

The song ends. They all return to the table. Grayson goes to his mother. Kissing her on the cheek, he whispers in her ear. "It's getting late. Beth and I are turning in. We'll see you at breakfast." Walking over to Chad and Rachel, he thanks them for coming. "I hope the two of you will stay through the rest of the holidays." Looking at Chad, he offers his hand. "It was nice meeting a long-lost relative. Be sure to come around more often." Turning to Rachel, he kisses her on the cheek and says, "Wow, you work fast. You're already married to this guy." He laughs and gives her a big hug. "Good to see you again." He turns to Beth as she walks up and, puts his arm around her. "I know this one wants you to stay around for the holidays, so I hope you two can stay."

Beth gives Rachel a big hug. "Can you stay for a few days?"

She looks at Chad for consent. When he nods yes, she says, "Of course. We would love to."

Beth picks up the shot glass that was left on the table for her and downs it. Grayson looks at her and says, "Okay, I like that," and downs his too.

Hand in hand, they leisurely stroll as they walk back to her suite. Approaching her door, he swings her around, backing her up against the door. Putting his hands on the sides of her neck, he pulls her in for a passionate kiss. She responds with the same eagerness as he moves to her neck. Enjoying the fuzziness, the shot is now evoking, heat rises in her. Turning swiftly to unlock the door, she pulls him inside. She pushes his jacket off and throws it on the floor. Taking the hint, he removes his tie and unbuttons his shirt. Following, she turns for him to unzip her dress. The dress falls to the floor as he removes it from her shoulders. She is now in her lingerie.

Grayson stops dead in his tracks. Her breasts are heaving from her heavy breathing. Running his finger over the mounds, he says, "Damn, you are beautiful."

Using her forefinger, she gestures for him to follow her to the bedroom, backing her way there. He follows, unzipping his pants. She could see he has already hardened. She stares directly from his groin to his eyes. Lust is written all over his face. Kicking her heels off, she turns back to him as he approaches. Pulling her bra strap down, he kisses her shoulder. Heat rises in her abdomen. He reaches behind her and unsnaps her bra. It falls forward. Throwing it on the chair, he kisses her deeply as his fingers wrap around the tip of her nipple. She moans and pushes down his briefs. As he bends to remove them, his lips take her nipple in his mouth. Tickling the tip with his tongue, her nipples harden. Falling on the bed, their lovemaking takes them to heights of love and exhilaration. Each time, they seem to reach a new peak in expressing their love and unbridled bliss.

Laying in one another's arms afterward, they are wrapped in the afterglow. Out of nowhere, he says, "How could you ever doubt my love for you?"

Shocked that his mind went there, she replies, "Sex doesn't always mean love."

He lifts his head and looks her square in the face. "I did not just have sex. I just made love with you," he says, emphasizing the word 'I.'

A tear rolls down her cheek. "I'm sorry, I didn't mean to belittle our lovemaking."

Shaking his head, he looks deep into her eyes, "I love you, Beth. I have never been in love before, but I know I love you." He wipes the tear from her cheek.

"I love you too, Grayson. Please give me time to get used to this. Give me time to become secure with our relationship. It's all so new to me."

His reply is instantaneous. "No. I will not give you time." He kisses her delicately. "It's time for love, Beth. Right now, no doubts, no questions. Just let yourself go. I don't want to be in this alone."

Hearing his words, she knows the time has come to let go. She feels it, so why not live it? Kissing him lightly she repeats. "Yes, Grayson, it's time for love."

They fall asleep wrapped in each other's arms. A peace settles over Beth that she has never experienced before. She somehow knows it seals their love. Before falling asleep, she studies the face of the man who has finally captured her heart. She says a silent prayer to herself, thanking God for bringing him to her. She falls asleep thinking this is the best Christmas ever.

CHAPTER 19

THE MERRIEST CHRISTMAS

Waking as the sun is rising, Grayson quietly gets out of bed. He puts on his bathrobe and rings for coffee and toast. Feeling a slight headache, he needs to get the caffeine right away. In only a few minutes, a soft peck alerts him to go to the door. Rolling the cart in, he thanks the attendant for the early visit.

"It's no problem, sir. Guests are already rising."

"Merry Christmas, James."

"Merry Christmas to you, too, Mr. Vanders."

Closing the door quietly, Grayson rolls the cart to the bedroom. He finds Beth is still sound asleep. Setting the coffee at arm's length, he climbs back into bed.

Feeling his body move up against hers, she gradually comes out of her stupor. "Good morning."

"Good morning, love. How's your head this morning?"

Taking stock, she says, "Not bad. I expected a headache after the shot and alcohol I consumed, but I don't."

Nuzzling, he says, "That's good." He kisses all around her nipples, but not touching them.

Being playful, she says, "Oh, I do have a headache after all."

Raising his head from her bosom, he maintains, "That's too bad. I had something in mind I thought you would appreciate."

Trying not to respond to his tongue running across her nipples, she quivers as she declares, "Oh, my head is really hurting." She pushes him off her. "Behave yourself. I can't go downstairs and look everyone in the face when all I have accomplished the last hours is making love."

He replies, "I can."

Hitting him, she jumps out of bed and runs to the shower. He goes to his suite to get dressed.

An hour later, they are dressed in their Christmas best. Beth is wearing a dark green dress that hugs her perfectly proportioned body. Grayson whistles when she enters the room.

He dresses in a black suit. She asserts, "Wow, I love that suit. I don't think I have ever seen you wear that one. Out of all the suits I see you in at work, I have never seen this one." She kisses him on the lips lightly, wiping the lipstick off his lips afterward.

"Really? I have never worn this before?"

"No, not that I recall." Searching for her keys, she suggests, "We had better get down to breakfast. It will be a room full today."

Grayson is dusting his suit, pulling it out like he's confused.

Beth turns back and says, "Come on silly. I love the suit."

"Do you really?" He draws out the jacket, inspecting it and making a pretense of dusting it off. He reaches into the pocket and plucks out a miniature box. "Oh, what is this?" Grayson is smiling, mischievously.

Beth stops dead in her tracks. Getting ready to say something frivolous, she pauses as he reveals the tiny little box. Looking back at Grayson, she inquires, "What are you doing, Grayson?"

He crouches down on one knee and opens the package. Looking at her astonished face, he declares, "Beth, I love you." Rolling his eyes, he continues, "I know, I have said those words a lot lately, but I do love you." He watches for her reaction. Seeing her stunned expression and silence, he asks, "Beth, will you marry me?"

The diamond is magnificent. Her hands go over her mouth. Looking from him to the box, she remains there, powerless to speak. The words are trapped in her throat. Hoarsely, "Grayson." Looking back down at the diamond, then back to him again, the tears spill. Running to him, she draws him up and drapes her arms around his neck. "I love you so much."

He draws back and inquires, "Is that a yes?"

Laughing, she replies, "Of course. Grayson, are you sure this is what you want?"

He brushes his nose against hers, "I have never been more confident about anything in my life. I want you to be my wife!"

She restates the word. "Wife."

He removes the ring from the box and places it on her left hand. It's a perfect fit.

Holding her hand up to study the ring, she asks, "This is a long engagement, right?"

His response is quick and pointed, "Hell, no. I want you to marry me immediately."

"Immediately? Grayson, you need time to think about this."

"No, I don't, Beth. I know my devotion to you and I want you as my bride now."

Looking surprised, she inquires, "Now? How soon is now?"

He hadn't honestly thought of the exact date. All he knows is that he wants it soon. Thinking about it for a minute, he answers, "I think we should get married on New Year's Eve."

"What?! Are you teasing me? That's not sufficient time to organize a wedding."

He acknowledges a bride's desire to have a large wedding but counters. "Look, everyone is here on New Year's Eve. The estate is already decked to the hilt and all of our family is here for the last holiday event of the year. The only action needed is to get the preacher and a dress. The rest is magic."

"You really aren't kidding, are you?"

He takes her in his arms, "Honey, I don't want to be away from you. I have to rectify my dilemma of not being capable of living without you anymore. Of course, we can wait, but to be genuine, I don't want to." Adding humor to the tense situation, he adds, "You know how we spoiled rich kids always get what we want."

She slaps his arm for that comment. Gazing into those dark penetrating eyes, she recalls their night of lovemaking and the life they could have together. Laying her hand on his jaw, she maintains, "If you want to, then I want to."

He hoots and picks her up, spinning her around. "Okay, in six days!"

She laughs the whole time he is twirling her around.

They embrace and seal the deal with a kiss.

He grabs her by the hand and says, "Come on, we need to get to breakfast. I'm going to need all the strength I can get to pull this off."

The dining hall is already crowded. They quickly find their seats and sit. Rachel and Chad are placed directly across from them.

Beth looks at Rachel, "Good morning."

Rachel says, "Good morning. I was beginning to think you weren't going to make it."

"Sorry, we were delayed exchanging presents." Beth rolls her eyes down to her ring.

Rachel squeals.

Beth puts her fingers over her lips. "Shhh. I think Grayson wants to tell his mother first."

Rachel composes herself and takes a bite of her eggs. She mouths, "I am so happy for you, Beth."

"Thanks, Rachel. I'm overjoyed."

As breakfast ends, the tone of the room converts into high gear. Children are begging to open Santa's presents. Everyone moves to the sitting room where the large tree is located. Only minutes after entering the room, Santa arrives with a big "Ho, Ho, Ho!"

The squeals are ear piercing. Children are jumping up and down with excitement.

Beth turns to watch Grayson, who's grinning adorably. Watching the children, his excitement builds. Pulling out his phone, he records everything. Getting up, he goes over to help a little girl who is struggling with the ribbon on her package. Rubbing his hand over her head he assists, then leaves. He records her successfully getting the rest of the wrapping off. A scream of excitement bursts from her as she sees the doll in the box. Grayson grabs Beth's hand and squeezes it. He asserts, "This never gets old. The emotions on their faces are priceless." He stares at Beth, who is gazing at him affectionately.

"I didn't realize you were such a mushy guy."

"Are you kidding me? Since I met you, I have lost all sensibility. I'm now mushy like a lovesick puppy." Smiling, he pecks her on the lips, "You have crushed this hard, unfeeling louse."

Rubbing her hand across his jaw, she is surprised by someone grabbing her hand. Looking up, she sees Mrs. Vanders.

"What is this?" She holds Beth's hand up toward Grayson.

Grayson says, "Mother, stop. You knew I was going to ask."

Smiling, at her son, she counters, "Yes, but I didn't know you had already proposed."

Gazing at Beth, he replies, "I couldn't resist her charms a minute longer."

Mrs. Vanders grabs Beth and hugs her. Whispering in her ear, "I couldn't be happier. You have been like a daughter to me. Now you will be."

Beth almost cries as she squeezes her extra hard. She has never had a happier day in her life. "You have no idea what you and your family mean to me."

Mrs. Vanders is watching her son, who is shaking hands with Chad and hugging his father. "I think I have a clue. Some things are just meant to be."

Beth watches Grayson as he receives slaps of congratulations on his back. For the first time, she understands how thrilled he is. He's laughing and receiving the noose jokes without phasing his demeanor. Understanding his pride in their announcement gives Beth a moment of unbridled joy.

Rachel gives her a hug. "You look happy, Beth." She glances at Grayson, then back at Beth. "The only remarkable part is how the two of you didn't get along at all in the beginning."

Beth laughs. "I know, go figure." Allowing the beaming to leave her face, she asks Rachel, "Should I tell him everything? I feel like marrying him with all the secrets is not a suitable way to begin our marriage."

Rachel gets serious. "Beth, it's not your secret to tell. That is between Mr. and Mrs. Vanders to share with their son." She looks at Chad. "I almost lost Chad because of the truth."

Beth declares, "But you didn't lose him. If anything, it has brought you closer."

"Beth, Mrs. Vanders was his aunt, now his mother. That would be difficult for anyone to comprehend. Relieving your guilt of the knowledge may hurt him irrevocably."

Thinking about it, she agrees. "I know you're right. Maybe someday I can take him to visit you and Chad in the past. That could be the opening of doors to his understanding."

"I would clear it with Mrs. Vanders. Beth, she has a lot to lose if this gets out. If Grayson is angry and shares the knowledge of all of this, it could hurt her."

The logic sets in. "I agree. I'll let Mrs. Vanders decide if she wants to share it."

Grayson walks up between them. He asks, "Rachel, do you think you and Chad can stay until New Year's Day? I know Beth would love for you to attend our wedding."

Beth adds, "Rachel, I want you to be my maid of honor. Please say you'll stay."

Rachel glances at Chad. He is thoroughly engaged in a conversation with Mrs. Vanders. Looking back to Grayson, she replies, "I think we can stay for that long. I'll check with Chad. If he has no pressing issues at work, we can stay." Looking back at Beth, she replies, "I would love nothing more than to be beside you as your maid of honor on your special day."

Grayson raises his eyebrows at Beth. He kisses her temple. "See honey, getting married so quickly while all of our family is here will work out perfectly." He puts his arm around her waist.

Beth says, "You are so wise. Wise beyond your years."

He counters, "You are too. Anyone agreeing to marry me is a genius."

Throwing her arms around his neck, she states, "The best decision I have ever made." This has been the merriest of all Christmases.

CHAPTER 20

WORDS YOU CAN'T TAKE BACK

During the next week, Mrs. Vanders and Beth have the conversations about Beth entering their marriage with the secret. Mrs. Vanders informs her that they took Grayson aside and told him about time travel. He was really zooming in on Chad and Rachel and the portrait. What he doesn't know is that originally, she had not been his mother. Years ago, they had decided that was not the important facts. Fate had stepped in by landing Mrs. Vanders back to when she met Nathan. They made that choice when she conceived.

Beth asks quizzically, "Shouldn't he know everything?"

Mrs. Vanders replies, "I think he does. We're not lying about his parentage. I'm his mother and Nathan is his father."

"I understand. I suppose I can understand that there is nothing to be gained by telling him."

Mrs. Vanders quietly says, "I agree."

They hug each other, agreeing that it's best to let the remaining knowledge be a secret. A day later, Beth is summoned into the library by Mrs. Vanders. She walks in to see Mr. And Mrs. Vanders seated with Grayson. Mrs. Vanders asks her to have a seat. She sits beside Grayson on the long leather couch. Mr. and Mrs. Vanders are perched on the two chairs opposite the couch.

Looking at Beth, she nods, signaling what she is about to do. "Are you sure?" Beth asks, now feeling unconfident about whether it is the wise thing to do at this point. She has finally brought her around to their way of thinking. However, they surprise her with this last-minute decision to tell him.

Mrs. Vanders looks at Grayson and begins. "Grayson, we have shared with you about who I am and the history of my journey to this century." Hesitating, she continues. "Well, I want to make sure we explain everything to you."

He glances at Beth, then back to his mother as if to say, "Beth will never understand all of this. What are you doing?"

Mrs. Vanders glances toward Beth and reacts. "Beth already knows, son."

Looking at Beth, he asks, "You do? Why didn't you say anything?"

Looking back at Mrs. Vanders, she answers. "I only learned yesterday that they had told you."

He looks at his mother, "Okay, but why are we going over all of this again?"

Mr. Vanders says, "Son, we wish to make certain you and Beth enter into this marriage with no secrets between you." He reaches over for his wife's hand. Looking back to Grayson, he continues. "Let your mother explain." Squeezing her hand, he adds, "It's her story to tell."

Mrs. Vanders looks at Grayson and begins. "I'll repeat everything I told you about me being Adrianna in the past, and how I was unhappy with my life there." Squeezing her hands into fists, she continues, "When I woke up in this time period, your father and I lived a beautiful life together." She stares at Nathan.

"He is the best thing that ever happened to me. It was when Beth and Rachel came to the estate that everything shifted." She stops to look at Nathan again. He nods, encouraging her to go on, and she does. "I was constantly confused about how those portraits got into the photo gallery. When Rachel showed up looking identical to me in my youth, I soon found my answers. In the past, Rachel is somehow me."

Grayson goes, "Wait a minute, are you saying Rachel went back to the past to be you?"

"That is precisely what I'm saying. Son, you just saw Chad Grayson and Rachel together this week. She is Adrianna in the past, and he is the real Chad Grayson."

"Is that why she vanished from the face of the earth?"

A nervous smile crosses Mrs. Vanders face. "Yes."

"Did you force her to go back to be you?"

Surprised by the question, she emphatically replies, "Absolutely not!

"So, she just out of the blue figured out, on her own, that time travel is possible and took over your life?"

"No, it began when she saw herself on the portraits. As a journalist, her curiosity won over after that. I confess I suggested that there were rumors of a time portal on the estate. I bantered with her that the portrait was truly her. She took it from there. I didn't even know she was going to the past until one day she told me she has been to the past, where she fell for Chad Grayson. She confided the pictures were definitely her."

Getting up and walking around, he runs his fingers through his hair, then asks, "So, you're saying anyone can travel through time, not just you?"

Beth interjects, "Yes Grayson, I have traveled too."

"You what? You've traveled to the past?"

"Yes, I traveled back to see Rachel. It's absolutely possible."

Sitting back down, he looks at his mother, "Go on."

She begins. "After I gained clarity on how things transpired, I took a trip back to the past where I attended Rachel and Chad's wedding. When I returned, I found that my cancer had diminished. I discovered that going to the past, had turned back time in my body."

Grayson adds, "That's good."

"Yes, it's wonderful. But after that, I became obsessed over how time and travel could transform life events. I wanted more than anything to let my parents know the truth. I missed them more than you could know." She looks at Beth then continues. "That's when during one of our meetings, Beth and I wondered if we could go back before the switch. I wanted to tell everything to my parents. We also investigated how to return not at my age now, but before, when I was Rachel's age."

Grayson again adds in, "Interesting concept. Go on."

"We gathered all the facts of our current travels and what would be required to be different to return not at my age but in my youth. We came up with a strategy that actually worked." Mrs. Vanders grabs Nathan's hand again.

Nathan nods for her to continue, "It's okay, tell him."

"Tell me what?"

She continues. "We did things differently this time when I returned, and it worked. I returned to my youth, back in time before Rachel went there. I told my parents about it. Of course, they didn't believe me, but I took them to the room as I departed. When they watched me disintegrate, they had no choice but to believe me. Unfortunately, when I returned home, because I was in my youth again, I returned to when I first arrived here and met your father."

He seems relieved. Looking at everyone he says, "Okay, so that's a good thing. Why are you so apprehensive about telling me this? I have heard all about the romance between you and dad."

Again, searching for encouragement from Nathan, she stares at him. Once again, he nods to go on.

"So, I had a choice to relive this life with your father or go back to the current ages. I chose to relive it. The reason I relived it is that in the past, your father died two years ago."

Grayson again rises and paces the floor. Running his hand through his hair, he says, "So, the first time, father passes away earlier in life. Then why are you here?"

Nathan replies, "Because your mother knew my illness and promptly took medical steps to stop it from happening. It was a type of cancer that could have been stopped if we if we had discovered it earlier. The first time around, we caught it too late."

Sitting beside Beth, he takes her hand in his. "Well, this is all good news. Why are you acting like I will not like this?"

"The whole point of this is to tell you that you were not born to me originally. You were born to your aunt. Alex was your brother, not your cousin as he is today."

Flabbergasted, he exclaims, "What?"

Not wishing to make this too uncomfortable for him, Mrs. Vanders replies, "They don't know anything about this, so it doesn't matter."

"It matters to me."

Mr. Vanders intercedes. "That's not what is important here, son. To help you understand, your mother and I have determined that it was your soul that was next to be born. In the first life, we didn't have children. In this second life we did. Your soul went to your mother this time. It feels like history is correcting itself. You were meant to be our son."

Grayson sits in dumbfounded silence.

Beth says, "Grayson, your parents shared this today because they didn't want you and I to marry with secrets between us. This is a major sacrifice for them."

"So, you knew?"

"Yes, up until days ago, when our times came back together. I woke up to a new truth. It was when your mother left, and because I was there, my memory wasn't changed. Time caught us up and shifted our reality. What is astonishing is that no one else knew the difference. It was only me who experienced the transformation. Maybe it was because I was a part of it. I knew everything both past and present outcomes. So did Rachel, and of course your mother told your father."

He rose. "And you didn't feel the need to share this with me?"

Mr. Vanders strongly inserts his opinion. "It was not her place to tell you, Grayson. That belonged to your mother and me."

"Well, I'm so glad the three of you decided what was best for me." He storms out of the room.

CHAPTER 21

LOVE BEYOND TRUTH

It is three days before the wedding. Beth doesn't know if the wedding is still on. She hasn't heard from Grayson in two days. Waking alone in bed, she hugs the pillow, struggling to decide what to do. Maybe she was mistaken wanting his parents to tell him.

There's a knock at the door. She crawls out of bed to answer it. Opening it, she hopes to find Grayson standing there. To her dismay, it's Rachel.

"Hello sleepyhead." Rachel is so chipper in the mornings. It's enough to make you want to punch her.

Turning to walk away and let her enter, she replies, "Yes, that's me, sleepyhead."

"What's wrong, Beth? You should be on top of the world right now."

"I think you may have been right, Rachel. We told Grayson everything."

Her eyes widen. "Yikes, how did he take it?"

"Well, we haven't seen him since. It's been two days."

"Oh no, that's not good."

Beth declares, "What's worse is that we are supposed to marry in three days, and I don't even know if the damn wedding is still on. I'm finding it kind of hard to focus on a dress when I might get stood up at the altar."

Rachel tries to soothe her. "Don't give up yet. Consider Grayson's feelings. It's a lot for him to take in. Give him space. One thing is for sure. He loves you."

"Does he love me beyond truth?"

Rachel shrugs her shoulders and says, "Part of genuinely loving someone is to accept everything about them. If you consider it, Beth, he could never marry anyone else. You know the whole truth about him and his family. You two should feel closer for that reason alone. It worked for Chad and me. It took him forever, at least, it felt that way to me. However, he ended up thinking I was truly destined for him because to travel beyond time to discover the kind of love we have, could never be matched."

Beth sighs. "I know. Your love story is for the ages."

Grinning, Rachel says, "Yours will be, too. Have faith in what the two of you have found."

"I know, but I feel guilty for insisting the truth be told. If I hadn't, we would be happily planning our wedding day together."

"You have three days left. That's plenty of time to pull it all together. What's left to do? Let me help."

Pointing to a rack of wedding gowns, she says, "Well, if you could help me select a dress, that would be a start."

Rachel rushes over to the garment rack. "Oh, they're gorgeous." Turning back to Beth, she motions for her to get up and help her go through them.

One by one, Beth tries them on. It would have been impossible to get them on without Rachel's help. It is the second to the last dress that overwhelms both Beth and Rachel. Standing in front of the floor-length mirror, Beth can't believe her eyes.

The body of the white gown is made of silk. At mid-thigh, sheer lace flows out. It's not just one layer of lace, but six. Each section underneath is longer than the last one until it touches the floor. Across the chest, the same thin lace meets the bust area of silk. The long slender arms of lace go just past her wrists. Holding out her hand with the ring on it, perpetuates the look she's going for. Twirling, she faces Rachel, "I love it. What do you think?"

Rachel has her hand over her mouth. Pulling it away, she responds, "That dress was made for you. You're stunning." Rachel walks over and hugs Beth warmly. "I hope this is the best day of your life."

Coming back to her present situation, Beth quietly replies, "I sure hope so."

Changing out of it, she puts it away. If Grayson were to show up, she wouldn't want him to see it. That being completed, the two dress for lunch. Having missed breakfast, Beth is famished.

Seeing Mrs. Vanders first, she sits next to her, asking if she has heard from Grayson.

Laying her hand on Beth's, she answers, "Yes, he came by last night."

Excitement builds in Beth. "Oh good. How is he?"

Concerned, she asks Beth, "He hasn't been by to see you?"

"No, nothing."

Squeezing Beth's hand, she asserts, "He's coming around. It's a lot to absorb."

"I know. I regret asking you to tell him."

Mrs. Vanders replies quickly. "No, Beth. He deserved to know. We don't regret it for one minute. In fact, Nathan and I were discussing it last night. Grayson responded the same way when we shared that I am from the past. Once he got over the shock, he asked if he could watch me the next time I go."

"Well, I do feel a little better hearing that. I just wish he would contact me. The fact that he has approached you, but not me, scares me."

"In due time, my dear. He loves you." Mrs. Vanders recalls all the other unimportant relationships Grayson had been in. He was never committed and broke many hearts. It was not until Beth that he changed. "Beth, the two of you have a love that will carry you beyond this. Be patient with him. If we need to postpone the wedding until he's ready, we can do that."

That thought never crossed her mind. Panicking, she counters, "If he wishes to postpone, I will cancel it completely."

"No dear, please don't make a rash decision. He'll calm down."

"Andrea, he cannot hold something against me that was never in my control. The fact that he has turned away from me for two days has caused me to reexamine what we have. We will have many obstacles in our marriage. He shouldn't be so hasty to turn away from me."

"But this is unique, Beth. This has nothing to do with you. His identity is in question. He's struggling to figure out who he is. Can you see how complicated that can be for him?"

Beth just doesn't want to analyze it anymore, so she replies, "I hope he's okay. Well, I need to run some errands." Finishing up her breakfast, she tells Rachel that she'll see her later.

Rachel replies, "Okay." Looking at Chad then back to Beth she says, "I'll make some plans with Chad then. I need to show him what this century is all about. If you need me, you know how to find me." She gives her an expression of sympathy.

"Thanks Rachel, I'll be fine." Leaving the room, she contemplates her next move. Deciding to work out her frustrations, she puts on some jogging clothes and running shoes. Donning a big sweatshirt, she goes out onto the property for a strenuous run. Getting to the Gazebo, she leans over, catching her breath from the brisk pace. While standing to take in the fresh crisp air, she notices Grayson. It surprises her to see him sitting in the corner. Still unable to understand why he hasn't come to her; she turns to leave without a word.

"Wait, Beth."

She stops but doesn't turn around. "What do you want Grayson?"

"I'm sorry I haven't been to see you in the past few days. I've had a lot to think about."

"It didn't stop you from reaching out to your mother."

"Mother told you?"

"Yes, I asked about you this morning."

"Beth, I love you. This has nothing to do with us. I'm struggling to understand who the hell I really am."

She turns sharply. "And you thought you couldn't come to me for support? Is that what marriage and a partnership means to you? Is it entirely on your terms, Grayson? Did you consider for one minute that you were hurting me by staying away? Or, is it all about the rich kid who is spoiled and thinks of nothing but himself?"

"That's unfair!"

"You damned right it is. And frankly, I'm not prepared to share my life with someone who shuts down when they have a problem instead of coming to me for comfort." She runs off and doesn't look back.

Getting back to her suite, she's breathless. Part is from her heart pounding anger toward Grayson, and part is pure exhaustion. Sleep has been sparse these past couple of nights. Shedding her clothes, she jumps in the shower and allows the tears to flow. What was she thinking? Trying to fit into this family was a mistake. After drowning herself in tears and water, she turns off the shower and puts on a bathrobe. As she blows out her hair, she decides makeup is not happening today. Walking into the living room, she stops when she sees Grayson. "What are you doing here, Grayson?"

"I'm taking you at your word. You said I could come to you, so here I am. Maybe you can sort this all out for me."

Thinking back to her remarks, he's right. She needs to listen. She sits on the chair opposite the couch. "I'm listening, but I must tell you, I am too furious to be of much help right now."

Shrugging his shoulders, he runs his hand through his hair. It's an action she has learned he does when stressed. He begins.

"First, I'm sorry. I should have come to you. Hell Beth, I'm about to marry you and I don't know who the hell is offering you this life. Everything I thought I knew about my life has changed in an instant."

"I understand it's a shock."

"No, it's impossible to hear. The shit that was revealed to me doesn't reconcile to who I assumed I was." He thrusts his hand in the air and gets up. "Beth, all my life, I have worked my ass off to be the best at business. I worked my way up from the mailroom as a teenager to be better than anyone else. Now, I'm looking back, asking if this life was handed to me on a silver platter? Were my parents so overjoyed to have a kid, they showered me with things I don't deserve?

Shocked that he even has those concerns, she counters. "Grayson, no one handed you a damned thing. I conducted the research on you, and whether Mrs. Vanders was your aunt or mother, she gave you nothing but what you deserved. You made yourself what and who you are today. You have eclipsed all of my expectations in business. You are business savvy and frankly took our business where I could never have alone. We are what we are in our own rights. Mrs. Vanders wanted me to exceed. That's why she gave me the best. She knew we didn't like each other. She saw past our impediments and made the hard judgment to give me the best person who could bring my dream and this business back to life." Getting even more ticked, she continues, "I thought you knew her better than that. She loves you, but she doesn't love you in spite of yourself. She loves you for who you are. What you don't know is that even when you were her nephew, you were special to her. She wanted us together then too." Shaking her head, she adds, "You need to get over yourself. This has been just as painful for her and your father as it has been on you. They have lived their entire lives under an umbrella of secrecy. Love them for it and consider them special in every way. That's how I see them, especially her.

I respect her far beyond anyone I have ever met. She has been like a mother to me."

Sitting down, he lays his head in his hands.

He doesn't respond right away. Finally, he hoarsely says, "You're right. I'm a complete ass!"

Calmly she states, "Yes, you are."

He looks up at her and laughs. "Well, leave it up to you to call me out. I must admit, you're pretty good at putting me in my place."

"Unfortunately, I have had good practice with you. In the beginning, you were arrogant and obnoxious." Softening, she continues. "But you eventually brought out the kind, loving man that I fell in love with." She adds, "I want him back."

Going over to her, he pulls her up from the chair. Taking her hand in his he says, "I love you, Beth. I'm not as arrogant as you think I am. This threw me for a loop. I didn't know if I was good enough for you, anymore."

"Grayson, you went from being a nephew to a son of the woman that has transformed my whole life. That is a step up in my book. Now, because of you, I get to be her daughter. Because of you, I have a successful business that is making me rich beyond my wildest dreams. Because of you, I am the happiest I have ever been in my life! What else do you want for proof?"

Finally laughing, he pulls her in close. "Kiss me like you mean it."

She kisses him tenderly. Not passionately, but affectionately and reverently.

"Do you think that kiss will convince me I'm the man?!"

"No, but this will." She moves her tongue into his mouth for a passionate kiss that follows with a long embrace.

They spend the rest of the evening sitting on the couch talking about all of it. Beth starts with the story from the beginning until now. It was hours before they stopped talking. Ordering dinner in, they ponder their life together and make some decisions on future plans. They talk about where they will live, how many children they will have, and all the details they hadn't focused on about their future until now. They slept soundly that night, full of peace about tomorrow and the path they will pursue. They have found love beyond the truth they have unearthed. The intensity of their commitment is heightened by the sheer fact that they believe that destiny brought them together.

CHAPTER 22

BECOMING THE STORY

Waking alone on the day of her wedding allows her to contemplate her future. Getting up and walking around her place, she realizes it's the last morning she's waking up as a single woman. Her whole future is about to shift in hours. Brushing her teeth, she watches herself in the mirror.

She says, "Girl, you're about to become Mrs. Grayson Vanders." A full smile crosses her face, and then she does the happy dance. Not in a million years could she have ever believed she would marry into this family. Thinking back to the day she walked through these doors, she accepts how blessed she is. It's not about the wealth, the lifestyle or the grandeur for her. It's about the love that has developed within these walls. Mrs. Vanders is like a mother to her. Grayson is an unexpected surprise. Moving from that first interview to today is a miracle. She smiles. The warmth he brings to her heart is palpable.

To avoid running into Grayson, she orders breakfast in her suite. The food arrives just as Mrs. Vanders approaches. Beth allows the waiter to take it in. She says, "Good morning" to Mrs. Vanders and invites her in.

"Good morning. How is the bride-to-be this morning?"

"The bride-to-be is very happy." She smiles at Mrs. Vanders.

"Grayson came by to let me know the two of you worked things out."

"Yes, we did. I'm glad he felt safe enough to talk to me about it."

Mrs. Vanders agrees. "Well, I knew he would come around." Looking at Beth with a serious expression, she asks, "Forgive me, but I would not be a good mother if I didn't ask. Are you genuinely in love with Grayson?" She lets out a nervous giggle. "You aren't going to break his heart, are you?"

Examining Mrs. Vanders for the seriousness of her question, she sees no smile crossing her face. Reaching over, she lays her hand on hers. "I love Grayson, but the question that should be asked is if he will break mine?"

This produced a smile. "I think you two are made for each other." Looking at Beth, she gets serious again. "I think of you as a daughter. I have already given Grayson the speech I'm here to give you. I ordered him to protect your heart. Cherish every day that you have together, taking nothing for granted. You are together, because I believe destiny put you here. You, Rachel, Nathan, Chad, and Grayson all had a part to play in the chain of events that have brought us to this day. I found Nathan, the love of my life. Rachel found Chad, the love of her life. Now, Grayson has found you, the love of his life."

"He is the love of my life, too."

A tear trickles down Mrs. Vanders face. "Beth, this is the culmination of all of my dreams coming true. I love my son more than you ll ever know. I want nothing but his happiness." She pats Beth's hand and adds, "I couldn't be happier about the woman he picked to share his life."

Beth goes, "Ahhh, Andrea, you're going to make me cry." A tear trickles down her cheek. Wiping it away, she says, "It's a good thing I haven't applied my makeup."

"Beth, just for this one moment between us, call me Adrianna."

Beth loses it. Tears pour as she responds, "Adrianna, I can't wait to be a part of your family. I am the luckiest girl in the world, getting two for the price of one. I love you both so much."

Standing, Mrs. Vanders tries to pull herself together. Beth also gets up from her seat, grabbing a tissue to wipe away the happiness falling from her eyes. As she wipes, she says, "These are tears of joy."

They embrace and stand in silence. No further words are needed between them. Both are welcoming one another like family. Mrs. Vanders finally breaks the silence, "Well, I had better get used to having a daughter."

Beth replies, "I'm already used to having you as a mother."

Mrs. Vanders lays her hand on Beth's cheek. "You are so good for my son." With that, she turns toward the door. "I'll see you downstairs in a few hours. The ballroom is lovely, by the way. I know it's New Year's Eve, but we made it very festive for the wedding."

"Thank you for taking care of that on such short notice. I would never have had the time to do all of that, too."

Mrs. Vanders laughs, "I can do that in my sleep." Smiling, she says, "But, I will admit this one was rather special. I'll see you in a couple of hours." Blowing a kiss, she closes the door.

Beth walks to the window and gazes out, trying not to fall apart. Every dream she has ever had for her life is coming true today. She has a fabulous career ahead of her, and a life filled with love and possibilities. She thinks about having Grayson's children one day. She shudders. Thinking that far ahead scares her. The way she was going, to be honest, she didn't believe she would ever marry, much less have children. Grayson's handsome face comes to mind. She can imagine a son looking just like him.

There's a knock at the door. Opening it, she finds Rachel in a robe and a cup of coffee in her hand. Beth says, "Good timing. I was about to have breakfast." Opening the lid, she sees a smorgasbord of eggs, bacon, toast, and fruit. "There's plenty here."

Rachel says, "I would love to join you. Chad left to go with Nathan and Grayson. He didn't say where they were going, so I thought I'd come to get you for breakfast."

Handing Rachel a plate, she replies, "I ordered in, because I didn't want to run into Grayson before the wedding."

"That's wise." Placing eggs, bacon, and toast on her plate, she sits at the four-seater table. Deciding it is best to eat a hearty breakfast with no lunch, they both leisurely chat over the meal. Beth is forcing herself to eat. Her nerves are causing her stomach to flip-flop every time she thinks about the wedding.

Rachel notices her picking at her food. "Beth, having the wedding at 2:00 p.m. in the afternoon means you will get to eat after the wedding at dinner. At least, have a little more."

Beth nods and begins forcing the food in. After she eats, she admits she feels better, not so queasy. The toast is what she needs. The two talk for over an hour. Having Rachel show up just in time to be at her wedding is wonderful. They have become best friends. Not having family, Grayson's father is going to walk her down the aisle. Grayson's best friend Derek is his best man. He would have selected Nathan, but since he is walking Beth down the aisle, it worked out nicely to have his best friend at the wedding.

A knock on the door makes her glance at the clock. It's already eleven. She opens the door to find her hair dresser and staff to assist Rachel and Beth in getting ready. Rachel goes to her quarters to get her dress. Deciding on a black and white wedding, Rachel's dress is black. It is in a similar style to Beth's wedding dress, without the train.

While Beth jumps in the shower, Rachel gets her hair and makeup done. Coming out of the shower, she dons a robe. As she walks into the room, she sees Rachel being zipped up into her dress. She is in awe of her beauty. Rachel has long dark hair. Her eyes are a gray-blue that peep out from beautiful thick black lashes. She is so regal and elegant. Beth can tell she carries herself a little differently than she did when they first met. Being Adrianna back in time, she has assumed the character in its entirety. Beth says, "Rachel, you are stunning." Laughing, she adds, "Wait a minute, you aren't supposed to outshine the bride." Both Laugh.

Rachel replies, "Beth, that is one thing about you. You're not vain. I always say, you don't know your own beauty. Haven't you ever noticed that all eyes move to the blue-eyed blonde when we enter a room simultaneously? You are tall, slim and gorgeous. You could easily be a model." When Beth snorts during laughter, they can't get their breathe from laughing so hard.

Sitting in the makeup chair, she asserts, "Well, let's determine whether my makeup artist can transform me into Cinderella." Again, they chuckle.

At twelve thirty, fruit and snacks are delivered to her suite. She mindlessly snacks on some cheese and crackers. After finishing her makeup and hair, she strides over to her wedding dress. Pulling the skirt out, she embraces her selection. Feeling more anxious as the clock quickly ticks by, she faces Rachel. "Rachel, what am I doing? I'm marrying Grayson Vanders!"

Smiling, Rachel replies, "Yes, you are."

Continuing she asks, "How did I get from detesting him, to falling desperately in love with him?"

Rachel again replies, "It was destiny."

Beth says lightheartedly, "If you had stayed here and married him yourself, I wouldn't be in this situation."

Rachel laughs, "Yes, you would. The two of you were meant to be. I wouldn't have gotten past first base if you had reduced your hostility toward him."

Grinning, Beth says, "You're right, I was pretty nasty to him, wasn't I?"

"Yes, you were." Remembering how it was and how it is now, Rachel says, "You two are a perfect match. I have never seen a man so in love." She hesitates then adds, "Well, Chad too, of course."

More giggles erupt.

For the next hour, they talk back and forth about the initial days they arrived and what has befallen their lives since walking through those doors. How ironic it is that it didn't just happen to one of them, but both. Entering the walls of this estate changed both of their lives permanently.

Finally, Rachel looks at the clock. It's twenty after one. "We had better get you into that gown."

Taking the dress off the hanger and discarding her robe, she steps into it. Pulling it up, she turns so Rachel can zip it. As she looks in the mirror, the transformation stuns her. Her hair, makeup, and now the dress. Everything is overwhelming. She wants to cry. As she holds her palm over her mouth, the tears want to fall. She turns to Rachel, "Rachel, this is my wedding day!"

They embrace. "You are a stunning bride, Beth. That gown is beautiful, but on you, it looks gorgeous!"

"I feel beautiful, Rachel." Running her hands down the dress where the lace flows out, she does a half turn to look at the back in the mirror. "I feel like Cinderella." She looks at Rachel, "You must be my Fairy Godmother."

Rachel laughs, "I can be whatever you want me to be today." She goes over and picks up a bag off the table. Pulling out a diamond necklace and diamond earrings, she hands them to Beth. "This is something borrowed. Mrs. Vanders, loaned these to me when I married Chad. She had them locked away when she was Adrianna. She wore it when she married Nathan, too. She is loaning these to you to marry Grayson. She believes they bring good luck." Reaching in the bag again, she pulls out a beautiful diamond pin that attaches to the headpiece on her veil. "This is something new."

It's a beautiful piece. "Oh Rachel, I couldn't. It looks too expensive."

"Nonsense." Rachel says as she reaches up to attach it to the center of her headpiece. It fits perfectly in the middle. Reaching back into the bag, she pulls out a blue garter. Laughing, she swings it around her fingers, and says, "And of course the most important, blue."

Beth smiles. "I love it! You thought of everything."

"Well, I can't take all the credit. Mrs. Vanders and I discussed it. We came to a consensus on the gifts. You are like a daughter to her, Beth. The two of you have grown so close. I really wish I could stay here with the two of you, but I know Chad would never go for that." She rethinks the statement. "Actually, I was never happy here. We have a magnificent life in his time. I just miss you, Beth. You have become such a good friend. I have social friends, but not like you and me. Maybe it's because of our secret, but I can be one hundred percent me when I'm around you."

Giving her a hug, she declares. "I understand. Knowing the secret about you and Mrs. Vanders has made all three of us extremely close."

A knock alerts them that it's now time to go downstairs to marry the man of her dreams. Rachel opens the door. It's Mr. and Mrs. Vanders.

Mrs. Vanders, says, "Beth, you are stunning!" She walks over and hugs her. Pulling back, she peers at the diamond necklace. "I see Rachel has given you the necklace and earrings."

Touching them with her fingers, Beth replies, "Yes, thank you so much for allowing me to wear them."

Tears filling Mrs. Vanders eyes, she speaks in a not so steady voice, "Of course." She turns to the side and reaches for Rachel's hand. "This necklace and earrings have been on three Vanders women during in the most meaningful time of their lives. May this jewelry bring you the happiness it has brought the two of us. You are now a part of the story, Beth. You will be a Vanders. The two of you have completed the circle of life for me. I love you both."

The three embrace.

Nathan interrupts the joyous union by announcing, "We need to get down there soon, or there will be one less Mrs. Vanders."

Mrs. Vanders waves her hand at him and spews, "Oh nonsense! This wedding will definitely happen. Someone would have to run over me with a train to stop it." She reaches out for Rachel's hand and says, "Well, let's go down. It's time."

The two ladies lead, while Mr. Vanders and Beth follow. As they arrive outside of the ballroom, they see the doors are closed. Derek and Alex are waiting along with the wedding coordinator.

Seeing Alex there was a little weird, but not that uncomfortable. They have been crossing paths since her engagement and no awkward moment had occurred. She was not expecting him to be a part of the wedding party, though. She realizes as they line up that he is walking Mrs. Vanders down the aisle. Staying out of the view of the open door, Mrs. Vanders and Alex begin their trek down the aisle. Soon after, Rachel grabs her hand just before starting down with Derek. "We'll talk again later, when you are Mrs. Grayson Vanders."

Beth's heart pounds wildly. Nerves kicking in, she draws in a deep breath.

Nathan lays his hand over hers. "This is the beginning of the rest of your life. Enjoy walking toward the man that will cherish you forever."

Beth looks up at him, and the peace that settles over her is unexplainable. As they march down the aisle, Grayson comes into view. His handsome face is beaming, exposing those deep dimples that she adores. He has a twinkle in his eye she has seen in their most intimate moments. His tuxedo is black, which compliments his black hair and emphasizes his dark eyes. Smiling, back, she walks ever so gradually toward the rest of her life and the man who will fulfill all of her dreams.

"Who gives this bride?" The minister asks as they stop in front of him.

Nathan replies, "I do." Grayson walks up. Nathan takes Beth's hand and lays it into Grayson's. Backing away, he joins Mrs. Varders in the seating on the front row.

Their eyes meet. Grayson says, "You are stunning, my love."

Unable to speak, she just gazes at him. She has a lump in her throat. As they turn to the preacher, Rachel takes Beth's bridal bouquet. From that point on, Beth is in a daze of matrimonial bliss. Taking her vows, she holds the hands of the only man she has ever loved. This day could not be more perfect.

More than once, they say "I love you" to each other, even though the script didn't say to do so. The room bursts into laughter each time they say it. Grayson just smiles and raises his eyebrows at her each time.

They take the steps out as husband and wife. She notices a figure appear at the end of the aisle as they are heading toward it. Disbelief registers across her face as she grips Grayson's hand tighter. "Do you see that, Grayson? Is there a man standing in the hallway at the end of the aisle?"

Grayson looks. "Yes, there is. I don't know him. Who is he?"

A tear slips down her face. "It's my father."

CHAPTER 23

THE NEW YEAR

The festivities of the night are both the New Year celebrations and their wedding. There is so much partying and excitement that the walls are vibrating with laughter, music and dancing. Their departure is joyous as the crowd sends them off in style with bird seeds and fireworks.

The planned honeymoon is exquisite. The flight leaves at nine. It's a brief helicopter ride to Mountain High Lodge. They rent the honeymoon cabin to stay secluded for days. The place has developed into an intimate love nest for them. As they stand on the balcony with a glass of bubbly champagne, snow begins to fall. The silence in the air as the flakes fall softly, is mesmerizing. Toasting to the rest of their lives, they clink their glasses then take a sip.

Setting the glasses on the small table, Grayson takes her in his arms as they view the mountain peaks. The snow gets heavier as they snuggle into each other for warmth. The cold cannot penetrate the embrace between them. Leaning his head down to hers, he kisses her gingerly. "I love you, Mrs. Vanders."

"Oh my God! I'm Mrs. Vanders!"

Grayson leans back and responds, "Yes…" He is examining her revelation.

"No, you don't understand. I have repeatedly called your mother Mrs. Vanders. Now, I'm Mrs. Vanders."

"Would you rather be Mrs. Grayson?"

"No silly, that's Rachel."

Finding that amusing, he acknowledges the rationale. "So, how shall I address you?"

Kissing him seductively, she replies, "Call me, my love, my darling, my one and only, better yet, my wife."

Returning the kiss, he replies, "I can do that."

He picks her up and carries her into the room. Sitting her down, he nuzzles her neck. They had removed their wedding attire when they arrived, getting into the plush robes. He walks her to the bathroom. There is a tub of hot water with candles all around. Rose petals are floating on the water. Undoing her belt, he pushes it from her shoulders. She steps into the warm water. After being in the cold outside, the warmth seeping into her bones feels wonderful. Grayson throws his robe to the floor and joins her. She lays back into his arms. He hands her a glass of wine, then takes one himself. They discuss the wedding and all the adventures during the night.

She twists and says, "My father had a smile on his face. I think he's happy about our marriage."

Kissing her lips gently, he replies, "I felt that, too."

Turning toward him, she straddles her legs over his. She grabs the soap and sponge from the dish and starts washing his chest. As she rinses each section she washes, she leans in and pecks it with her lips.

When she has completed his chest, he says, "My turn." He takes the soap and sponge and washes her neck first, kissing and biting softly. He moves further down to her breast mounds, where he rinses, then reaches in to kiss them. As he runs the sponge over her nipples, they harden by the touch. His smile broadens, "You like that, do you?"

He takes her nipple in his mouth, provoking her to moan. She answers, "Uh, huh." They skillfully wash and tease each other.

Not willing to discipline himself any longer, he stands, pulling her by the hand out of the tub. Picking her up, he carries her to the bed. Laying her soaked body on top of the bed, he climbs in. Leaning over, her suckles her breast nipple with intensity. His desire explodes for her.

Leaning in to his body, she moves against him, feeling his hard loins and the heat of it. She grinds against him, with the need for him to enter her as he continues fondling her breasts with incessant teasing. His fingers find her hot spot and he rubs it feverishly. She sighs with pleasure as he strokes her. She succumbs to the spasms that overtakes her body.

Feeling her release, he moves between her legs entering her gradually. He groans as her flesh encircles his and takes him in. Rhythmically, they ride the wave of ecstasy and lovemaking that defies logic. It is an out-of-body experience that propels them to a realm of satisfaction and fulfillment. Their love tonight reaches the sphere of undying love and commitment. Each embrace is given and received passionately. Their kisses are gentle yet wild. Caresses are soft yet fevered. They become one in the purest sense. They are now one heart.

Day after day, their love and laughter grows. Staying in their room the entire time, they talk about everything. Time travel, his mother, Rachel, and what all of it means. Their love grows deeper with each confession of their struggles in life as they discuss their vulnerabilities. Discussing past relationships seems silly because none compare to what they have. Both admit they never knew love until they found each other. They manage to laugh over their not so pleasant beginnings. Rubbing her face, he admits being drawn to her even then. "I always thought you were beautiful. And the fact that you could simply dismiss me intrigued the hell out of me." He glances at her, "I'm not suggesting I'm all that, but many women want what comes with being with me, not just me. Let's just say they appreciate the Vanders' wealth and notoriety. I could see through them instantly. They'd allow me to treat them like shit. I would constantly want to scream at them to have some dignity, for God's sake."

Laughing, she concedes. "I recall being attracted to you and becoming furious with myself for having you in my thoughts at all."

He asks, "Isn't it mysterious how unknown forces drive us to fulfill our life's destiny?" He gazes into her eyes. "You are my true north, Beth. You are my purpose for this life. There is no confusion for me. We belong together."

"I agree. The path we began was a sure-fire way to never get together, but we were chased by those unknown forces, or our destiny to turn to each other."

Kissing her on the lips, he asserts. "Or, my mother had a significant part in it. I'm so glad we found our way." He shakes his head. "The day my mother called me in to tell me what she was doing concerning the magazine and my part in it, I protested." Looking at her, he grins. "Not too hard, mind you. I realized it would be challenging with the dynamics of our relationship. I charged her at first as if she had lost her mind. Of course, she had all the proper answers for feeding my ego. She clarified that the business would fail if it didn't have my business savvy approach to sustain it."

Wrapping her arms around his neck and pulling him closer, she counters, "I'm so glad she lied to you."

He stares at her in disbelief! "Did you just say that to me, woman?"

Pulling him toward the bed, she suggests, "I could have survived just fine all on my own. I didn't want you or need you, then. Running her fingers along the side of his face and behind his ear. She whispers, "But, I want and need you now, and that's what's important. Don't you agree?" She leans her breasts against his chest.

He grins, "Well, Mrs. Vanders, let's see what we can do about that."

The morning of their departure is met with dread. Leaving their cozy hibernation causes an ever-increasing sadness. Going back to life is not looking good to either one of them. Enjoying each other without interruptions will be missed for sure.

The minute the chopper lands on the estate, they feel normal life seeping its way back in. It's a brisk morning, starkly different from the heated cabin and hot tub they took pleasure in. A car is standing by the helicopter to take them to the main house. A servant is waiting to get their baggage, taking another car behind them. It unsettles her that reporters are waiting as they touch down. They snap photos of them all the way to the car.

Beth watches, astonished that they are the focus of attention for the maze of reporters.

Walking into the main entryway, they are greeted by Mr. and Mrs. Vanders. Happiness is plentiful as Beth hugs her new in-laws enthusiastically.

Mrs. Vanders asks, "How was the honeymoon?"

Beth replies, "It was amazing." Looking at Grayson she continues, "We barely left our cabin."

Mr. Vanders gives Grayson a man slap on the back, and says, "Glad you had a good time."

Mrs. Vanders looks at Grayson and announces, "We finished your suite, just as you requested."

Beth looks at Grayson, seeking what she means.

Grayson kisses her on the cheek, "We hadn't considered the specific details of where we would live after we were married. I asked you to marry me and we were wed within the week, so we made no preparations beyond us getting hitched."

"I assumed as we discussed, that we would live in my suite until we decided. It's big enough for both of us."

"Yes, but your suite is not in the family section of the residence. Your suite is where we put guests." Kissing her again, "You're no longer just a guest."

Not able to dispute that logic, she shrugs.

Thanking his mom and dad, he grabs her hand, leading her upstairs. He walks her down a lengthy corridor she had not visited before. They arrive at a double door. Opening it just a bit, he turns to pick her up. As he carries her over the threshold, the vision astonishes her.

The living room is magnificent. It has lush white furniture arranged around the room. The walls are dark gray. Large dark gray and white pillows are strategically placed here and there on the white furniture. It offers elegance and comfort. A blazing fireplace is heating the room with warmth and coziness.

Sitting her down, he observes her for a reaction. "Do you like it?"

Turning to view every part of the room, she turns back to him and acknowledges, "I love it. Was this place here all the time?"

"Well, yes, the place was here, but it was not decorated like this." Glancing around the room he anxiously replies, "Honey, this is just decorated enough for our return. You can do whatever you want with the décor. This is your home and you are the lady of the house. We have this entire wing as ours. We even have our private exit to the parking area." Looking toward the bedroom, he continues, "I had them move everything from your bedroom here until you establish what you prefer to do with this area."

They walk to the bedroom, which is triple the size of hers. "Well, I guess we will require more furniture. Mine doesn't begin to fill it."

Kissing her, he notes. "We have all the time in the world." Pointing to other areas, he maintains. "We will both want to design our own offices." Taking her hand, he leads her to a grand kitchen. "You can cook, or we can employ a chef to do our cooking. Whatever you choose."

He notices she's not responding. "Honey, I apologize if I charged ahead without you. I wanted it to be a surprise. It took everything in me not to mention it on our honeymoon."

"You succeeded. I'm surprised. I don't know what I was expecting our life to be, but I never conceived all of this."

He peers at her as if she should have known. "Beth, you're my wife. Of course, we'll live like this." Taking her hand to go sit on the couch, he asks, "Should we have discussed what it means to be a Vanders?"

"I'm not certain I follow your meaning."

"You saw the reporters? Did reporters ever follow you before now?"

"Well, no, but that was just because they found out about our wedding."

"Yes, but now you are powerful news. You are the new Mrs. Vanders. You are in the headlines now. You may as well be royalty. Everyone is going to want to know all about you."

Nothing like that ever entered her mind. "Are you suggesting we will be like John Kennedy Jr. and his wife before they passed? They were pursued and hounded."

"I hope not, but yes, likely. I suspect people didn't know you and I were a couple until we married. We basically kept our relationship within these walls. You must admit it developed quickly. Engaged at Christmas, then married on New Year's Eve. No one had a clue a marriage was occurring in the Vanders family." Studying her seriously for a moment, he declares, "You, my lady, are big news right now. Prepare yourself for some scrutiny."

Comprehending his comments are accurate, she recalls how it was such an immense opportunity with her publisher. She understands the stories about the Vanders are big news for sure. She wonders why none of this popped in her mind before now. They had been remarkably private before so no one noticed. She realizes now that her life is about to transform beyond her imagination.

CHAPTER 24

BETH UNDER A MICROSCOPE

The next day, the newspaper provided by the staff, has the morning news plastered all over the front cover. In big titles, "Unknown becomes Mrs. Grayson Vanders." It speaks of Grayson and his position in the Vanders family. He is next to inherit the fortune and grand estate. It extends in vast detail about her, which honestly surprises even her. The article speaks of her youth and where she grew up. They reveal she attended Yale, graduating and ranking top of her class. They even speculate about the business. They make suppositions of how they met. Feeling stripped and exposed for the world to see, she slams the paper down and goes to the bathroom.

Grayson looks up from his paper to witness her storm off. Grabbing the paper, she has been reading, he reads the article. Allowing her time alone, he waits for her return. "Are you okay, honey?"

Beth is struggling not to respond like an inexperienced girl who doesn't get a newsworthy story. "I'm fine. It's just difficult reading all about yourself on the front page!"

Grabbing her hand as she passes, he pulls her on his lap. "I'm sorry we didn't discuss this before, to prepare you for it. To be honest, since my existence had become all about work and no play, the stories had died down about me. I didn't consider what a shit storm this would cause and how it would affect you. I realized it once our chopper landed, and I saw the reporters. Let's discuss it now."

She nods, "Yes."

"Any news regarding the Vanders, good or bad, can be a front-page story. We are an established, well-to-do family in New York. It comes with sacrifices and undeserved scandal. We are never able to live a secluded life. Sometimes I fear if I shit, it will be in the newspaper the next day." He sets that out there so she would laugh.

A slight giggle escapes. "Go on, shit man."

He leans his head back, laughing. "My father and mother are the patriarchs of the family. Anything about them is newsworthy. I'm their only son, so of course, everyone demands to know what the spoiled rich kid is going to do." He stares at her and asks, "Admit it, that's what you thought when you met me, right?"

Feeling guilty, she acknowledges, "Yes, but it was because you acted like an ass at our first interview. You were in my eyes, fulfilling my theory of you."

"Right…." He gets a sad expression on his face. "Beth, I wish I could take that day back. I hate you ever thought that of me, but it is what it is." He continues, "I have gained a reputation of a womanizer and heartless bastard." He points his finger at her, "I have already explained that. Those sickening women who were social climbers or fawns, running after a fantasized image of what life would be like with me, instead of who I am. It soured me on relationships. I can admit that. It was you who finally opened my heart and gave me a kick in the pants. You didn't let me get by with my shit and called me out on it."

She never realized her not liking him was awakening a giant. Understanding how unusual she must have been in his eyes is presenting a new light on who she thought he was versus who he actually is. "I'm sorry. I admit I was defensive."

"Are you kidding me? You had every right to put me in my place. I was an ass."

Kissing his cheek, she replies, "Yes, you were."

They laugh, and he tickles her waist.

"All of that said, you are about to enter into the spotlight like you have never imagined. You snagged the most eligible bachelor in New York. They are going to want to know who you are and how you did it."

Finally, coming to terms with her new reality, Beth asks, "Okay, so give me the lowdown. How do I act, what should I say, or what precautions should I take?"

Pulling her close, he tells her, "Just be you. Everyone will love you, just like I do."

"Come on, Grayson, be real. What are the pitfalls I can fall into?"

"Okay, here are the guidelines. Never give more information than they ask. Never give an impromptu interview. Know your source and its reputation for honest newsworthiness. Being too elusive will cause them to chase you more. Giving a scheduled interview with an appropriate source, is crucial."

"Well, that's simple. I'll do an article in our magazine."

"They will consider that biased or self-serving."

"We can't win."

He smiles. "Yes, we can. I'll put in a call to a source I know and trust, and we can give them the interview together. Are you okay with that?"

Hesitating, she ponders the suggestion.

"Beth, the media is coming. Let's handle them on our terms."

"You're right. Schedule it."

"In the meantime, let's get started on a new story. Let's go make babies."

Laughing all the way to the bedroom, he chases after her. Running around furniture and jumping ottomans, she sprints to their haven of love. Slowing to allow the seeker to find, she falls into his arms willingly, surrendering to his touch. His smile and those dimples, makes her fall prey to his desires.

Routine returns to their daily lives. Getting back to normal is a priority. Her new normal entails being a married woman and running a conglomerate. She misses Rachel, who has now returned to her own time. Beth and Mrs. Vanders have continued writing the novel. It's so incredible hearing the details of her life as Adrianna. She can understand how Rachel had to adjust from her current behaviors to those of the past.

Rachel on the other hand has started a newspaper back in her time, which is becoming very successful. Covering politics and newsworthy stories, the newspaper only prints facts and has become another success story in the Grayson family tree. Mrs. Vanders is helping Beth understand the posture they need to uphold as a family and how closed off they need to be. Beth considers herself lucky to have the guidance of such a wise woman. The devotion she feels for her is a motherly respect and admiration.

Adrianna is a tower of strength. She has overcome being who she genuinely is to establish a new reality of her existence. It helps Beth to discover incidents that made Mrs. Vanders fear that her secret would come out. Questions regarding the resemblance of her and the portrait of Adrianna in her youth were constantly mentioned. Guilt plagued her over that portrait. Many times, she almost took them down to erase the forever reminder of who she was and what she gave up. Every time she thought things would calm down, something would occur to startle her.

After meeting Rachel for the first time, she panicked again. Who was Rachel and what did she want? At first, she consumed her every thought. It was not until Rachel had confided in her that she time traveled and met Chad Grayson, that peace fell over Mrs. Vanders. All of this history shared by Mrs. Vanders was an aid to Beth falling into the history books of the Vanders gracefully. Someday, the future will look back and write about her past, just like she does now.

Grayson was true to his word, setting up a scheduled interview with a reputable source. They set it up in their own living room. Sharing a piece of their life should satisfy the insatiable interest in their lives as a couple. Instead of an article, though, he sets it up for a news story for tv.

The morning of the interview, Beth is so nervous, she throws up. Trying to soothe her, Grayson tells her he will answer most of the questions if that helps. Thanking him, she says, "Let's just see how it plays out." Trying to reassure both herself and him, she adds, "I'll be fine."

Sitting in front of the cameras and bright lights, Beth feels panic stricken. She wants this over with. Grayson sees the expression of dread on her face and clutches her hand. As the camera's start rolling, she looks down at Grayson's hand over hers. A calmness overtakes her.

The interview goes extremely well. Grayson does not withhold his devotion to his new bride. The camera falls in love with their relationship, as the two gazes into each other's eyes with adoring affection. Panning the room with the cameras after the interview, the channel displays their life as a couple. It provides a glimpse, for the world to get to know the new Mrs. Vanders They shed light on the new Grayson Vanders as a husband. The world had not met this side of Grayson before.

Having been characterized as the wealthy bachelor who was not always pleasant to the ladies, the interview puts a fresh spin on his personality. Leaving his bachelor days behind, they now revere him as a successful businessman who has matured into a loving husband. He couldn't have written the outcome of the interview better himself.

After the interview is aired, Beth couldn't be happier. Her nerves have calmed down a bit. When she is out in public, she's treated with respect and dignity. Articles are favorable on the stunning blonde who captured and tamed the rich kid from New York. She is always pleasant, waving at the cameras as she passes, producing a smile of acceptance of them.

All of her publicity generates more enthusiasm in her book. Before she knows it, her book is on the bestseller list. Money is pouring into her bank account because of sales. They complete the time travel book in late spring. They publish it under an assumed name, and it also sky rockets to success. Renewed interest in the company and what it produces ramps up sales in all categories of their publications. It becomes a known fact that novelists with Olsen Vanders Publications are it, and sales increase. Realizing the name should be changed to Vanders Publications, Grayson brings it up.

"Beth, what are your thoughts about revising the name to just Vanders? I'm asking because I know you may wish to keep your identity with the publishing company as Olsen. I'm fine with your decision either way."

When the question is brought up, initially she gets defensive. The last sentence, relaxes her response. "Can I think about it? I know we are both Vanders now, but what happens if we divorce? That would give you complete autonomy in the name."

At first, wanting to get his back up with her defensive answer, he draws back. "Beth, that is why I'm asking you. I'm not insisting on anything. It's your name, your decision. However, I must admit, the term divorce coming out of your mouth doesn't set well with me."

Realizing how it must have sounded, she tries to defend it. "Grayson, I love you, but life can turn on a dime. I'm an outsider who could be exiled from the family if you decide I'm no longer desirable as your wife."

"Well, you are out of luck with that thought process. You, my dear wife, are until death do us part." He gets up from the conference table and kisses her before leaving.

Surprised, yet excited that he displayed affection at work, she yells after him, "It's your death that departs us!"

He chuckles as he strides out the door.

Each night, they leave the office at the office. They have hired a chef to do the cooking, so when they arrive home each evening, dinner is prepared. They invite Mr. and Mrs. Vanders over frequently on Saturdays for an intimate family dinner. The large galas still go on as traditional, with commitments of elaborate dinners and celebrations. The family uses any excuse to bring those together that matter. Mrs. Vanders still handles the events, as if she still lived in the past where these communal events could make or break anyone in society. If an individual is invited to a Vanders' event, they are considered to be of the upper echelon.

Spring turns into summer as the heat arrives in spades. Grayson and Beth enjoy late walks in the summer evenings as the night air cools. Sitting on the terrace of their suite is an evening event they enjoy. Grayson wraps her in his arms as they watch the moon rise. Many evenings end in silly cat and mouse chases and lovemaking that cements the bond of their commitment.

One evening, Beth is not feeling well and retires early. She wakes in the middle of the night to throw up. After an hour of hurling, she crawls back into bed. Grayson doesn't move, so she quietly turns over to fall back to sleep. In an hour, she is roused again by nausea. Running to the bathroom, she produces nothing but acid. Her stomach is empty, and there's nothing left to throw up.

Hearing her, Grayson gets up to check on her. "Honey, what's wrong?"

"Something didn't agree with me at dinner. I've been throwing up all night."

Pulling her hair out of her face, he can see the perspiration on her forehead. He takes his hand and feels for a temperature. "Beth, your head is burning up. I'm calling a doctor."

Grabbing his pajama leg, she says, "No, wait, Grayson. I think it's just the flu or something. I'm going to stay home today, and get some rest. If it's food poisoning, it will pass. If it's the flu, it will be over in a day or so."

"Beth, are you sure? Honestly, you have a fever. At least get someone to verify that its nothing serious."

"Please Grayson, I'll be okay soon."

He relents to her request, but insists that she call him, and the doctor if she doesn't feel better.

She agrees.

Grayson dresses and plants a kiss on her forehead as he leaves the room. She closes the curtains to black out the sunlight. With little sleep, she falls asleep as silence takes over her room. Waking periodically, she is grateful the nausea has subsided enough that she is no longer throwing up. She gets up once to eat some crackers and drink some ginger ale. Getting back into bed, she falls fast asleep again. It's like all of her strength is zapped from her body. Sleep comes peacefully and gratefully.

She is awakened by Grayson. It's after six o'clock. "Beth, have you been in bed all day?"

Moaning she doesn't respond.

Grayson awakens her again. It's now seven o'clock. "Beth, this is doctor Price. I want him to check you over."

Not responding, she falls back to sleep.

The exam goes off without Beth's interaction with the doctor. Walking outside the room, the doctor informs Grayson that she appears to be dehydrated. "If this continues another day, we would have to get her to the hospital for some fluids intravenously." He admits it could be the flu or food poisoning. Grayson replies, "I ate the same thing she did. It's not food poisoning. I would be sick, too."

"Then, my assumption at this point is the flu. That's something you have to wait out. Keep her hydrated if you can. If not, she will need fluids. I can set her up here for fluids in a day or so if she's not better."

After the doctor leaves, Grayson follows his instructions and puts a cool rag on her head. The next morning, she's still asleep. She doesn't stir as he leaves for work. He calls in the nurse on staff, asking her to stay in the suite with her today. He wants to be notified of any developments. Working without her at the office feels like his life has paused. She consumes his every thought. He feels lost without her, and can't focus on anything. He leaves early. Upon arriving, the nurse informs him that she tried to throw up once, but only had dry heaves.

Grayson furrows his brow. "I guess, there's nothing left. She hasn't eaten for two days." He calls the doctor again, who sends over an IV for the nurse to set up, stating it couldn't hurt to get some liquids in her.

Again, the next morning, Beth is still asleep. He decides not to go in today. He stays by her side. Sitting in a chair next to the bed, he handles the critical work things that demands his attention He can handle most things from home. His mother wants to come to visit, but Grayson insists that they not come, because he wouldn't want them exposed. They are getting up in age and he wants to be cautious.

Grayson falls asleep in the chair, holding her hand. Movement startles him awake. He sees Beth's weak eyes open, looking at him. "Hello there, sleepyhead."

Looking around the room and its darkness, she asks, "What time is it?"

He glances at the clock on the wall, "It's one o'clock in the morning."

"What are you doing up?"

"I'm babysitting."

A perplexed look passes over her face, telling him she is not entirely herself to get his joke. "You've been very sick. I've been sitting with you while you sleep."

She recalls throwing up earlier. "I know it was something I ate for dinner. I'll be okay by morning." She looks at his tired face, "Come to bed, honey."

He reaches over to kiss her forehead. "You have had nothing to eat for days, Beth. It's not food that has made you sick."

Shocked she asks, "What day is it?"

"It's Wednesday, or should I say Thursday morning? You began throwing up Monday night."

As she tries to sit up, she finds herself too weak to do so. She lays back down on her pillow. "Oh, my goodness. What in the world has happened to me? I'm so weak I wanted to black out."

"Honey, you have been sick for days. Would you like something to drink? Ginger ale?"

Feeling her dry mouth, she says, "I would love that."

Returning with a small cup of ginger ale, he pulls her up enough to lean on him. "Here, drink this."

She sips it, feeling the cold drink slide down her raw throat. Handing him the cup, she says, "That hit the spot. I'm so thirsty."

"Do you want more?"

"No, thank you." She wraps her hands around his arm. "You are so good to me, Grayson."

Smiling, he answers, "I know, I'm special."

Rolling her eyes up at him, she responds cynically, "No, that's just taking it too far."

Laughing, he responds, "There she is. That's my girl. I know you're on the mend now." He gets up and fluffs her pillow. "Here, lay back down and get some rest. I think you'll feel much better in the morning."

Feeling her hair, she goes, "Oh no, I must be a fright. My hair feels matted and dirty."

He laughs at her vanity. "You have never looked better."

She again rolls her eyes at him in disgust.

Laughing, he says, "You've got that natural look going on. You know, the swollen eyes, sunken cheeks and pale complexion."

"Grayson, I'm too weak to slap you right now, but I will be better soon, and you better be ready!"

He kisses her forehead, "You are my beautiful baby. Get some sleep. I look forward to our battle."

With that, she's asleep. He rubs his eyes and yawns. Going to the bathroom, he washes his face with a warm cloth. Changing into his PJ's, he climbs into bed beside her. Laying there, he listens to her low breathing. Listening to her, he marvels at how he could have ever lived without her. She is everything to him. Her getting sick makes him realize how she completes his life. He rolls up next to her and kisses her shoulder. Laying his head on part of her pillow, he falls asleep spooning the love of his life.

CHAPTER 25

HAPPILY EVER AFTER

Beth makes a complete recovery, and life moves back to normal. Grayson doesn't take her for granted as she goes back to her vibrant self. She attacks life with a vengeance. The book she and his mother co-wrote, called *"Timeless"*, is a whopping success. The adventures of the novel are complemented by the expert representation of every character, tying the heart of the readers into the love stories that bond each personality to their space and time. Beth writes a note to Rachel to let her know of the book's success. She also informs her that Mrs. Vanders' cancer has gone into full remission. Beth knows the truth, that time travel has healed her.

Beth's life with Grayson is adventurous and satisfying. They're both consummate perfectionists in running the business. The profits rolling in on the books are staggering. The magazine division of the business is also thriving. Hiring talented reporters and writers, has increased the popularity of the magazine.

An entertainment TV show is going up for sale. Floundering ratings allows Beth and Grayson to make the deal that's far below the show's worth. They discuss the pros and cons. Having brought the publishing company from the brink of extinction, they feel they have the bandwidth to do the same for this investment. Talking it over with Mr. and Mrs. Vanders, they are assured they have their backing. As they get ready to make an offer, the same sickness takes hold of Beth again.

Waking up one morning, she realizes she has the same consuming nausea. Beth throws up again and again. Fear racks her this time because, despite Grayson's insistence, she did not get tested last time to evaluate the source. Now, if this is cancer, she has let it go longer than she should have. Grayson wakes to her retching.

This time Grayson demands she go to the doctor for some tests.

Simply afraid, she agrees it's the wise thing to do. "Just let me see if this passes today, it may be just a mild flu or food issues," she argues.

He agrees that she wait only a day. She eats some crackers to settle her stomach. It helps a little, and she goes back to bed to sleep it off.

Waking at ten o'clock, she throws her legs over the side of the bed. Waiting to begin retching, she inhales to dismiss the nausea. She scuffs her way to the kitchen to get some coffee. Looking under the lid of the tray on the counter, she finds warm biscuits. She puts a small amount of strawberry jam on it, then goes to the living room to grab her laptop. Finding emails that require her attention, she absorbs herself into the work. Looking at the clock, she finds its four o'clock. Traipsing to the bathroom, she takes a nice hot shower to bring herself back to life. As she's dressing, she hears the front door open.

Looking up from tying her sneakers, she sees Grayson with a worried look on his face.

"How are you feeling?"

"I feel fine. I ate a biscuit earlier, and now I feel like I'm starving. What's for dinner?"

"That depends on what you think you can keep down. Still feeling nauseous?"

"No, I feel fine. In fact, I was just about to go for a run."

"Oh, no you don't." Looking at her with concern in his eyes, he reminds her, "Beth, this is how it started last time. You start out throwing up, then as the days pass, you get worse."

Walking over to him, she kisses his lips tenderly. "Grayson, you worry too much." Feeling sensual, she loosens his tie. "Would you like me to show you just how good I feel?" She lays his hand on her breast, "Doesn't that feel good to you, Mr. Vanders?"

Dimples deepen as his grin broadens. "HHMM, you do feel good."

She asks, "How do you feel, Mr. Vanders?" She unzips his slacks. "Oh, you feel swollen and warm. Do you have a temperature?"

Leaning into her neck, he moans his delight as her hand encircles his manhood. "Yes, I am very sick, feverish in fact."

Pushing her backward to the bed, he grabs her tee-shirt and pulls it over her head, staring as her chest heaving from excitement. Breathless, he unsnaps her bra. It falls to the floor. He doesn't take his eyes off of her as they continue to undress. She pushes him back onto the bed. Crawling on top of him, she positions herself to rub her spot on his manhood. The friction excites him as well. He leans up and takes a breast in his mouth. As she shivers from his suckles, she guides him inside her. His touch makes her feel warm with a surge of lust. She feels a higher level of sensuality. Both find their rhythm and enjoy heights of desire. Moaning his pleasure as they both reach the pinnacle of blissful orgasms.

Falling on top of her, she says, "Yes, you do feel better." He kisses her. Looking into her eyes, he declares, "I love you, Beth. Do you know that you are my world?"

"Yes, I do." She pecks his lips, then says, "Because you are my world, Grayson. I love you more than life itself."

Lying beside her, he gazes into those gorgeous blue eyes. Running his thumb over her nipple, he says, "You are beautiful, Mrs. Vanders. You are all I need."

Grabbing his neck, she pulls him in for a passionate kiss. Feeling her nipples harden again, she yells, "Stop! We have to get dressed for the ball tonight. We'll be late."

Slapping her rear as she exits the bed, he follows her to the shower. They wash each other's backs, then assist with wardrobes. Walking into dinner, you would never guess they just barely made it.

That night, they dance a few, then call it a night around eleven. Falling into bed, Grayson falls fast asleep. Beth lays in his arms and says a silent prayer of thanks. She's the happiest she has ever been in her life. Looking at his sleeping face, she counts her blessings for the day she strolled into this estate. She cherishes her mother-in-law and admires her father-in-law. Having seen two sides of how life could have turned out, Grayson being Mrs. Vanders son is exactly the way it should be. The contentment in this family is that of the purest of love.

As she falls asleep, she is peaceful and happy. Waking at dawn, she again faces nausea. Running to the bathroom, she chucks her dinner. Shaking, the sweat pores from her face. Unable to quell the nausea, she continues to hurl until the dry heaves begin.

Grayson runs in. Pulling her hair back, he asks, "Beth, are you alright?"

"Grayson, no I'm not. I think we need to go to the hospital. I'm not feeling well again. It's just like the first time."

"I agree. Something is seriously wrong, Beth." Leaving the room, he brings her a sundress that will slip on easily. He helps her into her thong undergarment. She patiently waits for him to get his clothes on. Grabbing a cracker from the kitchen, she trails behind Grayson to the car. The morning is already getting hot as the sun comes up full strength.

Grayson lays his hand on hers as they make their way to the hospital. Pulling up in front of the hospital, he walks her in, leaving his car in the entryway. Getting her checked in, the hospital puts her in a cubicle. As they take her vitals, Grayson runs out to move his car. While doing so, he calls his parents.

"Mother, something is very wrong. She continues to get terribly sick."

"It's going to be alright, son. We'll be there in a few. Get her settled into a room." His father adds, "She will not come home until we find out what's wrong. We'll have them run a battery of tests." As they hang up the phone, Mrs. Vanders has this sense of apprehension. These are the symptoms she had with pancreatic cancer. She fears that due to her returning in time to heal, the penalty transferred to Beth to have it in her place. The guilt and fear of the outcome consumes her on the way to the hospital.

The doctor allows Grayson back into the room after the full exam. Writing notes into her chart, he tells Grayson he can't find anything distinctly wrong with her. He instructs her to have a healthy diet, and he is going to prescribe some vitamins. Signing the document of release, he says, "She's free to go."

It stuns Grayson. "What the hell are you talking about? Is it the flu or what? Someone needs to tell me why this keeps happening."

Mr. and Mrs. Vanders walk in at the tail end of the discussion. Trying to calm Grayson, Mrs. Vanders tells him to take a breather. She asks the doctor if it could be pancreatic cancer. He assures her it's not.

Grayson is frustrated. Beth gets off the table to go. He rushes to her side to hold her. "Are you okay, Beth? I can get them to admit you for further tests."

Pecking his lips with hers, she says, "I'm fine, Grayson. This time it was the drinking that I didn't handle well. We just got over excited. Since that first episode, we have been overly sensitive. We all get sick once in a while."

As she passes Mrs. Vanders, she winks at her. Immediately, reassurance and comfort take over Mrs. Vanders. Beth knows she's okay or else they wouldn't be leaving.

The rest of the day is normal. Beth asks Grayson to go out to fill her prescription. While he's gone, she texts Mrs. Vanders, then puts on one of her sexy dresses and heels. Spraying herself with the perfume she knows Grayson is partial to. She has dinner set with candles and the romantic works. Turning all the lights down low where only the flicker of the candle is lighting the mood, she stands as Grayson walks into the room.

Surprised, the worry erases from his face. "What is this?"

She points with her hand like she's Vanna White and responds, "It's a romantic dinner."

Smiling, he replies, "I can see that, but what's the occasion?"

"Do I need an occasion to have a romantic dinner with my gorgeous husband? I mean, any girl would be lucky to be married to a man as virile as you."

Laughing, he kisses her. "I couldn't agree more."

Giggling uncontrollably, she takes off his baseball cap, running her fingers through his hair. "Oh yes, you are the man of all men. Powerful, sexy, a sperm Lord!"

That breaking out of left field, he asks, "A sperm Lord huh?" Running his hands over her rear, he entices her to let dinner wait. "My sperm, who is as you just called him, Lord, wants to take over."

Looking at the table, she replies, "But, we must have dinner first."

Looking at her in her provocative dress, he adds, "I can wait for dinner."

Cuddling up to him, she giggles again. "Well, this romantic dinner cannot wait. We have a guest."

Not understanding for a moment what she is talking about, he asks, "Did you invite mother and father up for our romantic dinner?"

Acting as if she just remembered, she asks, "Where is my prescription?"

Going to the chair where he tossed it, he hands it to her.

She turns for a glass of water, "Can you open it for me, and give me one? I think that would be incredibly sexy."

Looking at her as if she has lost her mind, he asks, "So giving you a pill would be sexy?" Opening the bag, he says, "Okay, your wish is my command. Here I go, I'm being sexy." He smirks a little as he hands her the pill from the bottle.

She asks, "Can you make sure they gave you the right pills?"

Still confused, he knows he will play whatever game she's up to. He reads the label out loud. "Prenatal Vitamins." He looks up at her. "What?"

Tears are now streaming down her cheek. She says nothing, because of the lump in her throat.

"Are you?" Looking back down at the bottle, he starts again, "Are you pregnant?"

Nodding her head yes, she says, "We have a guest for our romantic dinner. There are two and a half here tonight."

He howls so loud she knows the entire estate could hear him. He picks her up, and swings her around. He kisses her face, her lips, her nose, then settles his face in her neck.

They hold each other in silence while he allows her tears to release. He says, "I got you, babe."

Through her tears she says, "I know you do, Grayson. This is the second happiest day of my life."

He picks her up and carries her to the sofa. "Are you feeling, okay? Can I get you a blanket, water, another pill? What can I do?"

Kissing him passionately, she mumbles, "I think you've done enough, Mr. sperm Lord!"

He laughs as he connects what she was attempting to communicate. He stands and beats his chest, "Me, Sperm Lord!"

She pulls him back down beside her. She says, "One thing that occurs when a woman is pregnant is that her hormones go crazy. At the beginning of the pregnancy, there is a higher level of lust that is insatiable." Her tongue goes into his mouth as she releases the heat built up in her body.

Grayson responds accordingly and replies, "I really like these hormones you speak of."

She snickers, "Oh, but wait until the end of the pregnancy. A different kind of hormone will be released." She gives him a warning look, "Be afraid, be very afraid."

He pulls back. As he returns to undressing her, he says, "I'll think about that later. I'm going to revel in this phase."

They break the cardinal rule of not making love on the white couch.

EPILOGUE

The announcement reads, "A son is born to Mr. and Mrs. Grayson Vanders at four pm on Saturday, November 24th. Weighing in at six pounds 2 ounces, he is named after his father, Grayson Adrien Vanders, II. The Vanders family celebrates his arrival on this glorious day of the Lord."

Mrs. Vanders reads the article as she sits with Grayson, Beth, and Nathan in the sitting room. Beth gets up and walks to her. Handing Adrien to his grandmother, she says, "Adrianna, would you like to hold your grandson, Adrien?"

Smiling, she holds out her arms for the bundle. Gazing into the sweet face of her grandson, she can see both Grayson and Beth in his features. Looking back at Beth, she replies, "He's a Vanders, through and through."

THE END

ABOUT THE AUTHOR

Linda Mayo

Completing the third book in the "Time Series" has been inspiring. Writing in my spare time outside of a fulltime job, has been challenging. It took dedication and commitment. I triumphed! I have completed four novels now and it is exhilarating. In 15 days, I retire. I can't imagine what journey my imagination will take me on next.

Thank you for reading my book(s). My writing is dedicated to those who want to escape day to day routines and imagine the possibilities.

Blessings to you!